WHEN IT RAINS
AN AGE GAP ROMANTIC DRAMA
CHERYL TERRA

Bang It Out Writing

Contents

A Note on Trigger Warnings and Content

Full content warnings can be found on my website
(*cherylterra.com/trigger-warnings*)
Please note that this book is written in Canadian English, which has rules
and spellings from both UK and US English.
While this book is not considered a dark romance, it does contain
mentions of heavier topics and some items that may be triggering
to some readers. I have tried to address those topics here without
spoiling the story, however if you have concerns about any of the items
listed and wish to know more, please reach out to me via email at
info@cherylterra.com.

This book is intended for adults and features sexually explicit scenes. It
features a semi-taboo age gap relationship. A character within this story
experiences emotionally abusive family relationships as well as bullying
and the emotional consequences of this treatment leads to scenes that
include self-doubt, self-consciousness, body dysphoria, and shaming.
Cheating, though not by the main characters, occurs.

CHAPTER ONE

NOW

THEY SAY RAIN ON a wedding day means the marriage will last because a wet knot is harder to untie.

They also say rain on a wedding day means beautiful wedding photos, stories to tell for years afterward, and a great atmosphere.

They say a lot of things to make brides feel better about the sky opening and ruining all the girlish daydreams of sunbeams and gentle breezes in romantic fields full of sunflowers and daisies.

Before the ceremony had even started, my mom had said all those things and more to my sister. On the third or fourth repeat of how lovely the photos would be with the drizzle in the background, Chelsea snapped.

"I swear to God, Mom, if you say one more thing about the rain, I'm going to lose my mind."

"I'm just trying to make you feel better about it!"

"I wasn't feeling bad about it in the first place!" shrieked Chelsea. "Stop talking about the fucking rain!"

She slammed the door of the bathroom and the dull echo wove through the tension in the small hotel room. Mom swallowed, plastered a tense smile on her face to cover how hurt she was, and patted the photographer on the shoulder.

"Well, I think the photos will turn out just lovely with a bit of rain in the background."

The photographer nodded skeptically and Lisa, one of the bridesmaids, matched my mom's plastic smile.

"She's not usually like this," Mom said. "Just the stress from the wedding."

It took everything in me not to burst into gales of laughter. I covered the small snort of disbelief that escaped by coughing, though Mom still turned to me.

"Go check on your sister, Maid of Honour." She was trying to sound upbeat and light-hearted, but there was a pleading undertone to her words.

"Give her a few minutes," I muttered. "She'll be back out."

"Jocelyn." Her voice cracked and a surge of guilt rushed through me. "Please, will you go check on your sister?"

There weren't many people I'd do that for. Unfortunately, my mom was one of them. I sighed, marched to the bathroom door, and knocked.

"Leave me alone!" came the annoyed, muffled response.

"I'm coming in," I said unenthusiastically.

Chelsea never bothered locking doors behind her, and this was no exception. I heard her bound across the bathroom to lock it before I could swing the door open, but I was faster than she was. Still, it was a narrow miss: I was halfway through the gap in the door when Chelsea threw her body weight against it, almost crushing me against the frame.

"What do you *want*?" she grumbled.

"Mom asked me to check on you." I stalked past her and sat on the edge of the tub. "If you don't want to talk, fine. Just let me hide in here with you."

"And why should I do that?"

I raised my eyebrows at her, the answer already clear between the two of us. Chelsea glared at me a moment longer, then huffed as she turned to the mirror.

"Fine."

When Chelsea finally felt like leaving the bathroom and resuming the photos with her bridesmaids as they got ready for her big day, I trailed behind her. The photographer insisted on taking a few shots of me adjusting Chelsea's dress.

"Maybe we could try one with you smiling?" the photographer asked.

"I'm just so emotional right now, I don't think I can smile," I said listlessly.

The photographer tried to laugh. It was more of a grimace. "Well, how about one of... we'll, um, take it from the back, then."

She took a few more where my face wasn't visible and moved on to Mom and Chelsea. There was a slight moment of tension when Mom almost popped a button off the back of Chelsea's dress, but the recovery was swift. The photographer captured at least one where Chelsea didn't look like she wanted to kill Mom, and Mom's tears almost looked like happy tears instead of distressed ones.

The rain didn't let up once we were ready to trundle down to the limo. The driver, along with a frazzled-looking concierge, ran back and forth between the waiting vehicle and the lobby, escorting each person one-by-one under an enormous umbrella.

Well, except Chelsea. The concierge escorted Chelsea and me at the same time so I could have the honour of holding her skirt up behind her, preventing it from dragging across the puddle-soaked cobblestone. If we were as close as sisters should be, it would have been an adorable, joyful photo of us scurrying through the rain.

In actuality, I got the back of my dress wet and had to spend half the limo ride trying to fix my dampened hair as Chelsea lamented about how horrible I would look in the photos.

The day didn't improve. Our limo arrived at the church on time, but Mateo, the best man, texted me frantically five minutes before the ceremony was due to start because they were stuck at a train crossing. I alerted the wedding planner and the priest, who distracted Chelsea with more pre-wedding father-daughter photos.

That distraction lasted all of ten minutes. Then Chelsea was sniffling and looking up at Dad with big, watery eyes.

"He's late, Dad. What if we get behind schedule? What if..." She paused, hand fluttering to the mole on her throat she touched when she was nervous, though we all knew it was an act. "What if he doesn't come?"

"He'll be here," Dad replied. "He knows damn well what the consequences will be if he isn't."

I rolled my eyes and wandered off, peeking down the aisle at the people waiting for the wedding to start. I caught sight of Lawrence sitting near the back. He must have felt my eyes on him because he turned and caught my eye. With a quick glance around, he shot out of the pew and towards me.

"They break up yet?" he asked.

"Don't be a dumbass," I said. "Mateo texted and said they're stuck in traffic. Isaac's freaking out and Chelsea's being a drama queen to get sympathy from Dad."

Lawrence chuckled. "And the day just keeps getting better, don't it?"

"Doesn't it."

He frowned. "Yeah, that's what I said."

"No, you said... never mind."

I sighed, closing my eyes briefly. Lawrence touched my shoulder, fixed a piece of hair that was out of place on my forehead, and brushed his lips against mine.

"Who's watching?" I asked against his mouth.

"Isaac's dad," he murmured.

My eyes reopened and I glanced down the aisle. Sure enough, Derek Thompson was turned in the pew, hazel eyes filled with concern. Torn between the irrational pang of embarrassment caused by Derek seeing me kiss Lawrence and the pang of longing that was highly inappropriate, considering he was Isaac's father, I smiled grimly at him. He raised a hand in a strange sort of shrug, the question clear.

What's going on?

I jerked my head towards the door in response. *Come here.*

Derek turned to his daughter and said something before hopping out of the pew and striding down the aisle. Of course, the sight of the father of the groom leaving the church raised some suspicions, and a room full of curious eyes followed him as he strode towards us.

Well, most of the eyes were following out of curiosity. A fair number were following because Derek Thompson probably hadn't worn a suit since his own wedding, and damn if he didn't clean up *incredibly* well. The calluses on his hands and the tattoo on his neck were the only hints of the rough tradesman beneath the tailored edges of the suit, a man so different from his son that if they hadn't looked so much alike, people would question if they were related. As it stood, Isaac shared the same rectangular face and strong jaw, the same sparkling eyes—though Derek's were more hazel and Isaac's were more green—and the same thick, dark hair. The main difference was their height: Isaac towered over me by at least five inches and Derek was even taller than that.

Of course, all those thoughts were completely inappropriate. I tried telling myself that thinking Derek was hot was just a normal appreciation for an aesthetically pleasing man, but even I didn't buy that bullshit.

"What's happening? Where's Isaac?" Derek asked as he walked up.

"Stuck in traffic," I said. "Chelsea's freaking out. I guess Isaac must be, too."

"Do you need any help?"

I shook my head. "The wedding planner said we'll give them five more minutes and then make an announcement. I guess starting fifteen minutes late is standard for weddings."

"That's probably killing Isaac. You want him to show up on time, you tell him a time that's half an hour later than it starts, otherwise he'll be there fifteen minutes early."

Smirking, I nodded. "I remember. If I ever get married, I'm starting things five minutes early just to fuck with everyone."

"We're in a church," mumbled Lawrence.

I rolled my eyes at him.

"I don't think we've met," Derek said casually. "Derek Thompson."

"Lawrence Pitt." They shook hands, though I noticed a fleeting wince on Lawrence's face as Derek squeezed a little tighter than necessary.

"How long have you two been together?" Derek asked.

"A couple months," I said before Lawrence could respond. "Chelsea and Isaac were, um, kind enough to let me invite him last minute."

Derek smiled tightly. "The least they could do, I guess." He patted Lawrence on the shoulder. "You take good care of this girl, understand? She deserves the best."

My heart was floating somewhere in my throat. I swallowed hard, trying not to turn too red. Isaac's dad wasn't supposed to make me blush.

"Jocelyn!" my mom called from behind me, urgent and panicked.

I turned to see her beckoning me over. Behind her, Mateo was jogging through the foyer.

"They just got here," I said to Lawrence and Derek. "Gotta go."

Derek patted my back. "Good luck. You're gonna do great. And you look wonderful, Joss."

Lawrence nodded in agreement but said nothing, leaving Derek's words echoing in my ears as I rushed back to the wedding party.

I hustled into the room where Chelsea was waiting, dabbing at her eyes with the handkerchief she'd given to Dad as part of the bridal party gifts. Dad looked up, pressing his mouth into a straight line when he saw me.

"She was wondering where you were," he said.

"Letting people know not to panic," I said.

"You're here to support your sister."

I nodded and swallowed back what I wanted to say, which was that if she wanted someone to support her, she should have picked a different maid of honour.

"He's here," I said. "We can get started."

"We can't get started. I'm a mess!" she snapped.

So began the downward spiral.

It took two of the other bridesmaids to convince Chelsea that her eyes were not red and puffy, which she should have known because she wasn't really crying. When she finally declared she was ready to walk down the aisle, the flower girl threw a tantrum and dumped the basket of petals on the floor. While Mateo and I scrambled to pick the petals up, the wedding planner cued the music, not realizing we were not, in fact, ready.

We dumped as many petals as we could into the basket and had Mom escort the flower girl down the aisle to prevent yet another tantrum. Chelsea bristled at the last-minute change but was placated by Dad. The procession proceeded almost flawlessly until the ring bearer hurled the ring pillow at Mateo, sending the rings skittering across the floor.

While collecting the rings, Mateo hit his head on the edge of the piano. He smiled, insisting he hadn't hit it all that hard, but by the end of the ceremony there was a golf-ball-sized lump on the back of his skull. I exchanged looks with Lawrence from the front of the church, his hand strategically covering his mouth as he tried not to laugh.

That only made my predicament worse. I managed to cover my laugh by sniffing and turning just before Chelsea entered, as if overcome by emotion. I guess I kind of was overcome by emotion: whatever emotion someone feels when they're faced with the absurd, taking part in a strange pageantry of a show, where half the players knew it was a farce and the other half were too stupid to figure it out.

I avoided looking at Isaac. He was probably focused on the back of the church, waiting eagerly for the moment my dad opened the door and escorted Chelsea down the aisle, her dress floating behind her as she fluttered her eyelashes demurely and pretended to be the virgin we all knew she wasn't. Instead, I let my eyes wander around the other guests, eventually settling again on Derek.

His ex-wife, Isaac's mom Angela, was sitting beside him. The corners of her lips were turned up, but it couldn't be called a smile. Derek hadn't bothered trying to smile; he sat with a solemn expression on his face, observing the front of the church until his eyes caught mine.

Let no one say I didn't almost cry at my sister's wedding. When Derek gave me that look, that little half-smile that said so much with no words, I almost lost it. Swallowing hard, I tore my eyes away just in time to watch Chelsea walk down the aisle.

The puppet show continued. I took Chelsea's flowers. She said her vows beautifully with dramatic pauses at the right moments, her voice wavering as she finished. The bad luck continued. The priest announced Mr. and Mrs. Isaac and Chelsea Thompson for the first time, at which point Chelsea stumbled and grabbed Isaac's arm for support. The photographer caught the grimace of pain on Isaac's face, but not the moment after when he recovered and smiled at her adoringly.

The photos were a mess: Chelsea refused to do anything that might get her hair wet, meaning I had to hold an umbrella over her head in most of the pictures. One of the groomsmen huddled beside me with an umbrella over us, but I was still sickeningly damp by the end.

Chelsea, of course, got mud on her dress and had a meltdown. I was tasked with finding a rag to scrub the mud off her train and proceeded to get splatters of it all over the ugly-ass pink dress she'd forced me to wear.

Just before the grand entrance, one of the bridesmaid spilled champagne down the front of her silvery-grey dress.

At dinner, one of the buffet tables collapsed, sending salad and buns skating across the dance floor. The DJ was late, the bar ran out of red wine, and Isaac's sister Samantha cut her hand on a broken glass as she was congratulating her brother and his new wife.

Through it all, Isaac kept smiling. He smiled all throughout dinner, smiled as Chelsea kissed the side of his head and excused herself to the washroom, and smiled at me when I caught his eye a few minutes later. That smile was sadder, a bit more tentative, but I smiled right back at him, then decided that Lawrence had pretend-called my name so I could leave the head table and made my way to his table, only to realize he wasn't there.

Probably at the bar again, I thought, and turned towards it.

No Lawrence at the bar, either.

Bathroom, I thought, my heart pounding. He had to be in the bathroom, he *had* to...

The only person in the bathroom was Isaac's great-uncle, who nearly had a heart attack when I barged in.

When I returned to the hall, my mouth was dry. I glanced around again, just in time to see Mateo leading Isaac out.

"Rain's stopped, just taking a quick breather!" I heard Isaac call to someone.

Palms sweating, I tried to walk as though I wasn't freaking the fuck out, even though I was definitely freaking the fuck out. Isaac and Mateo were far enough ahead of me that the door to the church had closed before I reached it, and I pushed it open hard enough that it almost bounced back in my face.

"You *asshole*!" I heard Isaac shout.

That was when I started running, rounding the corner of the church just in time to see Chelsea drop her skirt from around her waist, a comically shocked "O" twisting the smeared lipstick on her mouth. Isaac grabbed Lawrence and threw him to the ground with far more strength than anyone who knew him would have thought possible.

Lawrence ended the evening with a black eye, a split lip, and a bruise that wouldn't have been quite so dark if Isaac's wedding ring hadn't scraped across his face. Mateo jumped in almost immediately, but it took every bit of strength he had to pull Isaac away from the cowering man on the ground. As soon as he had, Lawrence pulled himself up, and without so much as a glance at me, ran from the parking lot as fast as he could.

There was a sickening moment of silence as Isaac turned to Chelsea. Her lip trembled as she brushed the back of her hand across her mouth.

"I'm... I didn't... it was a mistake," she stuttered.

"A mistake," Isaac repeated.

She bit her lip. He stared at her until she nodded. Without saying anything, Isaac turned. He paused, staring at me and then just beyond, until I turned and realized there was a small crowd who must have heard the commotion like I had. Standing in front of everyone, his face colder than ice and twice as hard, was my father.

Isaac still said nothing as he started walking away.

"Wait," Chelsea called, her voice wavering. "Isaac, wait! Let me explain!"

She stumbled forward, pushing Mateo out of the way as he tried to stop her, and raced after her new husband. She grabbed his arm and he froze, then turned towards her.

"Explain? It's our wedding day, Chels." His voice cracked and my heart stuttered painfully. "We've been married for like eight hours."

"It's not... it was a mistake."

Isaac was silent. Then slowly, incredibly slowly, a smile spread across his face. He snorted, and then laughed, and then shook his head as he wrenched his arm out of Chelsea's grip.

"Fuck you," he chuckled. "I should have listened to your sister."

With that, he kept walking, leaving Chelsea staring after him and the rest of the wedding guests staring at Chelsea.

Well, except me. I stared at Isaac too, watching him saunter through the parking lot, passing by car after car until he reached the main road. Long after he started down the sidewalk, I stared at the place he had disappeared from sight.

I didn't realize she had moved until she spoke from just beside me.

"Jocelyn," she whimpered.

"What?" I snapped.

She recoiled. "You're mad."

"Mad?" I repeated. "Chelsea, you're cheating on him. On your wedding day. With my... my *boyfriend*. I don't think 'mad' is quite the right word to use."

"You're my maid of honour," she sniffled. "You're supposed to—"

"Maid of honour duties don't extend to defending you being a goddamn whore," I spat.

"Don't call your sister a whore," Dad hissed.

Just like Isaac had, I started laughing. "She is, though."

"She's your sister and—"

"And Isaac was my boyfriend, and she took him, and then I had to be in her wedding party even though that's super fucking weird, and after all that, she fucked my current boyfriend on her wedding day, *at the wedding* and I can't even call her a whore?!"

"She's your sister," he repeated.

"Jocelyn, I'm sorry," whined Chelsea, touching my arm.

I yanked myself away and slapped her. My dad gasped, half the witnesses winced and the other half smirked, and I walked towards the church without looking back.

CHAPTER TWO

THEN

I tried not to smile. "They, um, make the car stop. It's what provides the friction."

He nodded, adorably bewildered. "And that's what was making the noise?"

"Well, sort of. The brake shoe was coming in contact with the rotor, so…"

He looked lost and the smile at his confusion was even harder to hide.

"Okay, so in simple terms, you put your foot on the brake pedal. The pads make it stop. They're worn out, so the metal behind the pads is scraping against something it shouldn't. I mean, your car isn't supposed to make a screeching sound every time you brake. That's, uh… bad."

He nodded again, pushing up the glasses on his nose, then shook his head. "Yeah, I dunno. My dad would know this stuff, but… well, anyway. What's the damage?"

I raised my eyebrows. "Well, like I said, the pads were worn through, so… there was lots of damage. We had to replace them."

He startled me by laughing. "I mean, how much do I owe you?"

"Oh." I grinned, despite knowing my face was turning red. "Right. Well, the good news is you won't have to sell a kidney."

"And the bad news?"

"How often do you use your spleen?"

He clutched his chest dramatically when I told him the price. I watched, bemused, until he looked up and grinned.

"Nothing?"

"A little over-the-top, but hey, thanks for not screaming at me because your dad could do it cheaper or something."

He shrugged and grinned.

"All right, Mr... uh..." I flipped through the paperwork for his name, but he spoke before I found it.

"Isaac's fine."

"Okay, Mr. Isaac's Fine," I said. "How are you paying today?"

He laughed and held up his card. "Credit, Miss...?"

"Just Jocelyn."

"Miss Just Jocelyn. Or, um, Mrs.?"

"Dude, I'm twenty-three. Definitely not a Mrs."

"Me neither," he said solemnly, and I had to bite the inside of my cheek to keep from giggling.

I brushed my hand across my cheek as he put his PIN in the machine, then tried not to smile too wide when his fingers brushed mine as I passed him the receipt and he hesitated.

"Bring her back in if you have any more troubles," I said.

"Will do. Thanks, Miss Just."

"No problem, Mr. Fine."

He grinned. "Mr. Fine? I could get used to that."

I felt my face turn red again and he waved before leaving. It was still a hopeless shade of pink when my boss, Bretta, stormed out of her office.

"I can't believe you," she spat.

"What?!"

"You didn't give that boy your number!"

"I thought it was bad form to date customers," I said, putting his paperwork away. "Besides, he wasn't into me."

"Jocelyn, he was totally into you!"

"Oh, bullshit," I said. "He was cute, but come on."

"He couldn't stop staring at you. Though..." She picked up a rag, chucking it at me from the other side of the desk. "I guess it could have been the dirt smeared across your face."

I whirled around, checking the mirror that the receptionist kept hanging on her file cabinet, and groaned. Grit streaked across the entire left side of my face, from the bottom of my cheek up to my forehead.

"That's probably what it was," I said.

"Get off it, I'm teasing," Bretta said. "He'll be back."

"He better not be. I fixed his brakes, he shouldn't have a reason to—"

"He's going to be back with some 'mysterious' noise it's making that you won't be able to figure out. Within a week, I guarantee it."

"Yeah, right."

She shook a finger at me. "If he comes back in the next week, girl, you better give him your goddamn number. Otherwise, you're fired."

"One of these days, you're actually going to fire me and I won't take you seriously, you know."

She flipped me off before going back to her office. I grinned and went back into the shop, promptly forgetting about Isaac and his bright smile, his brilliant green eyes, and his nerdy glasses that slid down his nose.

Three days later, Bretta flew into the shop while I was trying valiantly to save an old and ill-maintained Grand Am.

"Jocelyn!"

I stood up from under the hood just in time for a rag to hit me in the face. "What the fuck, Bretta? What was that for?"

"Wipe your face, then your hands, then get your cute ass to the front because *someone's* car is making a mysterious noise!"

It spoke to how certain I was Isaac wanted nothing to do with me that I had no idea what she was talking about until I pushed the door open to the reception area and was almost face-to-face with him.

"Hey, Mr. Fine," I said cheerfully.

His face lit up. "Miss Just. You're, uh, *just* the person I wanted to see."

I snorted and leaned on the desk. "Brakes still giving you trouble?"

"No, they're great," he said. "It's just my car is, uh, making a weird noise again. Like a... clicking sound, but only sometimes?"

"Might be out of blinker fluid. Have you topped it up recently?"

He looked bewildered. "Uh, no. I've never topped it up. Is that bad?"

I bit back another laugh. "Nah, it's probably okay. So this clicking sound, when do you hear it?"

"Uh, not like, all the time. Just once in a while. I'm not sure..."

I could see Bretta through the small window to her office, watching intently. Taking a deep breath, I decided to go for it.

"Let me ask you something, Isaac."

"Sure," he said.

"This clicking sound started after bringing your car in the other day?"

"Yeah, I noticed it, uh, the next morning. I thought maybe it was just supposed to do that?"

I raised my eyebrow at him. "That's just so strange. Are you sure it's making a funny noise, or did you just say that so you could come back and see me?"

I had never seen a man get so flustered so quickly. Isaac stuttered, then chuckled, then stuttered again. Redness crawled up his neck and I couldn't stop the grin that crept across my face.

"Look, I'm just saying, if you were just coming back to see me, you might as well save yourself the hundred bucks it'll take for me to check out the car. You can use it to buy me dinner tomorrow night."

He laughed, shaking his head and grinning.

"You got me. It's a date, Miss Just."

CHAPTER THREE

NOW

INSIDE THE CHURCH, NO one seemed to know what had happened yet. The DJ was still blaring music, Mom was still splitting a third bottle of wine with my Aunt Sharon, and people were celebrating, oblivious to the train-wreck that had just happened.

I glanced around, not sure what I should do. Did I go over to Mom and tell her what happened? Did I go to the microphone, tell everyone the wedding—and probably the marriage—was over, and to leave? Did I go to the bar, grab a bottle of whiskey, and wait to see what happened next?

The last one was the most attractive option. I had just decided to pull a stool up to the bar and drink until the whole thing was funny when my eyes fell on Isaac's parents.

They were sitting together at a table near the back of the hall, chatting and sipping wine. When Isaac and I had been dating, he'd warned me his parents had a weird relationship. They divorced when Isaac was sixteen and his sister was twelve, but they were still best friends and, from what I could tell, loved each other. One of those strange cases of loving each other but not being in love, I guessed, but it seemed to work for them.

Less so for Isaac, but that was his own issue.

Derek glanced up while I was looking at them. He shot me another one of those little half-smiles, then raised his wine glass at me, the message clear. *Come have a drink.*

Well, I was looking for a drink anyway, and it wasn't their fault Isaac was stupid. They deserved to know what happened before the entire clusterfuck exploded.

"Jocelyn!" Angela beamed at me as I walked up to them.

"Pull up a chair," Derek invited. "You don't happen to have a banana, do you?"

"Shit, that's what I forgot," I said, settling next to him as he poured wine into an unused glass on the table. "No wonder this party sucks."

He chuckled and handed me the glass, clinking his against mine. "Don't think it's just the lack of bananas, but that might be a contributing factor."

"How are you doing, dear?" Angela asked. "Holding up okay?"

Part of me prickled at the question, though not in a bad way. It was more in a way that made me want to cry, a touching level of concern that no one else seemed to have. She didn't even know what I had just found out but was concerned enough about the fact that my sister married my ex-boyfriend to ask.

Angela had never quite gotten over our split and I knew she'd never warmed up to Chelsea the way she had to me. I was sure, until that very day, that Angela had hoped Isaac would change his mind about marrying Chelsea and beg me to take him back. She'd said as much after a few too many mimosas at the bridal shower. I didn't have the heart to tell her I would never take Isaac back.

It wasn't because he left me for my sister. I'd long since forgiven him for that. No, it just turned out that I didn't like Isaac, not like that.

Isaac loved Chelsea. He truly, deeply, completely loved Chelsea. There was no doubt in my mind of that, and no doubt in my mind that he had struggled with the fact that she was my sister. It hurt at first, back when

I still thought I liked him, but over time I realized he was never the one for me.

He wasn't the one for Chelsea, either, and that was what made it hurt now. Isaac was too good for her, and he just couldn't see it. As for me, I would have liked the chance to realize I wasn't in love with Isaac before she took him, but Chelsea would never have allowed it.

We were just too different. Sure, we were both a bit geeky, but Isaac was sweet and smart and tried to be a decent person. I was insecure and awkward. Isaac wanted a girl who was pretty and delicate. The most delicate thing about me was the fragile wall I tried to keep my emotions behind. He was idealistic; I needed someone realistic. I was derisive; he needed someone he could be romantic around without them snorting at the cheesiness of it all.

I didn't harbour any animosity towards Isaac, not anymore. I did have some animosity knowing that Chelsea wasn't the pretty, delicate, romantic woman he thought she was.

I also had some animosity knowing that all the things I liked about Isaac and all the things he didn't have that I needed were mixed together in someone else, and that someone else was twenty-some years my senior and my ex-boyfriend's dad.

Angela didn't need to know any of that, though.

"I, uh... yeah, I'm holding up okay," I said, sipping the wine that Derek handed to me. "I was, anyway."

Angela nodded. "It must be hard."

"It's a weird situation," Derek added. "Not gonna lie, it's a little... well, it's fucked right up."

I shook my head. "It's not that."

"No?" Derek asked.

I took another sip of wine, trying to gather my thoughts, and then took a deep breath. "So, I just wanted to give you a head's up that I think... well, um, I'm pretty sure, actually... I mean, I don't know for sure-for sure, but it seems to me like maybe Isaac and Chelsea are, uh... getting divorced."

Derek laughed, startling all of us. "They've been married for eight hours. I think that would be an annulment."

"Well, whatever. I don't think even Isaac is stupid enough to forgive Chelsea."

Angela looked stunned. "What... Jocelyn, what do you mean? It's... what happened?"

I didn't know how to phrase it nicely, so I didn't. "Isaac caught Chelsea, uh, fucking my, um... Lawrence in the parking lot."

Neither of them spoke. Angela gaped at me, her mouth opening and closing, punctuated by the occasional slow blink. Derek's mouth was pressed in a hard line, eyes wide.

I cleared my throat. "So, uh... yeah. I guess I'm also single if you know anyone who's looking. Not Isaac, though, no offense. That would be... extra weird."

Angela gaped for a moment longer before turning to Derek, her eyes wide. He stared back at her, then looked back at me. He took a breath, opening his mouth as if to speak, and burst out laughing.

"Yeah, that'd be a little fucked up," he said.

I glanced at Angela, my chin trembling. She pressed a hand to her mouth, suppressing the smallest of giggles, and seconds later, all three of us were practically falling out of our chairs. By the time we regained composure, there were tears in my eyes and I could barely breathe. I wiped my cheeks with the back of my hand and took a sip of wine.

"I told him she was bad news," Derek said, a thread of anger winding through his voice. "I told him she... well."

Angela touched my arm, her eyes full of sadness. "I'm so sorry she did that to you. Jocelyn, you don't deserve to be treated like that."

Something caught in my throat. Angela was sorry for me. For *me*. She was probably the only person who was going to acknowledge that. I nodded, the muscle in my neck twitching as I swallowed back whatever that emotion was called.

"Not like it's even the first time." Derek shook his head and put a warm, comforting hand on my upper back. "Are you alright?"

"Yeah. I... yeah. It's fine." I chuckled awkwardly, trying not to shiver at Derek's touch. If I did, he might move his arm, and it felt far too good for that to happen. "Like you said, it's not the first time. It's probably not even the last time. But I mean... I'm sorry too. For Isaac."

Angela nodded, her eyes downcast. "Me too, dear."

"I am," I repeated. "I know it's weird. Between me and him, I mean. This whole thing is messed up, I know that. But I didn't want him to get hurt, that's... you know? Whatever happened, happened. That doesn't mean... I just, I'm so sorry."

Angela reached out and squeezed my hand. "He's... is he still out there?"

I shook my head. "He, um... Isaac got a little... I mean, Lawrence's face was just..." An inappropriate laugh bubbled out at the sudden surge of pity. "Mateo pulled Isaac off him, and that's when everyone else got there."

"Pulled... wait, Mateo pulled Isaac off Lawrence?" Angela repeated.

"Uh, yeah. He beat the shit out of Lawrence and walked off."

"Did anyone go after him?" Derek asked.

I shrugged. "Mateo was still out there, so maybe. I don't know. I left after slapping Chelsea."

"You slapped your sister?" repeated Derek.

I nodded.

"And Isaac... beat the shit out of Lawrence?" Angela asked again.

I nodded. There was a long pause, a strange beat as Derek and Angela processed what I'd said.

"*Isaac* beat the shit out of someone?" Derek said.

Angela slapped the arm that wasn't around my shoulders. "He could beat the shit out of someone if he wanted to."

I mashed my lips together, chewing the inside of my cheek. The snort still escaped and again we dissolved into laughter, sad laughter, absurd laughter. It was only when I bowed my head that I realized I was crying, and moments later Derek was tightening his arm around me, his face close to mine.

"It's okay," he whispered. "You got this, you're okay."

"I'm fine," I said. I sniffed and pulled back, wiping my cheeks angrily. "I'm not crying."

Derek raised an eyebrow, but Angela nudged him before he could say anything. It was just in time, too, because that was the moment my dad stormed through the doors to the hall.

He paused like I had, glancing around. His eyes fell on me sitting with Angela and Derek, Derek's arm still around my shoulders and tears still stinging the corners of my eyes. A cloud passed over Dad's face before he straightened his shoulders and marched to the microphone set up near the head table.

"Oh no," I whispered.

The three of us watched him pick up the mic, Derek's arm resting against me protectively as Angela took my hand. Dad tapped it, a dull thud that grated deep in my chest, then glared at the DJ and flapped one hand at him in an indication to turn the music down. As the music cut out, the guests turned to my dad with expressions that ranged from confusion to annoyance at what they must have assumed was yet another speech.

"Thank you for coming tonight, everyone," he said once the hall was quiet. "Due to an... *unfortunate* incident, the wedding will be ending early."

"What?" My mom's voice was loud and bewildered, carrying over the sudden hiss of shocked whispers. "How early?"

"Now," Dad said. "Isaac and Chelsea send their apologies and—"

"What 'unfortunate' incident?" called one of the other guests. One of Isaac's cousins, I thought.

"Yeah, like… did someone get hurt?" asked someone else.

"Oh my God, is someone dead?" gasped a bridesmaid.

Chattering filled the hall, the restless disquiet of worry.

"It's nothing like that, nothing at all like that." Dad's face was turning red and he cleared his throat. "At this time, we won't be commenting further on—"

"It's probably 'cause the bride's a whore and was fucking someone else in the parking lot."

I don't think anyone ever figured out who said it. It wasn't me or Derek or Angela. It wasn't my dad, obviously. I didn't see Isaac or Mateo, and it clearly wasn't Chelsea.

It didn't matter, though: the damage was done. Mom shrieked, a hand flying to her mouth as she looked up at my dad, horrified. Angela cringed and shook her head. Shocked murmurs and aghast grumbles swarmed about the hall. I glanced around, watching faces go pale as the scandal shook through the families and friends gathered to celebrate a marriage that lasted less than half a day.

Derek's arm jostled against me and I glanced at him. He was covering his mouth with his hand, his eyes sparkling as he tried to hold in another inappropriate laugh. The sight of his face turning pink set off something inside me. I chewed the inside of my cheek, holding back a giggle of my own.

"Are you sure?" someone asked loudly.

Derek snorted. That was all it took to set me off, which was all it took to set him off.

I knew people were staring. I could feel their eyes on me, knew that every single person in the room was flabbergasted and stunned as the two of us tried to muffle our laughter. Tears threatened to spill down my cheeks again until I glanced up. Even from across the room, I could see the heat in my dad's eyes, the anger and frustration and hot, stinking shame flashing across his face.

I sniffed, a final chortle escaping before I cleared my throat.

"Sorry," I muttered.

Dad put the mic down, turned to the DJ and told him to pack his shit up, then stormed towards my mom.

There was a flurry of activity underscored by whispers, rumours, little breaths of stories that started to spread as those who had been witness returned to the hall. Angela got up to speak with Isaac's side of the family, leaving me sitting still as a stone at the table with Derek, tuning into the various conversations sparking around us.

"...fucking him in the *parking lot*..."

"...her sister's boyfriend?"

"...heard Isaac nearly killed him..."

"...and she *punched* Chelsea, right in the tit..."

"...bullshit, she didn't punch her, I was there..."

"...did slap her though..."

I tried not to make eye contact with anyone as I listened to the rumours fly. I pretended not to notice the pathetic, pitying glances out of the corners of eyes, ignored the persistent hisses of "Poor *Jocelyn*, first Isaac and now Lawrence, doesn't that just tell you everything you need to know about Chelsea, I mean, to do that to her *sister*, twice!"

Yeah, it certainly told everyone what they needed to know about Chelsea, except the fact that she hadn't just done it twice.

CHAPTER FOUR

THEN

"Shit," Isaac swore as I pulled up in front of his house.

"What?" I asked unnecessarily.

In the driveway was a really nice motorcycle. I wasn't especially knowledgeable about motorcycles, but Bretta was obsessed with them and I'd learned a bit here and there. The one in the driveway was the type I knew Bretta favoured, somewhat vintage-looking and well-maintained by the tall man standing beside it, a helmet on his hip as he looked towards my car.

Beside him stood a woman with long blonde hair and a bright, familiar smile. She waved excitedly and Isaac groaned.

"How weird would it be to meet my parents right now?" he asked.

I still lived with my parents and I knew he lived with his mom, but we hadn't discussed meeting each other's families yet.

"I mean, we've been dating for what, three weeks?" I said.

He groaned again.

"It would be weirder if I just dropped you off without saying hello now that they've seen me," I pointed out.

"I know," he sighed. "Okay, quick crash course. My mom's name is Angela, my dad's is Derek. He left my mom a few years ago and, for some reason, they're still like best friends. Mom'll question you until she's pried every last bit of information from you. Dad'll make fun of me for knowing less about cars than you do, and please give me another chance before you run away screaming from my weird family."

"I won't run from yours if you don't run from mine," I said.

Isaac snorted and shrugged. "Let's do this, then."

The moment I opened the driver's side door, there was a loud, excited squeal. Isaac grimaced.

"Hey, Mom," he said. "If we could act, you know, normal…"

She ignored him and raced down the driveway, grinning as she extended her hand.

"You must be Jocelyn," she said.

"Nice to meet you, Ms. Thompson," I said.

She dropped her hand and put both on her hips. "Nope, that won't do," she said sternly. "It's Angela, dear."

My face must have turned red because she started laughing and yanked me in for a hug.

"I'm joking, I'm joking," she giggled. "Not about calling me Angela, of course, but you don't need to look so terrified. I'm so happy to finally meet you. All Isaac talks about these days is 'Jocelyn this' and 'Jocelyn that', and I just had to see this woman for myself!"

Rather than feeling overwhelmed, I found her enthusiasm touching. As she released me from the hug, I smiled. "It's nice to meet you, Angela. I'm both Jocelyn This and Jocelyn That."

She howled and lightly slapped my arm. "A funny one, Isaac! I like her already."

Isaac was trying to hide his smile, but he couldn't hide the pleased glint in his eyes. "I do too, Mom."

She put an arm around my shoulder. "This is Isaac's dad, Derek."

My first thought was that aside from the tattoos and the casual jeans-and-T-shirt combo he was wearing, he looked a lot like Isaac. My second was that if I was seeing a glimpse of Isaac's future, *damn* was

I lucky. My third, and the one I had the most control over, was that I understood why Isaac seemed bitter about his dad leaving his mom.

Angela was pretty. I never understood the fascination women had with appearing younger than they were, and Angela didn't seem to, either. She looked her age, and she looked gorgeous, her cheerfulness lending a natural aura to her beauty.

Derek, on the other hand, was hot. There was no way to talk around it; Angela exuded a sweet loveliness, and Derek exuded sex appeal in a way that was completely inappropriate for me to think about.

"Nice to meet you," I said, shaking Derek's hand.

"And you," he said pleasantly.

"Is that a Thruxton 900?"

Derek turned to Isaac, his eyes sparkling. "Keep her around, kid," he said, pointing a finger at him, then turned back to me. "You know your shit?"

I laughed. "A little. My boss is obsessed with motorcycles, so I've picked up a bit here and there. I still like cars better, though."

"A little is better than nothing," Angela said. "He just got this one and while I'm thrilled to listen to... whatever it was you were saying, Derek, you should tell Jocelyn about it, since she'll probably understand more."

Before I knew it, I'd been standing in the driveway with Derek, Angela, and Isaac for nearly forty-five minutes. Derek was like a kid at Christmas, pointing out all the features of his new bike and overjoyed that I understood what he was talking about.

"Well, if you ever want to take it for a spin..." he said.

I shook my head. "I don't have a motorcycle license, and besides, you've got... what, a foot of height on me? My toes wouldn't even reach the ground."

"Why don't you drive and take her with you?" suggested Angela.

I glanced at Isaac. He smiled, though it didn't quite reach his eyes.

"That's a great idea," he said, clearly not meaning it.

"Maybe some other time," I said. "I have to get back home pretty soon."

I don't know if Angela just missed the silent cues from Isaac or if she was just that excited to meet me, but she scoffed. "You'll love it. Derek, take her around quick! Jocelyn, you can borrow my helmet."

As much as I liked Isaac, I wasn't about to turn Derek down. Part of it was that I was trying to make a good impression on his parents, but the other part of it was that I really wanted to go for a ride. When Isaac didn't protest, I shrugged and nodded.

Just a few minutes later, I was climbing on the back of the Thruxton and Derek was seated in front of me.

"There are grip handles, but you're probably gonna be more comfortable if you hold on to me," he said.

"Probably," I said. "I usually hold on to Bretta when she's driving."

"Good." Derek smirked. "You're so small you'd float away on the breeze if you flew off."

My laughter was drowned out as he started the bike. I might have been short, but I didn't think I was especially dainty. Wrapping my arms around Derek's waist, I held on as he pulled out of the driveway.

If it had been inappropriate for me to think about how hot Isaac's dad was before, the ride on his bike made it even worse. When I rode behind Bretta, she often teased about how her bike was just a fancy vibrator, and I would laugh and tell her to cool down or I'd have to have words with her girlfriend. She would joke that Leigh would be into it and maybe she should just drive me back to their place to find out. I wasn't into women, but I couldn't deny that there was something kind of enticing about being on a motorcycle with my arms around someone else.

When that someone else was Derek, who was really attractive and definitely not a woman, it got... well, complicated.

The ride wasn't long. He drove down the block and onto the main road, zipping through traffic as the wind raced past us. The bike purred beneath me, and we hit a couple of bumps that jostled me against Derek's back. I bit my lip, telling myself to stop enjoying the feel of his body against mine so much.

This is your boyfriend's father, I told myself furiously.

Derek pulled into the parking lot of a nearby park, slowing down to a stop. I let go of him, thankful for the break so I could collect myself, and he turned in the seat.

"Doing okay?" Behind the visor of his helmet, hazel eyes were sparkling at me.

I grinned. "Yeah, it's great! Runs smooth."

Derek grinned and flipped the visor up. "I gotta ask," he said. "Your tattoo. What does it say?"

"It's... wait, did you just ask what it says?" I repeated.

"Yeah," he said. "I can tell it's Gallifreyan, but I can't read it."

"You nerd!" I laughed, delighted.

"I'm the nerd?" Derek feigned offense. "You literally have a Doctor Who tattoo."

"I didn't say I wasn't a nerd." I held my forearm out so he could look at it more closely. "It's one of the best pieces of advice from the show."

"New series or the old ones?"

"New."

Derek thought for a moment. "Is it that one about being the optimist and dreamer of impossible dreams?"

I snorted. "Nah, that's far too positive."

He chuckled, taking my arm into his hand and studying the tattooed circles. "Hmm... we're all just stories in the end?"

I shook my head. "A bit more light-hearted."

"Always take a banana to a party?"

"Yep."

Derek laughed, then looked up at me. "You're not serious."

"Seriously. 'Always take a banana to a party.'" I pointed at the last circle on my arm. "This one says 'bananas are good'."

He was laughing so hard that I thought he might fall off the bike.

"You'll have to show Samantha that when you meet her," he said. "Isaac's sister. She got me into the damn show. She'll love that."

Derek let go of my arm and went to put his visor back in place. He stopped, looking over his shoulder at me.

"Gotta say, Jocelyn," he said. "Ange said you and Isaac have only been dating a couple weeks, but I hope you two stick together. You're good for him."

By the time we got back to the house, my blush had faded, but I hadn't stopped smiling. After hopping off the bike, removing Angela's helmet, and ruffling my short hair, I looked at Isaac.

"Have fun?" His voice didn't betray his nerves, but his eyes did.

"Had a blast. Apparently, your sister and I are gonna get along, too."

Isaac relaxed somewhat, though he didn't ask for clarification. Instead, he put an arm around my shoulder.

"Well, thanks for the ride," I said to Derek, then turned to Angela. "I should get home. It was wonderful to meet you both."

"It was great to meet you, dear." Angela was beaming. "Derek, give me a hand in the house for a sec."

"Oh, I was gonna take off. It looks like it'll start raining... oh." It took him a moment, but he got the hint. "It was nice to meet you, Joss."

Isaac and I watched as they walked into the house, silent until we heard the front door close. Once it had, he let go of my shoulder and turned to me.

"I'm so sorry," he said. "I had no idea they'd be home, and I know my dad gets intense about his motorcycles and Mom is overenthusiastic about everything. I hope you don't think we have to, like, rush into anything or like you feel pressured because you met them. I know, it's super weird, three weeks is, like, hardly any time but—"

He was still talking as I reached up and pulled his face to mine, only stopping when our lips pressed together.

"It's all good," I said when he'd gone silent and we parted. "Really, Isaac. Your mom is super sweet and your dad is pretty cool."

He scoffed. "He's all right."

I didn't respond to the obvious tension between Isaac and his dad, instead choosing to kiss him again and promising to text when I got home.

Over the next few months, I got to know Angela and Derek fairly well. Once the initial meeting had happened, it felt like there was a lot less pressure. With both of us still living at home, it gave me and Isaac somewhere to hang out that wasn't a coffee shop or a park or the movies. We both had plans to move out within the next year, once we'd each saved up a bit more money, but in the meantime, it was nice to just be able to hang out.

It didn't hurt that Isaac's room was in the basement, that Angela worked evenings a few days a week, and that Samantha was often out with her friends. As awkward as it was, it got even better after Angela sat down with us before going to work one night, said she knew we were both adults and to just be safe and keep it down, and if I was still there in the morning, did I want cereal or toast for breakfast?

"I'm so sorry," Isaac said after she left, his face still pink. "That was so awkward."

I laughed, shaking my head. "Better to be upfront and honest, I guess."

He was still cringing, though not enough to stop him from taking my hand and leading me down to his bedroom. By the time he'd slid my panties off and had pulled me into his lap, kissing me as I sank down on top of him, I was pretty sure he'd forgotten all about it.

That should have been it for awkward conversations, but after we finished and were lying in each other's arms, blissfully sweaty and breathless, he brought up the one thing I had been dreading.

"So, you've met my family," he started, his fingers dancing along my arm.

The tension that rushed through me was so sudden and thorough, Isaac stopped moving.

"Jocelyn?"

"I know," I muttered.

He shifted, moving down on the bed so he could look at me. "Is it something... like, is there something I've done that you don't feel comfortable—"

"No!" I interrupted. "It's not you, Isaac. I just... my family is weird."

He snorted. "Yeah, so is mine."

"Your family isn't that weird. Even if they were, it would be eccentric at best. Mine is... I'm a different person around my family."

He brushed his fingers against my cheek, running them through my hair. His hair was almost longer than mine, I realized.

"Why?" he asked.

"I just don't fit in with them all that well. My mom is fine, she just is... I love her to pieces, she just... she's the queen of guilt trips. My dad is... well, he's just not that... we're not close. And Chelsea..."

I trailed off, trying to think of how I could describe my sister. Isaac waited patiently, still playing with my hair.

"She doesn't like me that much," I said. "We used to be like best friends growing up. She was only a grade ahead of me in school, so we, you know, did a lot of stuff together. That all changed, though."

"I'd still like to meet them. I care about you a lot, Joss."

It was delaying the inevitable. I cared for Isaac, too. It was still too early to call it anything other than caring, but I cared enough that I could see it moving further than that.

"Let me think about," I said. "Please?"

"Okay," he said. "I'll drop it for now."

His hand had moved away from my hair, fingers starting to trail down the side of my face to my neck. I knew exactly why he was willing to drop it and confirmed it when his hand slipped beneath the sheets and cupped my breast.

"Stay the night?" he asked as he kissed me.

We hooked up again, then fell asleep watching Netflix. When I woke up the next morning, Isaac was lying on his back, practically dead to the world. I tried curling up beside him and falling back to sleep, but he didn't seem to like that and rolled away from me.

Still, I stayed in bed with him for a while longer, listening to the rain outside and thinking. Isaac wanted to meet my family. If I had any other family, I would have probably been excited about that. He was serious enough about me to want to meet my parents. Wasn't that the goal? And if they were weird, well, so what? He thought his family was weird and I still liked them. Angela treated me as if I was already part of their family, and Derek would sit and talk cars or sports or Doctor Who with me until everyone else was sick of hearing about it. Samantha and I got along, too, to the point that she'd asked if I would go with her to a concert in a couple of months.

The big difference was that Isaac liked his family, and his family liked him.

I should have been excited he wanted to meet my family, but all it did was make my stomach curl with dread. Wincing, I watched Isaac sleep for a while longer, wondering if he'd understand if I said no, if I explained to him why he couldn't meet my parents, and especially why he couldn't meet my sister.

After a bit, I realized the stomach pain wasn't going away, probably because I was hungry. I was considering leaving a note telling Isaac I just couldn't wait any longer and had gone out to get breakfast when footsteps started thudding above my head.

Was it weird for me to consider going upstairs and having breakfast with Angela while Isaac slept? Probably.

Was I too hungry to care? Yes.

Quietly, I slipped out of Isaac's bed and got dressed, flattening my hair before heading upstairs. A greeting was on my lips as I rounded the corner to the kitchen, seconds away from being spoken, and only disappearing when I realized it wasn't Angela walking around the kitchen.

It was Derek.

"Oh!" he said, surprise drawn across his face as he paused with a coffee pot just over a mug. "Jocelyn. Uh, good morning."

"Morning," I said, staring at him dumbly.

"Do you stay the night often?" he asked.

"Do you?" I shot back.

Instead of being offended, he burst out laughing. "No, and I didn't last night, either." He tilted his head at the patio door. "Ange asked me to build her a couple of new planters for the balcony. I was dropping them off before heading out on deliveries."

"What are you delivering?"

"Furniture, mostly. Saturdays are pretty busy for that kind of thing." He grinned as he finished pouring his coffee. "Ange's done a lot of great stuff for me but forcing me to start my business is definitely high up on the list. Coffee?"

"Please," I said. "I don't think I know what you actually do."

"Woodworking and furniture restoration," he said. "Once in a while I'll build a deck or something, but that's usually just for people I know. Cream or sugar?"

"Nope," I said, and he slid a mug of coffee over to me. "That's pretty cool. When did you start your business?"

"Hmm. I started it about a year after we separated, so not quite ten years now," he said. "Wasn't intending to, but Angela said she'd listened to me bitch about working construction for seventeen years and I should give it a go."

It must have been obvious that I was trying to do the math in my head because Derek laughed.

"Isaac was born a year before we got married. I started with a road crew while Ange was pregnant since there weren't a hell of a lot of good-paying jobs for a dumb eighteen-year-old who'd knocked up his girlfriend." He tilted his coffee cup towards me. "Not that I'd trade either of my kids for anything, of course, but we were too damn young and stupid to be parents."

"I didn't know that," I said.

Derek shrugged. "Like I said, wouldn't trade it for anything."

"Why'd you leave her?" I asked.

He raised his eyebrows and I grimaced.

"Sorry," I said. "That was..."

"Blunt?"

"Sure."

He smiled and shook his head. "It's okay. Ange and I were together for a long time, but we got together young. We just... we were both different people back then. I know we'll both love each other for the rest of our lives, but not the way we needed to for us to stay together."

I nodded, sipping my coffee. It wasn't really an answer, but he didn't owe me an answer. Either way, he didn't give me a chance to ask anything further.

"Back to my original question," Derek said.

I groaned and he started laughing.

"Would you believe me if I said it's the first time I've stayed over?" I asked.

"Anyone else, I'd say they were a damn liar," he replied. "You, though? Yeah, I believe that."

I shrugged and took another sip of coffee.

"Things are getting serious for you two, then?" he asked.

"I guess," I said. "Isaac wants to meet my family so... so yeah, I guess they are."

"You don't seem enthused."

"I'm not."

"Gonna elaborate?"

I smiled into my cup. "Isaac warned me a million times about how weird his family is. Once he meets mine, I think he'll have a greater appreciation for how nice you all are."

Derek chuckled. "Well, he's got a point. We are a little weird."

"Yeah, but nice."

"I'm sure your family is great." He tilted his cup towards me again. "Isaac's a good kid, Joss. Even if there're issues with your family, he's going to be understanding. If things are getting serious, he's not going to let a little thing like a weird family get between you two."

Long after Derek had left and the rain had turned to sunshine, I thought about what he said. I thought about it while Angela insisted on making a full breakfast of bacon, eggs, and toast, even though I said cereal was just fine. I thought about it after kissing Isaac goodbye and leaving, thought about it the whole time I drove home, and thought about it as I sat in my room until my mom called me down for dinner.

After sitting down, I sighed and brought it up.

"Can I bring someone by for dinner tomorrow?" I asked.

Mom's eyes shot up from her plate, an excited grin on her face. Dad glanced at her out of the corner of his eye, his face stony.

"Who?" she asked.

"My... boyfriend. Isaac."

Mom was practically vibrating with anticipation when she said yes and insisted on planning an entire Sunday night dinner. Chelsea raised her eyebrows, Dad nodded curtly, and afterwards, I texted Isaac to tell him we were having roast chicken the next night. After he responded, his excitement almost as palpable as my mom's had been, I put my phone on the nightstand and flopped back onto the pillow, certain I'd just put the beginning of the end into motion.

CHAPTER FIVE

NOW

ANGELA WAS TALKING TO who I thought was Isaac's uncle but might
have just been a family friend. From across the hall, I could see the anger
on his face, something caught between aggravation and rage, not quite
fury, but far deeper than annoyance. Each member of Isaac's family wore
a similar expression until Angela spoke to them, calming only as she
talked, then shaking their heads before leaving.

They were all offended on his behalf, all unquestionably supportive
and indignant. Aunts, uncles, cousins, friends: had Isaac been there,
he could have turned in any direction and found someone willing to
support him.

I wondered vaguely what that kind of unconditional love was like.

My mom was sobbing at a table and had been since some kind soul had
shouted that Chelsea was a whore. No amount of attention from Aunt
Sharon seemed to placate her. Dad had checked on her before deciding
the vitriol from the other wedding guests was preferable to handling his
wife's breakdown, so he was mirroring Angela's discussions with her
family.

The juxtaposition was kind of funny. Isaac's family was angry; our
family was plastic. Their expressions were practiced, drawn across their
faces to seem sympathetic but detached, already looking to distance

themselves from the scandal. Occasionally, someone would glance in my direction, pitying half-smiles on their faces.

When I couldn't take it anymore, I drank the rest of my glass of wine in one gulp and stood up.

"Where are you going?" Derek asked.

"Clean up." I motioned around the hall, which was slowly emptying out. "Might as well do it now so I don't have to come back tomorrow."

"Good idea." He rose as well. "I'll go get the storage totes."

I was too tired to protest, instead shrugging. Derek clapped a hand on my shoulder, then turned and headed out of the hall.

The banquet staff had already begun clearing dishes and glasses, but the decorations were the wedding party's responsibility. I had no idea where the wedding planner was—if she was smart, she'd high-tailed it out of there the second she heard what happened—but it didn't matter. The other bridesmaids and I were supposed to come back the next day to help clean up. It was tradition, apparently. I didn't know why the groomsmen couldn't pitch in and help, but in the interest of keeping the peace, I hadn't brought it up at the time.

There were eyes on me as I walked towards the head table. I could feel them, the strange, crawling tickle of awareness creeping up my neck. Ignoring it, I started removing the garland of flowers and ribbons that hung across the front of the table and coiled it on the ground. I had just begun blowing out the candles on the centrepieces when Dad stormed up to me.

"What do you think you're doing?" he hissed.

"Cleaning up," I said.

"Cleaning up," he repeated. "Right now. Really?"

Someone braver than me might have had a response, but my hands had started sweating and my mouth was dry.

"You can't wait until people at least leave?" Dad continued. "You have to cause more embarrassment in front of our friends and family?"

"Me cleaning up is embarrassing?" I asked.

"Of course it is!" he snapped. "Do you have to rub your sister's face in it? And yelling out that she's a... what she did, in front of everyone?"

"I didn't yell anything!" I said. "You can ask anyone. I was just sitting there."

"I'm supposed to believe that? I'm ashamed of how disrespectful you're being. You slapped her, called her names in front of everyone, then you're *laughing* in front of everyone about it. Now you're tearing down decorations while people are still—"

"That's a pretty surprising thing to be ashamed of, considering your other daughter got caught fucking someone else on her wedding day."

Derek strolled up casually, placing the storage totes on the ground beside me before straightening up and glaring at my dad.

"With all due respect, it's none of your business," Dad said through clenched teeth.

"With all due respect, your daughter cheated on my son." Derek folded his arms, raising an eyebrow at him. "I think that makes it my business, actually."

Dad didn't respond. His entire face was red, though whether that was anger or embarrassment, I didn't know. There was a strange hush around the hall, the few lingering groups of people falling silent as they watched the two of them glare at each other.

I chewed the inside of my cheek, glancing between them. Dad was an accountant. He fought his battles with words and actions, not with weapons.

Derek, on the other hand... well, he didn't seem like an aggressive kind of guy, but he didn't look like he was afraid to get his hands dirty. Though I knew him to be friendly and kind, the tattoo that peeked out above the collar of his suit made him look far rougher than he was. It didn't hurt that he was a few years younger and had a good few inches on my dad, not to mention that he was in far better shape.

I kept telling myself I didn't want them to fight. I refused to admit that I wanted to see Derek kick the shit out of him, not even to myself.

Just when the testosterone-fuelled tension was getting so strong it felt like it was going to boil over, Dad shook his head.

"That has nothing to do with this," he said.

Derek snorted. "Are you serious? Out of everyone here, Jocelyn is the victim. Yeah, even more than my kid. You know why?"

"I—"

"Her sister. Her boyfriend. Her ex-boyfriend." Derek counted off each thing on his fingers. "How can you argue that anything she's doing is worth being ashamed of? What kind of father are you?"

"That's uncalled for," Dad spat. "How dare you?"

Derek glared at him. "How dare you speak to your daughter that way?"

"You have no idea what you're talking about."

"Neither do you, apparently."

"Gerald, stop."

Derek, Dad, and I all turned our heads as Mom spoke up. I hadn't even seen her start towards us, but suddenly she was standing there with puffy red eyes, tears going from shiny to matte as they dried on her cheeks.

"She's just trying to help clean up," she whispered. "Let's just end this horrible day."

Dad glanced at Derek, then at me.

"We're leaving," he declared.

"Well, let's wait for Jocelyn to—"

"We're leaving," he said, and Mom fell silent. "You want to stay and clean so bad, stay and clean. Find your own way back to the hotel. Or don't."

He was halfway across the hall before Mom seemed to process what he said.

"Joss, I—"

"Just go," I said. "I'll take an Uber."

"Ange and I can drive you back," Derek said.

I wanted him to put his hand around my shoulder again, but he didn't. It was for the best; if he had, I would have very likely burst into tears, and I'd already broken my "no-crying-in-public" rule enough that day.

"Thank you, Derek," Mom said. "Joss, I'm sorry."

"Bye, Mom."

I watched her hurry off after Dad, very aware of the eyes that darted away from me as I looked across the hall. Once she was gone, I turned back to the head table, silently collecting the centrepieces.

Derek didn't say anything until we had packed up almost the entire table. By then, there were just a few stragglers left in the hall, people who were gleefully taking in every moment of melodramatic bullshit before they went back to their homes or hotel rooms to wallow in it. I put the last of the centrepieces into one of the storage totes and pushed the lid down.

It snapped closed, but before I could straighten back up, popped open again.

Sighing, I took the lid off, shoved the centrepieces down, and tried again. That time, the lid wouldn't even latch. Frustrated, I rearranged the contents again, then shoved the lid back on the tote.

I was about to give up when Derek reached down and pushed the lid on hard enough for me to latch it. Carefully, we both straightened up, eyeing the container suspiciously until we were certain it wasn't going to burst open again.

"It seemed bigger on the inside," I said.

Derek smirked but didn't laugh. I wasn't sure what else to say, so I turned to the stack of nested storage totes to grab another one for the fairy lights that were strung behind the table.

"Jocelyn, I'm sorry."

The words were so quiet I didn't register them at first.

Frowning, I turned back to Derek. "For what?"

His face was solemn, uncharacteristically serious. I was used to seeing Derek grinning or laughing, even at the worst possible times. He had a habit of laughing when he shouldn't, kind of like I did. Seeing him with that look on his face was one of the hardest parts of the day.

"I overstepped there," he said. "With your dad."

The corner of my lip twitched, a strange emotion bubbling in my chest.

"Don't be," I said. "Thanks for standing up for me."

"You don't deserve to be talked to like that."

The emotion stopped bubbling, instead catching as a lump in my throat that threatened to swell into tears. I tried to cough it away, instead making a weird, choked sound that might have been a laugh.

"I don't think anyone's ever defended me to my dad," I admitted. "Chelsea's the princess. I'm... well. He doesn't like me."

Derek's jaw was clenched and he struggled to hide his disbelief.

"That's not right," he said.

I shrugged. "It is what it is. He's still my dad. Family is family, right?"

"Yeah, but—"

"I told you my family was weird, remember? Back... that day, when Isaac and I were still... before he met them."

"I don't think 'weird' is the right word," Derek said. "Weird is being friends with your ex-wife or your kid's mom offering to make breakfast for his girlfriend the morning after. Your dad... that was just cruel."

"He's still my dad," I repeated.

"You shouldn't have to put up with that shit."

I made that weird, barking laugh again. "Dude, what you just saw was him being nice."

"Nice? That was..." He trailed off, then frowned. "Wait. Dude? Did you just call me dude?"

I snorted. Derek scoffed, and moments later, the lingering groups of people in the hall turned to us as we dissolved into another fit of laughter.

CHAPTER SIX

THEN

IF THERE'S A SOUND that is more uncomfortable than silence broken only by the scraping of cutlery on plates, I don't think I want to know what it is.

Six of us sat around the dinner table. It was supposed to be five, but Chelsea's boyfriend Brad, who no one had heard of prior to that day, had shown up just as I was introducing Isaac. Of course, as soon as Chelsea's boyfriend was there, that was where the attention went.

"Sorry," I muttered to Isaac as we trailed everyone to the dining room. "I told you this was a bad idea."

He squeezed my hand. "It's okay. It's going fine."

He was such a fucking liar. On the bright side, Dad didn't seem to like Brad any more than he liked Isaac at first.

"What do you do for a living, Brad?" he asked as Mom passed mashed potatoes around the table.

"I work at a liquor store," Brad said.

"Ah. Are you a student?"

"Nah, but my boss said he might make me full-time over the summer."

Dad raised his eyebrows. Chelsea smiled sweetly at him.

"He'll be running the place in no time," she said.

Dad snorted and ate a bite of chicken.

"What about you, Isaac?" Mom asked politely.

"I'm an accountant," Isaac said. "I work for—"

"Do you have your CPA?" Dad interrupted.

Isaac shook his head. "Still need a few more months of practical experience. I should have it by summer, hopefully."

"Hmmph," Dad said, but it was a less derisive snort than usual.

Cutlery scraped against the plates for a few minutes before anyone spoke again.

"Gerald is an accountant, too," Mom said.

Isaac glanced at me. "I didn't know that."

"You didn't tell your boyfriend he has the same career as Dad?" Chelsea asked.

"It must have slipped my mind," I mumbled.

Chelsea rolled her eyes. "Sorry, Isaac. That was rude of her."

I chewed on the inside of my cheek as my face turned red. Isaac was looking at me, but I didn't turn my head to meet his eye. He was waiting for me to defend myself, not realizing that I wouldn't.

"It's okay," he said. "I don't mind."

"She's forgetful," Dad said. "You'll have to keep that in mind."

I looked up sharply, as did Chelsea. Isaac just looked confused, but my sister and I could read a lot further into our father's words than he could. "You'll have to keep that in mind" meant he thought Isaac and I would be together for a while. Assuming Isaac and I would stay together meant he...

"You approve, then?" I blurted.

Dad raised an eyebrow at me and I felt my face turn red. He opened his mouth, but Mom spoke before he could say anything.

"Well, you seem very nice, Isaac," she said. "And you too, Brad. Jocelyn, you didn't mention how you and Isaac met."

Isaac laughed. "Well, it's a good thing she's the best mechanic in the city, because I am hopeless with cars."

I tried to laugh along with him. "He, um, came into the shop to have his brakes done."

"Well, that's nice," said Mom.

"That's not all of it, though," Isaac said, looking at me. "I chickened on asking for her number or anything, so a few days later I brought the car in again because it was making a funny noise."

"I see where this is going," Mom said, smiling.

I managed a small smile that time. "I told him I could either check out the car, or he could save his money and take me out to dinner."

"Aww," Chelsea squealed. "That's so sweet."

"My dad said if there's one good thing about me being clueless about cars, it's that I met Jocelyn." Isaac took my hand beneath the table, squeezing it.

I nodded, tried to smile, and hoped he didn't notice how clammy my hand was. The awkward silence fell over the table again. Isaac cleared his throat and let go of my hand.

"Uh, what about you and Brad?" he asked Chelsea.

"Oh, it was *incredibly* sweet," Chelsea said.

She nattered on about how they'd met for a bit, and then Mom made the mistake of asking Brad to tell us more about his job and he droned on about that for the rest of the meal. When we finished eating, I reached over to take Isaac's plate, but he picked it up himself.

"Let me help," he said.

"That's so nice of you!" Mom kept grinning as the two of us cleared the table, Isaac following me to the kitchen.

"Joss," he whispered when we got there. "What's going on with you?"

"What do you mean?" I asked.

He motioned to the dining room. "You're like a completely different person. You hardly talked at all!"

There were a million things I wanted to say at that moment. I wanted to grab his shoulders and scream that I'd told him it was a bad idea, that

I'd told him I was different around my family. I wanted to cry and tell him that yes, my dad always acted like that, that's just how he was and I'd learned to deal with it. That he'd said Isaac would have to keep in mind that I was forgetful and that was the closest he'd ever come to approving of someone or something in my life. That Chelsea had that look in her eye, that look that said she remembered what I'd done and wasn't going to forgive me and that meant something bad was going to happen.

"Can we talk later?" I whispered. "I just can't do this right now."

Instead of responding, Isaac pulled me to him, wrapping his arms around me. I closed my eyes, pressing my forehead against his chest, inhaling the scent of his cologne and trying to steady myself.

Chelsea had always been the pretty one.

She'd been Daddy's little girl, the perfect princess, a smart and beautiful overachiever who could do no wrong in his eyes. The older sibling, always top of her class, always the best at everything she did. She could murder someone in cold blood and Dad would have turned a blind eye to it.

I was the one that he had hoped would be a boy and when I wasn't, he seemed to lose interest.

That was probably part of the reason I'd grown up such a tomboy. Maybe it was just instinct from a young age. Dad wanted a son; he wanted a boy that would play sports and roughhouse and eventually follow in his footsteps and take over his accounting firm.

Well, I tried. I played sports and refused to let my mom put me in dresses. I screamed across the yard of our house and dug up the garden looking for pirate's treasure. I played with bugs and critters and tormented my perfect older sister by messing up her pristine dolls. As a teenager, I kept my hair short and dressed in baggy T-shirts.

It was never good enough. No matter what I did, Dad never looked at me the way he looked at Chelsea.

He always introduced us to people the same way: "This is my beautiful daughter Chelsea. She's the valedictorian of her class!" or "She's about to become a dental hygienist!"

And then me: "This is my other daughter, Jocelyn."

That was it. Just his other daughter. He never told people I played lacrosse and almost qualified for nationals one year. I mean, I didn't qualify. But I *almost* did, and doesn't that count for anything?

And he never told people I was a really good mechanic. Or that my boss made me her second in command. Or that I'd been interviewed for a cool article profiling our shop because we'd gotten a reputation for being reliable and trustworthy, particularly for female clients who felt they got talked down to at other shops.

I still tried, though. It was stupid, I knew that. There was no justification for putting up with my dad, other than the inherent need to get his approval. Everywhere else in my life, I was successful. I was a hell of a good mechanic. I had good friends. I knew I came across as blunt sometimes and while some people might call me gullible, I preferred to think of it as being trusting and seeing the good in people.

I just wanted nothing more than for my dad to see that, too.

Mom said he did. She'd told me a million times that he was proud of me and loved me just as much as he loved Chelsea, and that they just had a different relationship than he and I did.

I didn't believe that, and I think Mom knew that coming from her, it didn't mean much. Still, she tried, and I loved her for it. If it weren't for my mom, I would have walked out the door one day and never looked back. Doing that would have killed her, though. All she wanted in life was for her family to get along.

Mom said Dad and Chelsea were cut from the same cloth, and she and I were sliced from the same loaf. They were both tall, willowy, and slender. Mom and I could have made up the Little Teapot: she was short, and I was short and stout. It came with the territory for me: sports needed strength, and I worked a physical job. Being as short as I was, I felt like I was built more like an armchair than anything else. Chelsea was the pretty one with the perfect smile and beautiful, long hair. I was the one with the round face, the short hair, and the crooked tooth in the front.

I tried to explain all that to Isaac after the awkward, frustrating dinner, but he could only understand so much.

"I get it," he said. "I mean, I have issues with my dad, too."

When I said that his issues with Derek weren't like the ones I had with my dad, we had our first-ever fight.

I tried to explain it again when Isaac asked if we could hang out at my place once in a while, and again after he came over to watch a movie a few weeks later.

I don't remember what movie it was, probably because we were only about a third of the way through when Chelsea burst into the basement with tears streaming down her face.

"What's wrong?" Isaac asked, alarmed.

"Oh my God," Chelsea sniffed. "I didn't realize you were both in here. I'll go."

"No, it's okay." He paused the movie. "What's going on? What happened?"

She stammered an explanation, punctuating her words with dry sobs. Brad broke up with her, she said. Brad, the boyfriend no one had heard of until a few weeks earlier and hadn't seen since.

"I'm so sorry," Isaac said as I sat on the couch. He nudged me. "We're both sorry, right, Joss?"

"Yeah," I said.

Chelsea sniffed and looked at me, her eyes shining. "Thanks, sis. I didn't mean to barge in on your movie night."

She hugged Isaac before going to her room, wet-sounding sniffles fading away as she walked down the hallway.

"Jocelyn, what the hell?" Isaac asked, turning to me after we heard her door shut.

"What?" I asked.

"That was…" He trailed off, shaking his head. "Okay, you don't get along with your sister. I get that, but that was pretty cold."

He didn't think my explanation made any sense, and that was the day I knew I'd been right. It was the beginning of the end.

Two weeks later, it was the end of the end. My parents were out one night, Chelsea was partying with her friends, and Isaac had asked to come over.

One of the things I had liked about Isaac initially was how expressive his face was. It was that expressive face that told me why he was there the moment I opened the door. Still, I smiled, motioned towards the living room, and asked if he wanted something to drink.

"No, thanks. We need to talk," he started.

"Okay."

There was a brief pause.

"I don't know how to say this," he said.

"Just say it," I said sadly. "I know why you're here."

He sighed. "It's just not working for me anymore."

"Is it because you're in love with my sister?" I asked.

Isaac looked hurt by the statement. "Jocelyn. I wouldn't do that to you."

He wasn't lying. At that moment, he really believed he wouldn't do that to me. Things changed a month later when he stopped by the shop while I was at work.

"So, remember when we broke up?"

I raised my eyebrows, wiping oily hands on a towel. "Yeah?"

"And you asked if I was in love with your sister?"

"And you said you wouldn't do that to me?" I asked flatly.

Isaac shifted uncomfortably, but didn't say anything. I laughed, shaking my head, trying to ignore the feeling of my chest collapsing like a crushed can.

"Do what you gotta do," I said.

"I'm sorry," he mumbled. "Joss, I am, I didn't mean to... you know. It just kind of happened."

It didn't kind of happen. I wanted to scream that to him, to take him by the shoulders and shake him and tell him that it didn't just happen. She *made* it happen. She flirted and teased and wormed her way into his life. She made him think it "just happened" when every move she made was cold and calculated, and she only wanted him because he had been mine.

"She's going to hurt you," I said instead. "Just so you know. If you were half as smart as you think you are, you'd run from my sister."

"I know this is probably hard for you—"

I laughed again, cutting him off. "You're not hearing me. Chelsea is bad news. This isn't going to work out for you."

He took a steadying breath. "I can't choose who I love, Jocelyn. I'm sorry. I hope you can understand one day."

Love? Isaac and I were together for months and he'd never said anything about love. Now, a month after swearing he wasn't in love with my sister, he was saying he had no choice in it?

I looked at him for a long moment.

"Whatever, Isaac. Just don't rub my face in it, would you?"

He started to respond, but I didn't want to hear it. I threw my earbuds back in and went back into the shop, ignoring him as he stared after me.

CHAPTER SEVEN

NOW

"Well, I can make two trips."

We stared at the two storage totes in Derek's trunk. No matter which way they went in, there was no way we were getting all the totes in his car. We had shoved two totes in the back seat, but they were too tall to stack. Instead, we squeezed the glass vase Chelsea had used to collect cards on top of them, then piled a few oddly shaped items in the wheel well. Even though Angela's sister had offered to fill her car as well, plus take Angela home so Derek had a bit more room, there were still two more totes and a few reusable bags left inside the church.

"I think that's the only way," I agreed.

"Well, we can throw one of the totes in the front seat," Derek said. "To get these back to my place, it'll take about a half-hour round trip, if you don't mind waiting."

Given all the drama, I'd made the executive decision that the decorations would be stored in the highly specific locale of "wherever." Mom and Dad were staying at the hotel with everyone else, so we couldn't drop them off at their house. I didn't know where Chelsea was, but I didn't want to bring them to her and Isaac's apartment. Angela brought some of the decorations to her place, and Derek said he would store the rest in his garage until we figured out what to do with them.

I chewed the inside of my cheek. "I mean, if you have to come back anyway, can I just come with you? So I don't have to, you know, stay here?"

Derek hesitated. I cringed and shook my head.

"It's fine, I get it," I said.

"No, that's not—"

"Derek, it's cool," I said, laughing dryly. "You're already doing way more for me than you need to. I'll just, you know, wait inside. It'll be fine, I think pretty much everyone is gone and since we have the rental till two anyway, it's not like they're just going to kick..."

I trailed off as Derek silently moved beside me, a hand on my back guiding me to the passenger door.

"Good idea. I'll need your help to unload," he said when I went quiet.

He opened the door for me and I got in, smoothing the pale pink fabric of the dress on my lap to give my hands something to do while Derek walked around to the driver's side.

"She's still running good?" I asked as he started the car.

"Yep," Derek said. "Just like new. Should probably bring her in to get you to check out the brakes and everything, though."

"Drop by anytime. You get VIP service."

Derek raised his eyebrows. "VIP service, eh? Why's that?"

"Because you maintain your car, meaning I won't pop the hood and have to tell some indignant Karen that her engine seized because she's never changed the damn oil."

"And here I thought it was my strikingly good looks," he chuckled.

"Well, that doesn't hurt, either."

The words were out of my mouth without me even processing the thought. There was a beat, a single beat, and Derek looked at me, his face a mix of bemused curiosity.

I should have been embarrassed. I mean, it was inappropriate. Wasn't it? The panic was there, the moment of wishing I'd thought before I opened my mouth, but when my eyes met his, I shrugged.

"What?" I said. "You said it, not me."

He tilted his head for another moment, then smirked and started the car. "Just surprising. It's not every day some pretty young thing admits I'm devilishly handsome."

I snorted. "Watch yourself, Derek. My bullshit meter is pretty good."

"How many gorgeous women do you think tell me I'm the hottest stud they've ever seen?"

"I seem to be admitting to a lot more than I originally thought," I said. "And anyway, I have eyes, you know. You're laying on the 'pretty' and 'gorgeous' rather heavily to someone who looks like a burly cupcake."

"A *what* cupcake?"

"Oh, come on." I lifted the gauzy pink fabric of the skirt. "You've seen this thing. I'm pretty sure Chelsea wanted to make sure I looked like I fell into a cotton candy machine."

"Never pegged you for the type to go fishing," Derek said, glancing at me before turning out of the parking lot.

"What?"

"For compliments."

I scoffed. "I'm not fishing for compliments. This dress is hideous and I'm not exactly a sugar plum fairy to begin with."

"You know I think you look stunning," he said quietly.

I tried to chuckle, to keep the slightly-risque-but-mostly-innocent banter going, but the reluctant honesty in Derek's voice was sending things in a direction they just couldn't go.

We couldn't go there.

Could we?

Of course we couldn't, I chastised myself. I was stupid for even considering it. It had been a crazy day, an emotional day, and I was considering things I shouldn't.

Derek cleared his throat and chuckled. "Too far?"

Yes, I thought.

"No," I said. "Just... surprising. It's not every day some—what was it, devilishly handsome stud?—tells me I'm stunning."

He burst out laughing a little harder than necessary and shook his head.

"This has been a fucking weird day," he said.

"Tell me about it," I muttered.

"Well, first of all, it rained all morning, then—"

"Not literally," I laughed.

Derek smiled and we fell quiet.

"How are you doing, Joss?" he asked a few minutes later.

"Fine," I said.

"My bullshit meter might not be as good as yours, but I have a hard time believing that."

I shrugged, looking out the window. "I don't know what to tell you."

"You've hardly said anything about Lawrence. Aren't you... I don't know, mad?"

My shoulders tensed as he mentioned Lawrence. I shrugged, hoping he hadn't noticed. "We weren't together all that long, so... I mean, that doesn't make it better, it just... there's been a lot of other things to think about."

"When it rains, it pours," he said.

"I mean, it only poured for a bit. It was just drizzling for most of the afternoon."

"Smartass," Derek said, and I laughed. "For what it's worth, you seemed too good for him even before he pulled that stunt."

I smiled sadly. "Thanks."

"Your sister…"

"I don't want to talk about her," I said.

He nodded brusquely. "Understood."

We didn't speak again until we got to his house. I hadn't seen it when Isaac and I were together and was a bit surprised. Apparently, Derek liked to garden. There were flower beds around the front, carefully tended and maintained. The house itself wasn't as big as Angela's, which I knew had been their home before they divorced, but it seemed reasonable for one person.

"We'll put the totes in the garage," he said as he parked in the driveway. "Not enough room to park in there, though."

I understood why when he opened the overhead door: besides a workbench and some miscellaneous half-built pieces of furniture, there were three motorcycles in the garage, two of them in various states of disassembly. I smiled when I saw the Thruxton, as shiny and cared for as the day I'd first seen it.

"How many before it's considered an addiction?" I asked.

"Not sure," he replied. "Four seemed excessive, though, so I sold one of them earlier this year."

"And then bought another one?"

He laughed. "I might be looking into a couple of leads."

"Do you run your entire business out of here?" I asked, looking at the furniture.

Derek shook his head. "I have a shop for that. These are just personal projects."

We each took a tote out of the trunk and brought it to the garage, stacking them near one of the disassembled bikes. I went around to the passenger side and opened the back door without thinking. As soon as I did, the vase we had shoved on top of the totes tumbled down. It slipped from my hands as I attempted to catch it and shattered at my feet, glass spraying across Derek's driveway.

"Shit!" I exclaimed, stepping back from the car.

"It's okay," Derek said from the other side of the vehicle. "It's just a vase. We'll clean it up."

"No, not that," I said.

He came around the side of the car and went pale. "Well... shit. Let's, uh... I've got a first aid kit inside. Or... do you need a doctor?"

I stared down at the piece of glass embedded in my calf, my mind blank. "I don't think so. What are the fucking chances, though, right?"

"Okay, well, let's... uh, here, I can help you..."

"It's fine, I'll just..." I bent down and grabbed the piece of glass.

"Jocelyn, don't!" Derek exclaimed, but it was too late. I yanked it out of my leg, hissing as blood blossomed on my skin.

"Shit," someone said again. Probably me, but I wasn't entirely sure.

"Stay right there," he said, as if I was in the position to go anywhere else.

He rushed into the house and returned moments later with a roll of paper towels. His shoes crunched against the shattered glass as he pressed a stack of paper towels to my leg.

"Hold these," he said, moving my hand to the towels. "I'm going to pick you up."

Before his words registered, Derek was lifting me in his arms and walking towards the house as if I weighed nothing. I clung to his shoulders with the arm that wasn't holding the paper towels to my leg, twisted in a strange pretzel around his arms.

We didn't go far inside: he brought me to the kitchen and had me sit on the counter next to the sink while he grabbed a first-aid kit. He was only gone for the briefest of moments, but that moment was the one where everything caught up with me. Images flashed through my head: Chelsea deriding me all morning, Chelsea walking down the aisle to marry Isaac, Chelsea's fake tears as I scrubbed mud off her dress, Chelsea dropping the skirts of said dress as Isaac grabbed Lawrence and beat the shit out of him.

More followed: the feel of her cheek under my palm as I slapped her, the satisfying rush of enjoyment at the shocked look on Dad's face, the miserable silence as he berated me for something I didn't do. All of it crashed down at once, a wall shattered by a stupid piece of glass from a stupid vase.

When Derek returned, I was hunched over, shoulders shaking, the hand that wasn't holding the paper towels pressed against my eyes. I barely realized he was standing next to me until a gentle hand nudged mine away from the paper towels.

He didn't pretend I wasn't crying, but he also didn't draw attention to it. Quietly, he directed me to twist on the counter so my leg was over the sink, and patiently washed the cut as I choked on my tears. Once the blood was washed off, it didn't look quite so bad, but he still held pressure to it for a while before bandaging it up.

Once he was done, he looked up at me.

"Don't think it needs stitches," he said. "It's not that deep."

"Sorry," I whimpered.

"Why?"

I shrugged and gestured towards my leg, then vaguely around me as a wet giggle bubbled out of my throat. "It's been a fucking weird day."

He didn't laugh. He put his arms around me and let me cry, a hand rubbing my back as soft nonsense was murmured into my ear. Slowly, I regained my breath, the tears replaced by an embarrassed blush. It wasn't enough for me to be humiliated by my sister. It wasn't enough for me to drop a vase and bleed everywhere. I also had to have a complete breakdown in front of Derek.

I took a hiccupping breath and sat back. His arms loosened around me, but he didn't step away.

"Sorry," I said again, wiping my cheeks with one of the clean paper towels that had somehow appeared in my hand.

"Don't be. I'd be more worried if you weren't upset by all of this."

He wasn't looking at me with pity, only concern. There wasn't any judgement in his eyes, no condescending sympathy. He just looked like he cared, like he understood, like I was okay to be myself around him.

He didn't step back. He was standing right in front of me, the counter I was sitting on bringing us eye-to-eye, and his face was so close to mine, close enough that I could see flecks in his eyes and the lightest shadow of scruff on his chin.

There was no moment where I decided I was going to do it, where I debated whether I even should. One second, I was staring at his lips, and the next those lips were pressed to mine, and they were soft and warm and kissing me back. He didn't stop me, not right away. He stood between my legs, his body just barely touching them, and his hands rested on the counter on either side of my thighs. He didn't touch me, didn't grab me, but he did kiss me back.

There was no mistaking that.

That one second changed everything. One moment I was barely holding it together, and the next I was grounded, warmth lazily swirling through my body and down my legs, my hand trembling as I brushed my fingers against his neck.

It wasn't until I touched his neck that Derek stiffened and pulled away.

"Joss," he said, staring at me like he had just realized I was there.

"Oh no," I murmured.

"This, uh… you're upset right now. It's been a… tough day."

My stomach curled and surged. "I didn't… I wasn't—"

"It's okay," he said, stepping back. "I shouldn't have, uh… I could have stopped…"

"It's my fault." I pushed myself off the counter, Derek stepping back instinctively as I slid to my feet. "My bad. I'm gonna go now."

"I drove you here," he said.

"I'll get a cab."

"Don't be ridiculous."

Stubbornly, I pushed past him. Up to that point, the cut on my leg hadn't hurt, but I only made it three steps before stumbling and wincing. Derek grabbed my arm, steadying me. "You can barely walk right now. I'll take you to the hotel."

"Don't bother." I wrenched my arm out of his hand, limping towards the door.

"For fuck's sake, Jocelyn," he said, exasperated. "Think for a second. I don't want to be responsible for you getting hurt or something. Just let me drive you back."

"Responsible?" I stopped, turning to him. "Who the hell made you responsible for me, Derek? I'm an adult. I can be responsible for myself."

"You're upset," he said. "It's been a hell of a day and you were just in shock and you're not thinking—"

"Right, I'm just some poor, stupid woman who can't make decisions for herself because she's just hysterical about everything all the time," I said.

He glared at me. "I didn't say that. Don't put those words in my mouth."

I opened my mouth to snap another response at him, but the words didn't come. Tension hung between us, silent and electric, until I glared back at him.

"Fuck you," I said.

"Excuse me?"

"You're right, so fuck you." I turned around and started towards the door again. "I'm going."

He was behind me before I even had my hand on the door handle. "I'm taking you."

"No."

"Yes."

"Can you just let me suffer in peace?" I asked. "I said you're right, okay? It was a stupid day and I've made bad decisions and I'm embarrassed and upset and I just want to leave before I make even more of an ass of myself."

"Joss—"

"I know!" I whirled around and glared up at him. "It was inappropriate and wrong for me to kiss you and I should apologize for it, but I'm not sorry. I'm just embarrassed, and isn't that even worse? Probably. But I don't care. I don't need a fucking lecture, okay?"

"Will you let me speak?"

"I don't want to hear it!"

"I don't give a shit if you don't want to hear it!" he snapped. "You're what, twenty years younger than me? You're my son's ex-girlfriend! Your boyfriend just fucked your sister, your dad is a horrible goddamn person, and it kills me to see any of that because you don't deserve this kind of shit. There's nothing about this situation that makes it right for me to want you, okay? Not a single goddamn thing, and then suddenly you're kissing me and I'm somehow supposed to tell you not to, knowing damn well I don't want you to stop and knowing damn well it's going to hurt you."

"'Somehow,'" I mocked. "You sure found a way."

"What should I have done instead?" His voice was miserably quiet. "Tell me. Was I wrong about anything I just said? You understand why we shouldn't do this?"

I did understand. He wasn't wrong. And there was nothing he could have done instead.

But he also said...

"You didn't want me to stop?" I asked.

"Come on, Joss," he said softly. "Don't pretend you haven't noticed."

There were a number of really good, really important reasons I should have agreed with him, let him drive me back to the hotel, and tried to forget how good his mouth felt against mine. He'd listed almost all of them, after all. I should have done the right thing and moved on, declared myself done with the Thompsons, insisted that going any further with Derek was only going to end in heartbreak. How else could it end?

Instead, I leaned back against the door and looked up at him.

"What if we just... forget about all that?" I asked.

He laughed, a startled bark that was full of disbelief.

"Forget," he repeated. "And then what?"

"And then you kiss me again."

He swallowed, glancing away from me for a split second before looking back. "And then what, Joss?"

I shrugged. Derek stared at me, then laughed dryly.

"This is a terrible idea," he murmured just before pressing his lips to mine again.

I couldn't say either of us forgot about all the reasons we shouldn't be doing this, but I could say I was ignoring them as he put his hands on my sides and I put my arms over his shoulders. He nudged me against the door, pressing his body against mine, and I could only vaguely wonder how, exactly, this could be wrong.

He moved tentatively at first, almost unsteady as he touched me, but that didn't last long. Apprehension drifted away and a thousand sensations rushed through my body, heat and desire prickling along my skin and to the tips of my fingers and toes. It was like I couldn't get enough. I needed more. I needed him more than I'd ever needed anything. He felt it, too, I was certain. He had to, with the way he was pressing against me and the urgency of his mouth as he deepened the kiss. His tongue slipped into my mouth, flicking against mine before withdrawing, making me whimper until he kissed me again and again.

I pulled him closer to me; he slid his hand up to my ribs, then brushed it against my breast. I smiled against his mouth and felt him smile against mine before cupping my breast more confidently. His fingers moved gently, squeezing and releasing, caressing me through the layers of my bra and dress.

Finally giving in to whatever was between us had broken down the flimsy walls we had created. I submitted to that passion completely, my body demanding his, my heart racing as he left me breathless. Derek's movements became more urgent, more intense, until it was obvious that the limitations of our position were frustrating him.

"I need you, Joss," he said, pulling back. "I can't... I just fucking need you."

I kissed him in response. He lifted me up for the second time that day and his lips only left mine so he could put me down when we got to his bedroom.

The urgency didn't die off there. Derek's fingers pulled the zipper of the dress down; I shoved his suit jacket off his shoulders. He pushed the sleeves of the dress down my arms and I stopped my work on the buttons of his shirt just long enough to let the dress drop past my legs and pool around my ankles.

The moment the dress hit the ground, he paused, seemingly forgetting he was in the process of loosening his tie. His lower lip curled between his teeth, his eyes raking down my body as his expression remained the same. He stared long enough to make me shift uncomfortably, biting the inside of my cheek until he looked back up.

"Are the panties part of the maid of honour get-up or do you always hide this beneath those jeans and coveralls?"

I snorted, a pinkish blush creeping along my chest. "I like cute underwear."

He yanked his tie off and dropped it to the floor, bringing his hands to the waistband of my panties. "I don't think I'd describe these as 'cute'," he murmured, hands trailing up my body to the matching lacy bra. "Sexy as hell, maybe. Shit, Joss. I never pictured you in something like this."

I smirked at him. "Do you, um, picture me often?"

A dry chuckle was the only response I received before Derek kissed me again. He didn't linger there for long; rather, he pressed his lips against my neck, then my collarbone, then between my breasts. I shivered as his tongue darted out, skimming along my cleavage, and then he dropped to his knees in front of me.

He kissed my stomach, his lips caressing every inch of skin he could find. I watched his head drop lower, felt his lips just above my belly button and then just below it, and gasped when his lips pressed against the waistband of my panties.

Moments later, he was kissing my covered mound. I could feel his breath through the fabric, hot against me, and when he kissed the spot on my panties that was rapidly dampening, my knees almost buckled. Derek put one hand on my ass to steady me, then used the other to push my panties to the side. He looked up at me, and I could see the sparkle of laughter in his eyes seconds before his tongue dipped into my folds.

The laughter in his eyes was followed by the strange, vibrating sensation of him chuckling against my pussy, unable to stop himself from reacting to the garbled noise I made when he started licking me. Entranced, I watched him bury his face against me, his tongue doing things I'd never experienced and couldn't get enough of.

He was going to make me come, I realized, and it wasn't going to take very long. The problem was that I didn't know if I'd be able to keep standing on my own two feet if he did. Urgently, I tugged at Derek's hair.

"Let me lie down," I begged. "I'm gonna fall."

He placed a lingering kiss against my mound and stood up. Before he could nudge me back onto the bed, I grabbed the front of his shirt and pulled his face to mine. His lips were slick, the taste of my pussy still on them as I kissed him and insistently unbuttoned his shirt.

"Thought you wanted to lie down so you didn't fall," he teased.

"I want this off first," I shot back. "You're wearing too many clothes."

Chuckling, Derek shrugged the shirt off, then nudged my hands away from the belt I was trying to undo. He unbuckled it far faster than I could have, though he let me push his pants down his hips before guiding me onto his bed.

The moment I was on my back, he parted my thighs and pushed his face back between my legs. I moaned, running my fingers through his hair as he resumed licking my pussy, one hand holding my panties out of the way and the other trailing up my thigh until he was teasing my dripping entrance with the tip of his finger.

"Oh my God," I whispered.

He might have laughed or he might have groaned. I wasn't entirely sure, but Derek made a noise of some kind that hummed against my pussy as he spoke. I shuddered, the telltale signs of pleasure building up in my stomach. Pricks of electricity danced along my skin, settling deeper and deeper inside me until I could almost feel it running through my bones. Gasping, I pressed my hands against his head, pushing my hips up into his face. When he finally pushed his finger inside me, I cried out, panting as the current grew and pulsated, until a final jolt ran through me and I tipped over the edge into bliss.

My thighs tightened around his ears and my legs shook as pleasure burst through me. Nothing else seemed to matter; I couldn't think, could hardly breathe, couldn't focus on anything except Derek's tongue against my clit and his finger curled inside me, pressing just the right way to draw out my orgasm. When I regained some sense of control, Derek withdrew his hand and placed a final kiss on my mound before sitting up.

"Oh my God," I said again.

He grinned, bringing himself over me and kissing me as I tried to catch my breath.

"You taste so good," he murmured against my mouth. "I could do that again, and again, and—"

"Don't tempt me," I said, nipping at his lip. "I want you inside me."

He groaned, nestling himself between my legs so I could feel the bulge of his cock pressed against me. Even through the fabric of my panties and his boxers, I could feel how hot he was. I pushed my hips up a bit, grinding against his bulge and eliciting another deep groan from Derek.

"Joss," he whispered. "Fuck, I want you so much."

I pulled his face down to mine, capturing his mouth and revelling at the feel of his body against mine. He slipped a hand beneath me, deftly unhooking my bra and pawing it away from my body so he could take my nipple into his mouth. I moaned, squirming beneath him again so his cock pushed against my pussy.

"Fuck," he said again, the word muffled by my breast.

"Please," I gasped.

He flicked my nipple with his tongue, then sat up so he could pull my panties off. He slid them down my legs, carefully moving them past the bandaged cut on my leg, and dropped them unceremoniously to the floor before removing his boxers. I bit my lip when I saw his cock, swollen and thick and throbbing.

"I have an IUD," I said awkwardly. "So if you're, um, good..."

"I am," he said, and brought himself back between my legs. His cock brushed against my thigh as he kissed me again. "You sure about this?"

"Yes."

His cock was pressed against my slit and he pushed his hips forward, letting it slide along my pussy. I moaned as his tip nudged my clit, unable to stop myself from raising my hips. With his lips pressed against mine, he reached down and positioned himself at my entrance.

"Joss—"

"Yes," I gasped. "Please, Derek."

I was so wet, his tip slipped inside me easily, but he was so thick that he had to slow down once it did. I tilted my head back on the pillow, my eyes closing as he pushed forward, the walls of my pussy stretching around him as he filled me.

"You okay?" he asked, pausing when he was about halfway in.

I could only nod. He brushed his hand through my hair, kissing me as he pushed the rest of his cock in. My lips parted, but no noise came out. Every inch of him was inside me, every inch of him stretching me and filling me, and I never, ever wanted to let go of that feeling.

"You sure?" he asked, his voice strained.

"Yes," I managed to say. "God, you feel good."

He groaned, pressed his lips to mine, and started moving. When I whimpered again and pushed my hips up to meet him, he pulled back, bringing his arms under my legs. There may have been a moment that my eyes rolled back completely in my head as he filled me even deeper than he had before, and that was the moment when I was lost.

I came twice on his cock: once with Derek rubbing my clit, and again when he let go of one of my legs so he could lean down to kiss me. Both times he swore, his thrusts staggering as my pussy clenched impossibly tight around him, and the second time he couldn't hold back any longer.

"I'm gonna come," he grunted. "Joss, I... fuck..."

I barely heard him, still floating somewhere in the white light of that place of complete bliss, though I felt it as his cock pulsed and spilled inside of me. He stilled, panting as he finished, and kissed me again.

If kissing him had been a terrible idea, I could only imagine how bad of an idea it was to fuck him. An even more horrible idea was curling up against his chest and falling asleep with his arms around me, his lips pressed to the top of my head, both of us knowing we'd just done something we couldn't take back.

The worst part, though, was knowing I didn't want to take it back, and knowing that moving forward was only going to make everything worse.

CHAPTER EIGHT

THEN

"...LOVIN' A CARBURETOR, LOVIN' it up while I wipe it down... lovin' a carburetor..."

"I'm eighty-six percent sure those aren't the lyrics," Bretta said.

I yanked the earbud from my ear, rolling my eyes at her. "What makes more sense, love in an elevator or loving a carburetor?"

"Uh, love in an elevator."

"Traitor," I muttered.

She smiled awkwardly rather than her usual cutting laugh, which was my first sign that something was wrong. The second was that she handed me a rag to wipe my hands instead of throwing it at me like usual.

"What's wrong?" I asked.

"Look, I wouldn't usually..." She sighed, glancing at the door to the reception area. "There's someone up front to see you, and I would have told him to piss off, but I think it's important."

I frowned, not sure who she meant. She shrugged and gestured to the front. Wiping my hands as I walked to the front, I hip checked the door open, then froze when I saw Isaac standing beside the reception desk.

"Hey," he said.

"I don't have time for this today." I turned to go back into the shop.

"Wait. Jocelyn, please. Just wait one sec."

He was pleading, practically begging. I clenched my jaw, almost continued into the shop, then cursed my weak will as I turned back to him.

"What do you want? Make it quick."

He grimaced. "Look, do you have time for a coffee or...?"

"A coffee?" I repeated. "With you? In the middle of my workday when I just said I don't have time for this shit today?"

"Please," was all he said.

I could feel the side of my nose flaring, twitching, an infuriating little flutter that betrayed how annoyed I was. There were only two reasons I could think of for Isaac to be in my shop, begging me to have a coffee with him. Based on what I knew, I didn't think he was there to tell me Chelsea had somehow broken his heart and admit I was right all along.

"You're buying," I grumbled. "Bretta, I'll be back in five minutes."

"Sure," she called from her office.

It was a little longer than five minutes, since it took about five minutes for us to get to the coffee shop and place our orders. We didn't say anything else until we each had our drinks: a plain black coffee for me, a hazelnut latte for him. In another life, I would have made fun of his drink choice, mocking him for having a fancy latte with cutesy art drawn on the top of it. In that life, he would have laughed good-naturedly, kissed the side of my head, and held my hand across the table.

Instead, I burnt my tongue as I sipped my coffee, staring at him as he nervously shifted on the other side of the table.

"You've got like two minutes to explain what you're doing here before I leave," I said.

Isaac took a deep breath. "I'm going to propose to Chelsea."

"Okay. And you're telling me because...?"

Relief mixed with dismay on his face at my lack of reaction. "I mean, Chels and I have been together for over a year now and I've seen you, what, three times?"

"I don't live with my parents anymore," I pointed out.

Chelsea didn't, either, but I knew she and Isaac had dinner with my parents at least once a week. I conveniently had a standing doctor's appointment that night.

I mean, it was Doctor Who, but no one needed to know that. It was better to let my parents think I was in therapy or something.

"I know," Isaac said. "I'm not saying… I just mean I didn't want it to come as a surprise or a shock or anything."

His consideration of my feelings annoyed me. It shouldn't have. I should have been appreciative that he even thought of giving me a head's up, but all it did was make me think he was a condescending dickhead.

"You still think she's God's gift to you, don't you?" I asked.

"Please don't," he said. "Joss, I just wanted to give you a head's up—"

"Jocelyn."

"What?

"My name's Jocelyn, Isaac."

He swallowed and nodded brusquely. "Right. Okay. I just wanted to tell you, okay? I love Chelsea. I want to marry her. I know that it's… I know this is weird, I get it."

"It's super weird."

"I know." He twisted his coffee cup in his hand. "I wish things were different."

"You wish you hadn't met me first, you mean."

Isaac looked more hurt at my words than I felt. "I wish things were different," he repeated. "I'm sorry I hurt you. And I'm sorry I'm still hurting you."

I took another huge gulp of coffee, feeling the searing burn as it travelled down my throat.

"It's fine," I said. "Really. I don't hold it against you. You know Chelsea and I don't get along. I'm sure she's bitched about me a million times—"

"She doesn't," he interrupted. "Joss, she... I mean, Jocelyn. She doesn't say anything bad about you, ever."

"Whatever," I continued. "We don't get along. You know that. But, as my mom would say, she's my sister and I have to love her, so I'm not bitter or angry or... whatever. I just don't give a shit anymore. You have my... I dunno, blessing or whatever it is you want. If you want to marry her, marry her."

I refrained from adding that it was his own funeral to do so, and Isaac smiled.

"Thank you," he said. "Seriously, thank you. You don't know how much—"

"You don't need to get all sappy."

He chuckled. "Okay. Well, thank you."

I tried to smile at him, but when I couldn't force my lips to turn up, I took another gulp of coffee.

"Whatever. Congratulations. I hope you both get the happiness you deserve."

He thanked me again, clearly not understanding what I meant, and I went back to work with my throat stinging.

I didn't know when Isaac was going to propose. I didn't care. Instead of thinking about it, I buried myself in work, arriving at the shop before anyone else and leaving long after people left for the day.

"You have to stop doing this," Bretta said one morning about a week later.

"I'm just getting a head start on—"

"I don't give a shit what the excuse is this time," she said. "One, you shouldn't be working on cars when you're here alone. If you get hurt, I'm gonna be fucked. Two, I can't afford to pay you all this fucking overtime."

"I haven't been claiming overtime."

"Three, if the labour board finds out you've been working overtime and not claiming it, I'm gonna be fucking fined." She put her coffee cup down on the counter. "Four, something is wrong. What is going on with you?"

"Nothing."

"Tell me or you're fired."

"You can't fire me," I said. "One, you have no cause. Two, I can report you to the labour board for letting me work alone and not paying me overtime."

She threw a rag at me. "Joss, you've been working here for what, four years? Almost five? You're not just my employee, okay? You're my friend. I'm worried about you."

"You have nothing to worry about," I said. "I'm just working through some shit. I'm not doing anything dangerous when no one's here, okay? I don't have anything up on the lift or whatever. Half the time I'm just doing paperwork."

Bretta studied me, then sighed. "Come have dinner with me and Leigh this weekend. Sunday?"

"Can't. I have a doctor's appointment."

"On a Sunday night," she said.

"Yes."

She rolled her eyes. "Saturday?"

I nodded begrudgingly and she went to her office, though I had a feeling she spent more time checking the security cameras to make sure I wasn't dead than she did actually working.

It was only by chance that I ran into him that afternoon: Bretta had insisted I take lunch and refused to let me sit in the break room, practically pushing me out the door and telling me to take a walk or go to the coffee shop or something, anything besides sitting around the shop. I did as she instructed, and if I hadn't, I wouldn't have seen him when I walked back in an hour later.

"Derek?"

He turned from the desk where he was trying to explain something to the receptionist, his face brightening when he saw me.

"Joss!" he exclaimed. "How's it going?"

It seemed natural to hug him. I didn't know why, because I wasn't much of a hugger to begin with, but Derek spread his arms and I reached for him without even thinking.

"I had no idea this was your shop," he said as he released me.

"What are you doing here?" I asked. "Don't tell me your car broke down."

He laughed, shaking his head. "I'm not too bad at working on my bikes, but I like to get someone to check the car out. Also, gotta get some new tires, so I need someone to mount them for me."

"I'm pretty good at mounting," I said without thinking.

He raised an eyebrow and I rolled my eyes.

"Get your head out of the gutter."

Derek grinned. "I didn't say anything."

"All right," I said, glancing over at the desk. "So you just want everything checked out and a tire change. Just on the rims you already have?"

"Yep. How long do you figure it'll take?"

I grimaced, glancing at the stack of papers I had waiting for me. "Honestly? We're slammed for the afternoon, but if you don't mind coming back around six, I should have it done."

"Don't you close at five?"

"For my best customer? I'll stick around until six. Not a second later, though, so don't be late."

He laughed. "Best customer? I've never been here before."

I glanced around the shop, making sure there were no other customers listening. "I know. That's what makes you the best one."

I overestimated my capabilities a bit. When Derek knocked on the locked front door a few minutes before six, I wasn't quite done with his car.

"This weather sucks," he said as I unlocked the door. "If it rains any more, we're going to flood."

"I don't mind it," I said, holding the door open for him. "It's refreshing. And I like the smell."

"It means the smell of dust after it rains."

"Petrichor," I said, laughing. "I'm running behind. It'll still be about fifteen minutes. Wanna come wait in the shop?"

"Is that allowed?"

"No, but Bretta's already fired me six times this week, so it should be fine."

We chatted idly while I finished working under the hood. The latest episodes of Doctor Who, theories on who the next Doctor would be, how Samantha and Angela were doing, how his business was doing. It wasn't until I closed the hood and we were standing at the front desk so he could pay that things turned serious.

"That's it," I said, handing him the invoice. "I'll open the overhead door and you can drive it out. Saves you a trip back out in the rain."

"Excellent," he said, then paused after picking up his key. "Look, this isn't any of my business, but you should know something."

"Is it that Isaac's proposing?" I asked.

He grimaced. "How'd you find out?"

I smiled, not able to meet his eye. "He came into the shop last week to tell me."

"Sorry," Derek said.

I shook my head. "Don't be. He didn't have to do it, but he did. I'm grateful for that. Takes some of the, you know, shock or whatever away. It was r-really nice of h-him."

It wasn't until I felt his embrace that I realized Derek had stepped around the desk. By that point, the tears were streaking down my face, cutting through the layers of dirt and oil that were scrawled across my cheeks. He didn't seem to care, holding me close as I cried into his shirt, finally feeling the pain I'd been avoiding, miserably mourning the loss of something that had ended more than a year and a half earlier.

"It's okay." His thumb rubbed my shoulder as he held me, a comforting back-and-forth that my heartbeat began to match. "You got this, you're okay. It's okay."

I took a shaky breath, pulled away, and roughly wiped my cheeks.

"I'm fine," I said, my voice squeaking.

"You sure?"

"I'm fine," I repeated. "I'm not crying. You're crying."

He laughed and let his arms drop from around me. "Sure, that's what happened."

"Sorry. It's stupid."

"It's not stupid. You liked him. At one point, anyway."

My cheeks tightened as I smiled. "I did, yeah. I didn't... I don't know if it would have lasted or whatever, but I wish Chelsea wouldn't have gone after him."

Derek nodded, his face serious. "It's definitely unfair."

"Do you know if..."

"What?"

I swallowed, willing myself not to cry again. "Is he really in love with her?"

Sighing, he leaned against the desk. "Yeah. I think he really is."

I had nothing to say in response, instead looking down at my shoes.

"It's her I'm not sure about," he continued.

That made me look up. He watched me with guarded eyes, trying to assess my reaction.

"Me neither," I said. "Chelsea is..."

"I know." Derek sighed, shaking his head. "I think he's making a mistake, but I'm the last person he'll listen to. Ange thinks he is too, but he won't even listen to her."

"Well, we all know he won't listen to me," I said. "I warned him before he even started dating her. But... well, I hope they're happy. I do. I want him to be happy."

"Me too." Derek smiled tightly. "We miss you, you know. Me and Ange."

His visit seemed to be what I needed. The next day, Bretta fired me for being twenty minutes late, and again when I told her I was checking out early but smiled when I flipped her off.

A week later, Mom called just as I finished work.

"Can you make it to dinner tonight?" she asked.

"Oh, I wish you would've called sooner," I said. "I, uh, have a date."

She squealed a bit. "A date?! Who is he?"

"Just some guy," I said. "It's not... it's our first date, so I don't know if anything'll come from it."

"What's his name?" she urged.

"De...an...iel."

"Daniel," she said, unimpressed. "Are you sure about that?"

"Yep."

"Are you making up a name and a date so you don't have to come to dinner tonight?"

"Mom!" I gasped. "Do you think I would do that?"

"Yes," she said bluntly. "Joss, please. I haven't seen you in weeks. I miss you."

"Well, why don't we have coffee or something this weekend?" I suggested.

"Your dad wants to see you, too."

I snorted. "Come on, Mom."

"He does," she said. "I know you haven't always gotten along with him but—"

"—but family is family," I finished, sighing. "Why can't you just accept that Dad and I will never see eye-to-eye? Like, maybe our family is stronger when he and I don't see each other very often."

"I refuse to believe that."

"Refusing to believe it doesn't make it any less true."

She didn't respond, and that familiar rush of guilt filled my stomach. Again, I'd said something that hurt my mom. Again, she'd guilt-tripped me, intentionally or unintentionally, and I was about to give up my own happiness just to appease her.

Maybe I should have changed some of those Doctor Who appointments to be with an actual doctor. Someone who could tell me why I was so hesitant to disappoint my mom, to where I'd put myself in uncomfortable situations and pretend like my father and sister weren't horrible, hurtful human beings. Then again, I knew why I did it: because my father and sister were horrible, hurtful human beings and my mom was the only one who wasn't disappointed by my very existence. Disappointing her meant I was losing the one person on my side. I didn't need to miss an episode of Doctor Who and pay someone two hundred bucks an hour to figure that out.

"What time?" I mumbled.

"Six," Mom said, trying to hide the thick wateriness of her voice. "Thanks, Joss. I love you."

"You too. See you in a bit."

I had just enough time to shower and get changed before heading to my parents. I took every precaution I could to make myself look as inoffensive as possible. Clean hair, small amount of makeup, one of the six pairs of identical jeans I owned, and my favourite Firefly T-shirt to lend a security-blanket-like comfort to myself. There was no question in my mind what was about to happen, especially once I saw Isaac's car parked in the driveway as I pulled up.

Despite having lived in the house for twenty-four years, I still knocked on the door before letting myself in.

"Jocelyn!" Chelsea cried as I closed the door behind me.

I frowned. That was far more cheerful than I was used to, and completely out of character for her. Chelsea's faux-kindness towards me was pathetically obvious at best, but she sounded genuinely excited. Maybe she was taking acting lessons.

"Hey," I said, stepping into the living room.

Isaac was sitting beside her on the couch, trying to hide the glimmering smile in his eyes. Dad sat in the armchair across from them and Mom was visible in the kitchen just beyond.

"Okay, everyone's here," Chelsea said, exhilaration winding through her voice. "Can we now? Please?"

Isaac nodded, Chelsea held up her left hand, and I plastered the plastic smile I had been practicing across my face. Mom shrieked and raced across the house, almost knocking Chelsea over as she hugged her. Dad took his turn after, hugging Chelsea before shaking Isaac's hand.

"You'd better treat my girl like the princess she is," he said.

"You have my word, Mr. Miller," Isaac promised.

"I think you can call me Gerald now," Dad said. "Congratulations, you two."

All four of them looked at me at the same time, standing a few metres away in the entrance to the living room. I widened the plastic smile.

"Congrats, guys," I said. "I'm happy you're happy."

Chelsea's face twisted. My chin trembled a bit before I realized she wasn't about to freak out at me.

She was fighting back tears.

"Thank you," she sniffed. "Jocelyn, you have no idea how much that... You're just so amazing, I can't... oh, just come here!"

I didn't, in fact, go there: Chelsea leapt forward and pulled me into a hug before I even had time to react. Startled, I hesitated, wrapping my arms around her and patting her back as she clutched me.

"Hey, it's all good," I said. "That's, uh, okay."

When she let go, she looked down at me, eyes still glistening. For the briefest of moments, I wondered if I'd been wrong. Maybe she wasn't with Isaac just to spite me. I mean, it had started that way, but maybe...

It didn't seem possible, but maybe Chelsea was truly, actually, completely in love with him.

"I have something very important to ask you," she said, still touching my shoulders.

Desperately, my eyes flicked from Chelsea to Mom to Isaac, then back to Chelsea. "Oh?"

"I know it might seem... weird," she started. "I know that, but... Remember when we were kids, and we pinky promised that when we got married, we would be each other's maid of honour?"

My heart was somewhere in the pit of my stomach, dread filling the place it used to sit in my chest.

"Um, I mean... yeah, I remember."

"Well, it would mean the world to me if... if you'd keep that promise," she said. "Will you please be my maid of honour?"

I wasn't sure if she would choose me as her maid of honour just to hurt me. It would hurt me, yes, but it would hurt her, too. She didn't like to hurt herself. I looked for the cold, calculated, hurtful Chelsea lurking behind the glimmering tears in her eyes, watching me, waiting for the gleeful moment that pain spread across my face, but I couldn't see her. I just saw hope, and that made everything ten times worse.

"Are you sure that's a good idea?" I asked.

"I can't think of anyone I'd want there more," Chelsea said. "Isaac and I would be so grateful, Joss."

From behind her, Isaac nodded at me hopefully. Mom pressed her lips together, her fingers entwined as she waited for me to respond. Dad watched stoically, eyes on Chelsea rather than meeting mine. The question hung in the air, everyone waiting for me to say yes.

"No," I said.

Chelsea raised an eyebrow at me, her lips parted just slightly.

"No," I repeated. "I'm sorry, but just... no. I can't."

"Why not?" Mom asked, the eager excitement replaced by shocked disappointment.

"That hardly seems reasonable," Dad said. "Your sister asked you to be maid of honour, Jocelyn. She wants you to be part of her wedding."

I glanced back and forth between everyone again. "No one else thinks this is weird?"

"It is weird," Isaac said. "But it's our wedding and we don't care what other people think."

"You're important to both of us," Chelsea continued. "We want you to be part of our day."

"Can't I just... I don't know, be an usher or something?" I asked. "Like, you're asking me to—"

"She's asking you to be her sister and do the right thing," Dad said.

"Gerald," Mom chided. She stepped past Chelsea and took my hand. "Joss, you don't have to do this if you really don't want to—"

"I really don't want to," I said.

"—but I think it would go a long way in healing whatever's happened between the two of you, and shows how strong of a family we are." She smiled at me, then at Chelsea. "Family is family."

Family is family.

What a stupid fucking saying. It didn't even mean anything. Family is family? Well, apples are apples. Water is water. Bullshit is bullshit.

I still had no idea if Chelsea was faking it or not. I had no idea if she was letting go of our past, if she was forgiving me, if she was finally going to stop being my enemy and start being my sister again. I was terrified to let myself hope that she was, to trust that this wasn't just another trap and be excited and grateful and happy. With four sets of eyes staring at me, ranging from coldness to hope to guilting to pleading, I sighed.

"Fine," I said. "But for the love of God, please don't make me wear pink."

Chelsea squealed and threw her arms around me again.

For the first few months after their engagement, I questioned everything. Chelsea seemed happy, truly happy, and even my cynical ass could see that she and Isaac were incredibly in love. I questioned if they'd always been like that, if the few times I had seen them since they began dating had been viewed through a lens of my own misery, and that their falling in love really was just bad luck.

Maybe it wasn't nefarious or malicious.

Maybe I was wrong.

Slowly, I let my guard down. It was little things at first: laughing at one of Chelsea's jokes, then cracking a joke of my own. Offering an opinion when she asked for one or complimenting her choice of shit I didn't care about, like flowers. Actually going to dinner at my parents, since Doctor Who was in re-runs anyway.

And I was... happy. I was starting to feel like I used to, like I still didn't fit in with my family, but that it was okay because I had my sister.

Chelsea's other bridesmaids were her actual friends, and they were initially as suspicious as I was about my involvement. Her friend Lisa was particularly sour that I was the maid of honour instead of her, probably because Lisa had known both of us since before high school and knew just how deep the animosity ran. Still, even Lisa began warming up to me, and when it came time to go shopping for bridesmaid's dresses, she came along with me, Chelsea, and Mom.

I was smiling as we walked into the dress shop, putting up with Mom's teasing that she was finally, *finally* going to see me in a dress.

"So, I have a vision," Chelsea said, cutting off Mom. "I think it's going to be perfect."

"You're the bride," said Mom. "What you say, goes."

I nodded, as did Lisa.

Even at the end of the shopping trip, I wondered how many of Chelsea's decisions were based on what would hurt me, and how many were just her not caring. I wondered why she was going to all that effort just to punish me, and wondered if maybe it wasn't hatred, but indifference. Indifference didn't support spending months making me think we were healing our relationship, but to put that much work into building me up just to tear me down...

The option I didn't want to think about was the most painful: that we really had been repairing our relationship, that she really had forgiven me, and that they were still so precariously fragile that the smallest moment of dissent could send everything crashing down.

The bridesmaids would wear matching dresses, she said. Cap sleeves, a square neckline, an empire waist and a flowing skirt in a silvery shade of grey that flattered all skin tones with a pale pink sash around the waist.

And for the maid of honour, the same dress, with the colours reversed.

I thought she was joking, so I laughed.

"What's so funny?" she asked, frowning.

"You can't be serious," I said.

"Excuse me?" Her voice took on that haughty, high-pitched tone. "Is there a problem with my dresses?"

The laughter faded and my mouth dropped open.

"Chels, I said... I mean, when you asked me, I said I just didn't want to wear a pink dress."

"Oh my God." She threw a hand in the air, glancing at Lisa, then Mom, then the saleslady. "Are you serious? You're going to make me change the vision for *my* wedding because you don't want to wear a pink dress?"

"It was literally the only thing I asked for," I protested.

"Are you sure, Chelsea?" Mom said. "I mean, she did say…"

"I knew it," she snapped. "I *knew* it. This whole time you've just been waiting to do what you do best, right, Jocelyn? Sneak in and make me think everything's okay, then pull the rug out from under me. I can't believe you're making such a big deal about this."

"If it's not a big deal, why can't we just reverse the colours?" I asked. "Why can't the bridesmaids wear pink and I wear grey?"

"Because that's not what I want!"

She turned to me, arms folded, tears welling in her eyes; real tears, not fake-Chelsea tears, which I could tell because the skin along her cheekbones was starting to turn red. That didn't happen when she fake-cried.

"I really thought things were getting better," she said, her voice cracking.

She saw the moment my heart broke, the fragile mending of our relationship splitting open. One of her perfectly arched eyebrows flicked up, just enough to ask me what I was going to do about it.

"It's fine," I said. "I'll wear the pink dress. I don't mind."

CHAPTER NINE

NOW

MY LEG WAS THROBBING. It was a weird sort of tightness, skin mending together but still fragile and papery, like it could tear at any moment. It pulsed in time with my heartbeat, slow and steady as it pulled me from sleep, and quickening as I took in the world around me.

I couldn't be sure of the time: at first, I thought it was early based on the cool light cutting through the gaps in the curtains, but the sound of rain against the window meant it could have been any time. The air in the room was cool, cold enough that the tip of my nose felt chilled, but the rest of me was shrouded in warmth. Thick blankets were pulled up to my neck, and beneath those blankets, powerful arms enveloped me. I was naked, embraced against his body, legs still entwined with his, and soft puffs of breath made my hair brush against my forehead.

Whether my heart was racing because I was horrified at myself for sleeping with my ex-boyfriend-and-almost-brother-in-law's father or because I was electrified to be waking up skin-to-skin with Derek, I didn't know.

It was probably both.

The fact that it was probably both made guilt crawl through me, a surging wave of nausea that rolled through my stomach so strongly, I unintentionally shifted in Derek's arms.

He must have been a light sleeper; I barely jostled him, but he inhaled deeply and his arms tightened around me. I held my breath, though I wasn't sure why. He had to wake up sometime, and it wasn't like I could untangle myself from him and sneak out of his bedroom with him none the wiser.

Of course, me holding my breath did nothing. Derek seemed to have the same slow sort of wake-up that I did, a few moments of blissful ignorance before he remembered who was in his arms and why, what we had done, and what we now had to face.

"Joss?" he murmured. "You awake?"

"Mm-hmm."

He took another deep breath, not quite sighing as he let it out. I thought he might stop holding me, that he might push me away from him as the panic and guilt set in, but he didn't. His arms loosened, but only so he could trail one hand down my back, calloused hands making me shiver against him.

He chuckled as he felt me shake.

"Ticklish?" he asked.

"No," I muttered.

He traced his fingers back over the same spot, and again I shivered.

"I don't know if I believe that," he said.

I smirked, but didn't say anything.

"Been up long?" he asked.

I shook my head. Derek twitched as my nose brushed his chest.

"Your nose is freezing!"

"Well, yeah. Why is it so cold in here?"

He shook the blankets away from one of his arms, bringing his hand up to my face and covering my nose. I burst out laughing, startled by the sudden gesture, and jerked back. Derek was looking at me, fighting back a smile.

"What are you doing?" I giggled.

"Warming you up," he said innocently. He held an almost-serious expression for a moment longer before dissolving into his own laughter.

It was stupid. We shouldn't have started the day like that, laughing like what we had done was perfectly normal. We should have been properly mortified to find ourselves in bed together. I should have stolen a sheet to cover myself and he should have averted his eyes while I dressed, and then we should have had a very serious conversation about why what we did was wrong and how we could never, ever tell anyone about it.

Instead, we came to the unspoken agreement that we were just going to forget everything for a little longer. We forgot everything just long enough for Derek's hand to move from covering my nose to cupping my cheek, just long enough for him to tilt my head up, just long enough for him to press his lips to mine and for me to melt against him.

One kiss turned into two, then to three. The fourth kiss was different: I could sense the sadness, the playfulness turning to a longing we knew shouldn't be requited. My heart ached as he lingered, his lips just barely on mine. My eyes were closed when he pulled away, though saying he pulled away was generous. I could still feel his breath, still sense his presence an inch away from me.

"We should talk about this," he said.

"Do we have to?"

"Yeah, Joss, we have to."

Reluctantly, I opened my eyes. He was looking at me, his eyebrows furrowed. There was something in his eyes: warmth, certainly, but also something that could have been pain or pity. Regret, maybe. The uncertainty of how to tell me to get out of his bed and never speak about this again.

"We don't," I said. "I get it."

I pulled back, holding the blanket to my chest as I sat up.

Derek looked surprised, propping himself up on an elbow as he stared at me. "Get what?"

"It," I said. "I get it."

"I don't know what 'it' is."

"It. This. It was a fun but stupid thing to do, you're now riddled with guilt about it, you're going to lecture me on the same things you did last night—blah blah blah, you're my ex's dad, blah blah blah, age difference—and ask me not to say anything to anyone. And I'm going to promise that I won't, and you're going to be happy about that, and we'll both just agree that it was a mistake."

I was pulling the blanket around me and reaching for my panties when Derek spoke again.

"Do you regret it?"

I stopped and looked back at him. "What?"

"Do you think it was a mistake?" he asked.

"Do I..."

I trailed off, trying to put what I was feeling into words. Did I regret it? Not a moment of it. Was it a mistake? Probably.

But did I *think* it was a mistake?

"No," I whispered.

"Me neither."

My heart was hammering inside of my chest, hard enough that the cut on my leg felt like it was going to burst open. "What about all the... problems?"

"Oh, you mean the whole 'I'm your ex's dad, blah blah blah age difference'?"

I laughed in spite of myself. "Yeah."

Derek sighed.

"I don't know. All I know is it doesn't make me want you any less." He paused, shaking his head. "I mean, it should. It really fucking should. I've got a kid older than you, Joss. And Isaac would... he barely tolerates me. He'd be livid if he found out."

I swallowed hard, staring down at the blankets. "But you don't regret it."

"No."

I fought the tears, my face twitching as I struggled to hold them back. "So now what?"

He was silent for a moment, then shook his head. "We can't do this again."

"I know."

"I'm sorry."

"Me too," I whispered.

"This fucking sucks."

I tried not to laugh. I knew if I laughed, Derek would hear the watery sound of my voice, that he'd know how devastated I was, and that he'd either feel horrible or start regretting having ever brought me to his bedroom.

Trying to suppress the laugh failed, though, and I made a strange sort of choked garble, clapping my hand to my mouth.

"Oh my God," I blurted, embarrassed.

He didn't say anything. He should have said something. At the very least, he should have stayed where he was. Instead, moments later, he was embracing me, pulling me into his lap as I sniffled, mortification creeping up my neck and turning my face red.

Then he was wiping my tears, the roughness of his thumb brushing along my cheek as he pleaded with me not to cry. I apologized again and he kissed the top of my head, then my forehead, then the trails my tears were still leaving on my cheeks, and then I turned my head towards his and his lips were on mine and he didn't pull away. He kept kissing me, kept holding me, kept letting me wrap my arms around his shoulders and kiss him back.

I shifted in his lap, my legs around his hips and my breasts against his chest. Derek groaned and clutched me. His tongue was in my mouth, flicking against mine, and already I could feel him getting hard. I squirmed against him, feeling his cock brush against my slit.

"Fuck, Joss," he groaned. "We just said…"

"Let's just forget," I gasped. "Just one more time."

He growled, nipped at my lower lip, and twisted so he could push me onto my back. I landed with a soft gasp, air puffing past my lips, hardly able to draw a breath before Derek was holding himself over me and kissing me again.

Lips trailed down my neck to my breasts, my nipples hardening as he lavished attention on them. He was incredibly thorough, his mouth tracing along every inch of skin, his hands cradling and fondling and squeezing. Every movement was a rush of arousal, a tingling that travelled over my skin and through my body, pooling between my legs.

He stopped quite suddenly, pressing a single kiss between my breasts before sitting up and staring down at me. His eyes raked down my body, taking in every inch. I bit the inside of my cheek, trying to will my self-consciousness to leave me alone for just a moment, but I couldn't control the warm flush that started on my chest or stop myself from shifting uncomfortably as he stared.

When I moved, he flicked his eyes up to mine.

"You're so gorgeous," he murmured.

I laughed uncomfortably. "Bullshit meter's going off."

He scoffed. "Don't play that game. You're absolutely stunning."

"It's not a game," I said. "You don't need to tell me I'm pretty. I'm… acceptable."

There was a moment where he seemed to be torn between thinking I was trying to get him to compliment me and thinking I really believed that about myself. He didn't say anything, just flicked his eyes down my body again and then back up to my face.

"Acceptable?" he said. "Joss, everything about you is perfect."

"Don't," I whispered.

"It's true. Who the hell told you otherwise?"

I didn't answer. Derek shook his head.

"Look at you." He skimmed his fingers along my skin, tracing every curve. "You have this perfect body, these gorgeous, perky breasts, this beautiful stomach, these amazing hips with this... you know, I had my face pressed against your pussy for quite a while last night and it was so fucking good, I didn't even notice you had another tattoo."

His fingers walked up the vines on my hip, another uncharacteristically-feminine touch that I kept hidden from almost everyone.

"I'm stocky," I said. "I'm built like an armchair."

"I've built armchairs. They don't look a thing like you."

"I know what I look like," I whispered. "You don't have to—"

"You clearly don't," he interrupted. "Jocelyn, look at you. Jesus Christ, you're... why do you think this is so goddamn hard? You're this amazing, sweet, hilarious woman who says shit that blows my mind, and all of that is packaged up in this perfect little shell."

There wasn't a trace of laughter on Derek's face. He was as serious as I had ever seen him, almost fierce in his insistence. I had no idea what he was seeing that I didn't, or couldn't, but all I could do was nod.

"Okay," I said. "I, um, I'm not an armchair."

He leaned forward, kissing me intensely.

"You are not an armchair," he repeated. "You are beautiful, Joss. You're incredible."

I couldn't agree with him about that. I'd spent my whole life looking in the mirror and seeing a girl who wasn't pretty, who wasn't perfect, who wasn't anywhere close to beautiful. For the moment, the best I could do was stop comparing myself to a piece of furniture, and that would have to be enough.

He seemed to sense it, but didn't press the issue. Instead, he showed me what he thought. He kissed every part of my body, his lips worshiping me until I couldn't take it any longer.

"Please," I gasped.

Derek's eyes flicked up from the place he was kissing, which happened to be a particularly sensitive spot on my inner thigh, a mischievous glint hidden beneath a raised eyebrow.

"Please what?"

"I need you."

"Mm," he said. "Is that so?"

"Stop teasing me," I grumbled.

He moved between my thighs, then surprised me by tugging me into his lap into a position similar to where we started. Kissing me, he leaned back against the headboard, then brushed a hand through my hair. I shifted on top of him, his cock sliding along my slick pussy, and moaned. I wanted him inside me, but I couldn't deny how good it felt to even just rub against him.

Derek didn't seem to mind when I rolled my hips again, making a soft noise as my wetness coated his cock. I did it again, shuddering as his tip brushed against my clit, and again when his hands gripped my waist. He let me continue to use his cock selfishly for a while, watching my face as I ground myself against him. I couldn't stop myself. A ball of pleasure was building up inside me, growing and pulsing. Every nerve in my body was poised to fire, every muscle prepared for the surge of bliss. I was ascending, meandering ever-closer to the tipping point, and I wasn't quite there yet when Derek moved beneath me, the tip of his cock breaching my entrance.

My mouth dropped open in surprise; seconds later I was crying out as I came, pleasure bursting through me unexpectedly. He buried his cock in me as my pussy clenched around him, and his hands held me still as I shook on top of him, unprepared but exulting in the sudden euphoria.

He was sucking on one of my nipples when I came down from the blissful high, his hands splayed across my back as he thrust up into me. My body was his to use, taken by him but freely given, gladly given, and I held on as he buried himself inside me again and again.

I took back some of the control after a bit, shifting my hips and starting to ride him. Derek moved away from my breasts and looked up at me, his eyes boring deep into mine before he kissed me. It was not the kind of look or the kind of kiss that we should have shared. The emotions that came with those actions should have stayed buried. They needed to stay buried, for everyone's sake, but we seemed to have forgotten about that, too.

His lips didn't leave mine when I came again; I cried out against his mouth, the sound muffled as my body shook. At the end of that orgasm, I could barely hold myself up, and Derek shifted me to my back with his cock still inside me. Once there, he moved inside me deeply, hard but not fast.

"Gonna come," he groaned, and I pulled his face to mine so I could feel his breath as he finished, feel the vibrating groan as he spilled inside me.

"We can't do this again," he murmured after we both caught our breaths.

"I know," I whispered.

He kissed me, and I kissed him back, and I knew it wouldn't be the last time.

CHAPTER TEN

THEN

"Jocelyn?"

I looked up from my beer to see a man with brown hair and lively eyes leaning against the bar.

"Mateo," I said. "Please don't tell me you're my blind date."

His face turned red. "Uh, no. Sorry, I didn't know you were on a date."

"I'm not."

Mateo winced. "Did you get stood up?"

I shook my head, draining my glass. "No, I just needed an excuse for why I'm drinking alone."

He chuckled. "If I buy you another, can I sit with you for a while?"

"Okay, but I'm not going home with you just because you're trying to get me drunk."

"I'm not—"

"I was joking," I said. "Isaac might be okay with marrying my sister, but I'd still find it weird to hook up with his best friend."

Mateo's smile was tense. "Fair."

He waved the bartender down and got a refill for me and a first for himself.

"So what are you doing here?" I asked.

"Full disclosure? I went to find you at the shop, and Bretta said you'd taken off early, but were probably here getting drunk."

I laughed dryly and shrugged. "The bitch knows me."

"Why the mid-afternoon day drinking?" he asked.

"The dresses came in. Chelsea wants everyone to go to the shop tonight to try them on for the first round of alterations."

He nodded. "I wanted to talk to you about that, actually."

"About the dresses? I had zero say in that, Mateo. You'd need to talk to Chelsea. Just a head's up, as best man, you'd probably have to wear the pink dress with the grey sash."

Mateo chuckled. "No, I meant about Chelsea. And Isaac."

I looked at Mateo. He was smiling, but there was tension in his neck and his eyes were wary.

"For fuck's sake," I said. "I swear to God, I'm doing the best I can. What more does Isaac want from me?"

"Uh, nothing that I know of," Mateo said.

"Sure, of course you don't. What else can I fucking do?" I took a huge swig of beer. "I don't hold it against Isaac, okay? I know he didn't do this just to screw with me or something, but I'm not going to sit here and start acting like we're buddy-buddy or something. He is just going to have to learn to deal with that. Chelsea... she's my sister. She... she's not a nice person, but she's my sister, as my parents keep reminding me. I thought she... Things were supposed to get better, but she's not... Look, I'm trying, okay?"

I could feel a lump in my throat and I gulped more beer, trying to force it down.

"You can go back and tell Isaac that I have put aside all pride here, okay? All of it. I'm over it, I'm over him, but I can't pretend like we're friends. I can't pretend to get excited about lilies and carnations and, I don't know, fucking boho-chic place settings and shit. I'm not a princess.

I'm a goddamn mechanic. And this whole thing is a sham in the first place."

"He didn't ask me to talk to you," Mateo said.

"Then why are you here?"

"I wanted to talk to you about the fact that Isaac's making a huge mistake."

I paused, staring at Mateo. He looked back, eyes determined and concerned.

"Explain," I said.

He sighed. "Isaac's been my best friend since we were kids, okay? You need to understand that. I have three brothers already, and they'd kick my ass if they heard me say this, but he's more my brother than any of them are. He listens to me, okay?"

"Okay."

"When his parents got divorced, I was the one who convinced Isaac not to just cut his dad out. I was the one who was there when he was fucking breaking down in college because of the course load. There is no one in the world Isaac is closer to than me."

"Where are you going with this?" I asked.

"Chelsea is bad for him," he said. "I don't know how he doesn't see it, but she is. He's so in love with her that—" He cut off suddenly, grimacing. "Uh, sorry."

"For what?"

Mateo looked uncomfortable and I rolled my eyes.

"I know he's in love with her. I'm not about to cry you a river over it."

"Right. Sorry." He cleared his throat. "So, uh, Isaac. He's blind to the fact that she's using him. She's already talking about becoming a stay-at-home wife and I'm like eighty percent sure that she's already cheated on him."

"Really? With who?"

"If I'm right, with her boss."

I snorted. "Must be. She's probably bored. I haven't dated anyone since Isaac and I broke up."

"She's bad news and Isaac's so drunk on love he can't even handle hearing the smallest amount of criticism about her. Like, you point out Chelsea made a mistake, and he almost loses his mind." He took a sip of beer before continuing. "If you think I haven't tried to talk some sense into him, you're wrong. The fact that I can't even get him to listen to reason... I'm desperate, okay? I've tried everything I can think of and nothing has worked."

"What do you mean, tried everything?"

"To get him to break up with her," he hissed. "I've tried being rational, I've tried pointing out the facts, I've tried begging—I shit you not, Jocelyn, I begged the bastard not to propose—and he won't listen. He told me if I bring it up again, we're not going to be friends anymore."

"And you think I can talk him into it?" I asked. "If he's a moron, that makes you a fucking idiot."

"Not him," Mateo said. "Chelsea."

"What?"

"We need to make Chelsea leave him."

"We?"

"Yeah. I need your help."

It was my turn to stare, my mouth hanging open. Determination was written across Mateo's face, from the glint of his eyes to the set of his jaw. He didn't even blink, just met my gaze with a steady, unshakeable sense of tenacity.

"No," I finally said.

"What?"

"No," I repeated. "I'm not... I mean, yeah, she's been a... I get where you're coming from, okay? But I'm not... family is family."

"You believe that?"

I chewed the inside of my cheek. "Yeah."

"You're so full of shit."

"So what if I am?" I asked. "Why the hell would I even help with this? I don't owe Isaac anything."

"You don't want revenge on your sister for taking him in the first place?"

"Fuck off." I glared at him. "Don't drag me into this shit, okay? I'm sorry your best friend is a moron, Mateo, but I'm done with him. I just want to get through this farce of a wedding and move on with my life."

"Think about it," he pleaded. "You know as well as I do that Isaac doesn't deserve to—"

"Seriously, fuck off." I got up, shaking my head. "You want to get Chelsea to break up with him, do it yourself. Isaac's life isn't my problem, okay? I don't want to be involved. Now, excuse me. I have to go try on a dress that makes me look like a fucking fairy princess."

Mateo's visit was the worst possible thing that could have happened prior to the dress fitting. If he had just left me alone, I could have had my drink at the bar, gritted my teeth, and spent the night pretending that Chelsea's passive-aggressive comments weren't getting to me. Instead, I was already balancing on the edge of breakdown when Mom picked me up, and that ledge started to crumble when we walked into the dress shop to see not just Chelsea, not just the bridesmaids, but Angela.

"Joss!" she said cheerfully.

I loved Angela, but the prospect of having yet another witness to my pink taffeta humiliation was almost more than I could handle. She didn't hug me, but put an arm around my shoulder in greeting as I walked up.

"Bianca, good to see you again," she said to my mom.

"You too, Angela." They smiled at each other politely, not friends but not necessarily enemies.

"Finally!" Chelsea groaned. "Jocelyn, you can't be late for stuff like this."

"I was the one who drove her," Mom said.

"It's no big deal anyway." Angela patted my back. "The seamstress is running behind. She said it should just be another few minutes."

Chelsea took a deep breath, not willing to disagree with her future mother-in-law about my lateness.

"I'm sorry," I said. "I didn't... I'll make sure I'm on time, next time."

"Good," she said, then turned back to the other bridesmaids.

I let out the breath I'd been holding. It wasn't a perfect reaction, but at least she wasn't yelling at me or berating me.

"What are you doing here?" I asked Angela. "Wait, that came out wrong."

She chuckled. "I understand, dear. Isaac and his father are having their suits fitted across the street, so he suggested I join Chelsea over here."

"That was a great idea," Mom said. "We should have you involved in more of the plans, Angela. You're about to be family, and family is family, after all."

I knew she was trying to be nice, but the words made my stomach curl. Mom seemed to notice the grimace I tried to hide.

"What's wrong?"

"Just a stomach ache," I mumbled. "I'm fine."

"Did you eat something? Do you need the bathroom?"

My face turned red. "I'm fine, Mom. It's just, uh, cramps."

"Oh, I might have some Midol in my purse. Let me check."

She plopped her handbag on a nearby table and started digging through it. I turned away, pretending to be very interested in a nearby rack of bridesmaid's dresses that all would have probably been preferable to the one I was about to try on. Moments later, three things happened almost simultaneously.

First, the seamstress and a saleslady came out of the back and walked over to Chelsea.

"Ms. Miller, it seems there's been an error with one of the dresses. It's a bit of a different style than the others."

Chelsea's face started turning red.

"Hey, baby!" called someone from the front of the store. I looked over to see Isaac walking towards us, grinning at Chelsea, and Derek following just behind him. "Are we allowed to see the bridesmaid dresses?"

Mom, not paying attention, pulled a small pill bottle out of her purse victoriously. "Jocelyn! I found some Midol. Are they one-pill cramps or two-pill cramps?" she asked loudly.

Derek glanced in my direction, looking alarmed. All I could do was start laughing.

"Oh sure, laugh again!" Chelsea snapped at me. "Thanks a lot, Jocelyn. Did you do this just so you didn't have to wear the damn pink dress, or are you just enjoying watching my wedding day go to shit?"

"I wasn't laughing at you!" I said. "I was laughing at—"

"Whatever," she hissed. "This is just like you."

Isaac looked like he regretted entering the store. "I'm sure it's fine, baby."

"How would you know?" she snapped. "And what are you even doing here?"

"We're done already," he said helplessly.

Even the other bridesmaids looked embarrassed. Lisa was staring at a wall, Mom's eyes were wide, and Angela looked furious.

That was the scariest part: Angela was the nicest person I'd ever met in my entire life, and it's true what they say: never, ever piss off a nice person. Never piss off the person who always has a cheerful smile and a kind word for everyone. Never upset them, because when they're upset, *damn* if it's not the most terrifying thing in the world.

Luckily, Derek had been married to Angela for long enough to recognize the look on her face.

"Hey now," he said pleasantly. "Let's all just take a breath here."

"Excuse me?" Chelsea said.

"I said we're all going to take a deep breath and calm the fuck down," Derek said.

Chelsea's mouth opened and closed. She looked at Isaac, her eyes burning. "Are you going to let him talk to me like that?"

"Considering how you just spoke to him, why the hell not?" Derek replied.

"Dad, stay out of it." Isaac walked over to Chelsea, taking her hand. "I'm sorry, baby. What's the problem? What's going on with the dress? Do we need to order a new one?"

Her face changed almost instantly: anger warped into a pathetic, simpering pout.

"There's not enough *time*," she whined.

"We'll figure it out," he promised. "If we have to buy a new dress, we buy a new dress. Whatever we need to do to have a perfect day, we're gonna do. So, let's figure this out."

She sniffed dramatically and I almost retched.

The saleslady finally piped up, her voice wavering. "It's the same fabric. It's just that the sleeves and neckline are a bit different on the pink one, and the bodice isn't form-fitted, and the skirt is just a tiny bit fuller."

"It's a completely different dress, you mean," Mom said.

The saleslady shrugged feebly.

"You know what? Why don't we just look at the dress before panicking?" Angela suggested.

I loved Angela. She was one of the sweetest, kindest people I knew. I reminded myself of that as the seamstress zipped the dress up and I looked in the mirror, knowing I was about to walk out in front of everyone wearing the ugliest thing I'd ever seen in my life. Before even opening the door, I knew Chelsea would force me to wear it. There wasn't a single doubt in my mind.

When I walked out in a dress the colour of bubblegum that had lost its flavour, with small puffed sleeves and baggy fabric drooping around my entire chest until it pinched in at the empire waist, I almost dared the seamstress to drop a pin. Mom's eyes were comically large, Angela's face was almost blank, Isaac looked like he was sorry he had ever been born, and Derek was fighting not to laugh.

Honestly, Derek's reaction probably hurt most of all, and that included when Chelsea squealed and clapped her hands together.

"I take it back!" she exclaimed. "Oh my God, Joss! It's *perfect*!"

"Yeah!" agreed Lisa, and the other bridesmaids murmured their fake approval. "It suits your... body shape."

I looked desperately at Mom, but she didn't seem to know what to do. Isaac smiled moronically.

"See? It all worked out!" he said.

The saleslady threw in free alterations for all the bridesmaids, and I was stuck staring at myself in a three-way mirror as the lady pinned and pinched and prodded the fabric until it was no longer just the colour of chewed-up bubblegum, but a shape that was reminiscent of it, too.

When I was finally allowed to change back into my jeans and TARDIS T-shirt, Chelsea was thoroughly distracted by Lisa's alterations. Mom touched my shoulder as I walked by.

"Are you okay?" she whispered.

"Yeah, I love looking like a bottle of Pepto Bismol," I muttered.

"It's not that bad, Joss."

It absolutely was that bad, and if I had to sit there for any longer, I was going to scream.

"Excuse me, I have to run for a sec," I said.

"What?" Mom said. "Where are you going?"

"Out for a smoke."

"You don't smoke," she hissed.

"I'm considering starting. I'm practicing by going out for smoke breaks to see if I like them or not."

Before she could say another word, I pushed past her and hustled to the front of the store. The door swung shut behind me and I turned to the left, following the sidewalk past a shoe store and a deli to the edge of the building. I rounded the corner, found myself in the back loading dock, and leaned against a green dumpster. Taking a deep breath to calm myself, I immediately regretted my choice to lean against the dumpster and tried not to gag as I moved to the wall of the building and leaned against that instead. Closing my eyes, I wondered if it would be overkill to fake my death before the wedding.

"You okay?"

I stiffened, hesitating before opening my eyes. Derek stood near the corner of the building, hands tucked into his pockets, looking far too good for someone I was angry at.

"Fine," I said.

"Oof," he said. "You sure? I think it just got about ten degrees chillier out here."

"Fuck off," I muttered.

"Whoa!" It came out as a stuttered sort of laugh. "We must have different definitions of 'fine'."

"We also seem to have different definitions of what's funny and what isn't."

Derek looked to the side, heaving a sigh. "I wasn't laughing at you."

"Sure, you were just laughing at the same thing everyone else was laughing at, which was obviously not the fucking pink abomination I was wearing. One of those 'you had to be there' things, right?"

"Joss, I wasn't laughing at you."

"You should've been," I muttered. "I suppose it would be funny to anyone who doesn't have to wear the ugly-ass thing."

He walked up and leaned on the wall beside me, hands still tucked in his pockets.

"I was trying not to laugh because about ten seconds before you walked out of the dressing room, Angela called out your sister for how she was speaking to Isaac."

"What?!"

Derek fought back a smile, shaking his head. "I mean, keep in mind that Ange doesn't say a bad word about anyone. While you were in there, Chelsea started complaining about how the dress mix-up was going to ruin the entire day and how miserable she was. The saleslady brought out the paperwork and wouldn't you know, *someone* filled out the order form incorrectly."

"Chelsea filled out all the order forms," I said.

"Yeah, and signed them in three different places saying they were right. So then Isaac goes, 'well, it's our mistake, so we can see how this looks and order a new one if we need to.' And Chelsea turns to him and snaps that he has no idea what he's talking about, and is he really blaming her for screwing up, and 'oh, I can't believe you'd do that to me over this, we're supposed to be a team!'"

His voice got preposterously high-pitched as he mocked Chelsea. I snorted back a laugh, and Derek grinned.

"So Isaac's embarrassed, right, and of course I'm pissed but Ange is shaking her head at me in that way that's like 'shut the fuck up, Derek, you're only going to make this worse.' And I'm not gonna fight with her because I know she's scary when she's pissed, so I keep my mouth shut. Isaac starts trying to calm her down and Chelsea tells him he's being stupid, and then Ange pipes up and goes 'if something as trivial as this is going to ruin your wedding day, maybe you're getting married for the wrong reasons.'"

"She didn't," I gasped.

"Oh, she did. And Chelsea's jaw just fucking dropped, Isaac probably would've loved if the floor just could've opened up and swallowed him, and Ange just says 'You know, even though Derek and I are divorced, I can't imagine I'd ever speak to him in such a way. I have far too much respect for him to do that.'"

"No way."

"Mm-hmm. Then the dressing room door opened and you walked out, Chelsea nearly knocked us all out with her mood swing, and when you went back with the seamstress she started sucking up to Angela and whimpering an apology to Isaac. He, of course, lapped up every word of it, but I'm pretty sure Ange is never going to look at her the same way again."

I pressed my lips together, but it was no use. I snorted again, Derek chuckled, and half a second later we were both laughing breathlessly.

"Too bad I missed it," I finally choked. "That might've made having to wear that stupid dress worth it."

"You're being far too critical," Derek said. "Seriously. It's not even half as bad as you think it is."

"I have eyes, you know. There were mirrors in there. I looked like a train-wreck."

"You looked stunning," he replied.

I opened my mouth to respond, but nothing came out. His words floated through me, uncomfortably affirming, meaning far more to me than they should have. I glanced at Derek, doubting the honesty of his statement, but there wasn't even a trace of insincerity in his eyes. There was a trace of something that shouldn't have been there, something that I might have been imagining was longing or desire, and my heart fluttered. I swallowed hard and tore my eyes away, staring back down at the ground.

"Seriously, Joss," he said before I could think of a cynical comeback. "You could go up there in a crumpled paper bag and you'd still look great. Don't worry so much."

"Guess there's no accounting for taste." I laughed weakly, hoping my face wasn't as red as it felt, and changed the subject. "I can't believe Angela said that to Chelsea."

Derek sighed. "You know it's bad when Ange says something. She said the other day she wishes Chelsea would just call it off. How fucking sad is that? Watching your kid get married is supposed to be exciting, and you know, even if we didn't like her all that much, we'd still probably support him. It's just that it's more than that. She's... she's bad for him."

"I'm sorry."

He shook his head. "No, I'm sorry. I shouldn't be saying shit like that to anyone. Would you do me a favour and not mention it? I'm already on thin ice with Isaac, and I don't want to... he's still my kid."

"What happened?" I asked. "I mean, what happened that made things so tense between you?"

He thought for a moment, staring at the dumpster across from us.

"When Ange and I got divorced, he was pretty upset. He was convinced I'd had an affair. I mean, you know he loves his mom, so he couldn't... he didn't understand why we'd split up. He wouldn't even talk to me for about six months after I moved out. He only stopped thinking that when it was clear I wasn't seeing anyone, and Ange told him he was wrong. She was ready to lose her mind, but we agreed that we weren't going to drag the kids into things. We didn't want them picking sides or turning against either of us, so we limited what we told them."

Pausing, he tapped his fingers against the wall, then laughed.

"You know, you hear all those horror stories about marriages ending and shit, and that's not what ours was like at all. For something that sucks so much, we had the best possible outcome, and we were certain we'd get through it without screwing Isaac and Samantha up. Sam was fine, probably because she was a little younger and adapted to things more easily. Isaac... well, I'd rather he take his anger out on me than on his mom, so it is what it is."

"It is what it is." It sounded like Derek's version of "family is family."

"It sounds hard," I said.

He shrugged. "I don't know if we'll ever be close again, but I can hope."

When we went back into the dress shop, the seamstress was just starting on the last of the alterations. Isaac was sitting on a puffy stool, elbow resting on his knee and chin in hand, and Angela was watching with her arms folded as Chelsea bossed the seamstress around.

"Are you alright?" Mom whispered as I came back in.

I nodded but didn't say anything. Isaac glanced up at me and tried to smile. Any other day, I might have felt a surge of guilty satisfaction at the hidden misery on his face, but really, it was just painful. Derek and Angela had maintained a friendship even after divorcing. Would it be that hard for me to at least be cordial towards him?

I took a breath and walked over to Isaac.

"How are you doing?" I asked, settling on the stool next to his.

He looked surprised, probably because I was actively choosing to talk to him, but smiled and seemed to relax.

"Okay," he said. "Sorry about the issues with your dress."

"It happens. How was your suit fitting?"

He positively grinned. "It was great. Dad and I are getting custom ones made."

We chatted about various things relating to the wedding for the rest of the appointment, and it was only when Chelsea stomped over to us that I realized they were done.

"Are you done distracting my fiancé?" she muttered at me.

Isaac stood up. "We were just talking, baby."

"Well, Jocelyn was *supposed* to be paying attention to the fittings and making sure we covered everything, but I had to do that myself."

"I was?" I asked. "No one told me that."

Chelsea took a breath. "It's fine. You know what? It's fine."

"Let's go home," Isaac said to her quietly. "It's been a rough day, we can just—"

"Rough day?" she repeated, staring at him with a disgusted look on her face. "What are you trying to say, Isaac?"

"Nothing, I just—"

"Why is everyone against me today?" she whined.

"I just meant you seem stressed and I thought we could—"

"Stressed," she sniffed. "You mean you think I'm a bitch."

"I would never say anything like that," Isaac protested. "You know that, baby."

She grumbled but allowed him to take her hand and kiss her, murmuring an apology. I stared, flabbergasted, wondering why Isaac was the one apologizing.

"I have to go pay the balance," she grumbled, shaking her hand away from him and turning on a heel to stomp towards the cash register.

Isaac stared after her, sighing just the slightest bit.

"Is she always like that?" I asked.

"No," Isaac said.

He didn't sound very convincing, but I let it slide, instead saying goodbye as the other bridesmaids began to leave.

"I'm heading out too," Derek said, striding up to Isaac. "Thanks for including me in this, Isaac. I appreciate it."

Isaac nodded and smiled. "Yeah. Thanks, Dad. It was fun."

He didn't sound convinced about that either, but shook his dad's hand.

"It was good to see you again, Joss," Derek said.

"Jocelyn," Isaac said.

"What?"

"Her name is Jocelyn," Isaac said.

Derek flushed. "Oh, sorry. I didn't know it—"

"It's fine," I said. "I don't mind. A lot of people call me Joss."

Isaac glanced at me, almost looking hurt.

"You can, too," I said to him. "I might've been a little pissed when I told you not to."

After saying goodbye to Derek, Angela was next. She asked Isaac to come out to the car with her because she had some of the wedding decorations and needed to move them over. With their departure, only Chelsea, Mom, and I were left in the dress shop.

"Listen, Jocelyn," Chelsea said as she came up to us after paying. "I don't know what you're planning but stay away from my fiancé."

"What?" I asked, shocked.

"I saw you sitting with him. He left you, understand? He will not be crawling back to you. We are getting married, and if you so much as look at him in a way that makes me think you're going to try something—"

"Stop being so paranoid. I'm not trying to steal back my ex-boyfriend that you're marrying, okay? We were just talking."

"That better have been it," she said.

"Girls!" Mom gasped. "Chelsea, your sister is allowed to talk to Isaac. I believe they spent most of the time talking about the details of *your wedding* to him."

Chelsea wasn't stupid. She knew when even Mom was calling her out on her behaviour, she had pushed too far.

"Sorry," she muttered.

"It's fine. Sorry I didn't help more with the fitting," I replied just as reluctantly.

"That's better," Mom said.

Chelsea nodded, still looking at me suspiciously as we left the dress shop. In the parking lot, she snapped at Isaac again, got into the passenger seat of his car, and folded her arms across her chest in a pout. The dejected look on Isaac's face as he pulled out of the parking lot was almost haunting.

It was so burnt into my mind that when Mom dropped me off at home, I couldn't stop thinking about it. I didn't know if Chelsea thought she loved him and was having a bad day or was just faking her love for him, but one thing was clear: if even I thought Isaac deserved better after he left me for her, standing by and letting him marry her was practically immoral.

It probably didn't help that Chelsea was accusing me of doing to her what she did to me, was putting me in the ugliest dress in the universe, and was treating me horribly. It definitely didn't help that I couldn't just drop out of the wedding, knowing my dad would lose his mind and my mom would never speak to me again.

Though, I did consider it. I loved my mom, but why did she think it was okay for me to put up with this? She turned a blind eye to all the problems between me and my sister, as if she just wished hard enough for us to stop being a dysfunctional family, it would become true. Maybe I should just take the plunge, finally stand up for myself, and be firm when I said I wouldn't be in the wedding party anymore. Maybe Mom would eventually forgive me. Maybe I'd be better off alone, anyway.

At the end of it all, I couldn't bring myself to do it. People make it seem so easy to just walk away from a toxic situation, but it wasn't easy at all. It was even harder because they were my family, and I loved them. Even Chelsea, as horrible as she was.

Leaving my family wasn't an option, but that didn't mean the wedding had to happen.

One of my tasks as maid of honour had been collecting everyone's contact information for various purposes. Invitations, coordinating events, general bridal party chats... communication was key. Because of that, I didn't have to look very hard for his number, though when he picked up, he still seemed surprised to hear from me.

"Jocelyn?"

"I'm in."

"What?"

"I'll help you get her to leave him, Mateo. What's the plan?"

CHAPTER ELEVEN

NOW

THE RAIN STOPPED MID-MORNING, just after Derek brought me to my apartment. I scrambled upstairs to change, then back down to his car so that if anyone saw him drop me off, it wouldn't seem quite as suspicious as it would if I was still in my maid of honour dress. When we got to the hotel, he pulled to the side of the building and parked.

"Joss, I—"

"I know, it was a terrible idea, we can't do this again, my lips are sealed."

"I was going to say I had a great time," he said gently.

"Me too."

"And then I was going to say that other stuff."

I snorted, smiling in spite of myself. "Goodbye, Derek."

I got out of the car before he could say anything else. I had to. The longer I sat there, the harder it would be to tear myself away. Limping only slightly, I made my way around the car to the side door of the hotel.

I wasn't quite strong enough not to look back. When I did, he was watching me. He lifted his fingers off the steering wheel in a half-wave, a small smile on his face, and I waved back before going into the building.

By the end of the day, I was wondering if I should have just said fuck it to what other people thought and stayed with Derek. Waking up in his arms was the happiest I had been in years. At what cost, though? My train-wreck of a family would react in one of two ways: either surprised but begrudging acceptance, like they did with Chelsea and Isaac, or complete and total disgust that got me cut off for good. Some might argue that would be for the best, but the thought of being disowned terrified me.

Derek stood to lose a lot more than I would. His relationship with Isaac was rocky at best, and I knew Isaac would have a problem with it. If I had been anyone else, it might have been okay, but I was Isaac's ex, and it wasn't like he needed much of a reason to be angry with his dad. That much was clear. Angela would probably be less angry and more confused, but she'd lose a lot of respect for both of us. And Samantha? Who knew, though she might have a problem with the fact that I was barely older than she was.

Still, even if Samantha was cool with it and for some reason Angela accepted what we had done, ruining Derek's relationship with his son was far too costly a price.

It wasn't an easy day. When I finally got home, Mom called almost immediately, telling me they had spent most of the day clearing Chelsea's things out of her and Isaac's apartment and bringing it back to their house, before begging me to come over for dinner.

"We need to get all the bad feelings out in the open and start to heal as a family," she said.

"Maybe we should wait a little bit," I said. "I'm a little on edge, what with the whole 'my-boyfriend-cheated-on-me-again' thing, Chelsea's marriage just ended, and it's... oh, look at that, it would've been her twenty-eight-hour anniversary just now. Dad's probably—"

"He will be apologizing for how he spoke to you yesterday," she cut in.

"Sure, Mom. I thought I felt a chill this morning when Hell froze over."

"He will," she repeated. "Joss, please."

"How many times am I supposed to forgive this?" I asked.

"She's your sis—"

"If Aunt Sharon slept with Dad, would you forgive her?"

"Yes."

I rolled my eyes. "You can't be serious."

"I would," she said. "At the end of the day, she's my sister, and family is—"

"I swear to God, I'm so sick of hearing you say that."

"Why are you being like this?"

"Sane, you mean? Why am I acting in a perfectly reasonable way given the circumstances?"

She didn't respond and I cringed as I heard the telltale sound of her plucking Kleenex from the tissue box.

"Don't cry, Mom," I pleaded.

"My family is falling apart and I can't do anything about it," she whimpered.

"Mom," I sighed. "Look at it from my point of view. Just for once, please. Can I at least have a couple of days to settle down? She slept with my *boyfriend*. At her wedding to my *ex-boyfriend*."

"She feels horrible," Mom said.

"I'm supposed to believe that?"

"You need to be the bigger person," she said. "Chelsea's not capable of it, but you are. Sweetie, please. For me?"

What little fire was left in me fizzled out. "What time?"

Dinner was tense. Chelsea mumbled a false apology, I mumbled a fake acceptance of said apology, Dad's apology started with "I'm sorry you were offended, but...," and then we sat around the dinner table not speaking.

"Where did the decorations end up?" Chelsea asked after Mom cleared the plates off the table. "I went back to the church but everything was gone."

"Derek and Angela took most of it last night," I said.

She sighed unhappily. "Great. You couldn't have gotten *anyone* to take it other than his parents?"

"I could've just left all that shit there," I said.

"Language," Dad muttered.

"That was all my stuff," Chelsea said. "Isaac will probably just throw it out."

"What are you going to do with a bunch of storage totes full of wedding decorations?" I asked.

"You wouldn't understand," she hissed.

"Well, Jocelyn can go collect it for you," Dad said.

"What?"

He raised his eyebrows at me. "You insisted on cleaning up. You sent the items home with the Thompsons. You can arrange getting it back from them."

"I don't remember volunteering to be a go-between," I said.

"I don't remember when it became okay to slap your sister and call her a whore."

"Oh, I remember when that happened. It became okay around the time I caught my boyfriend with his—"

"Enough!" Mom said. We all fell silent, startled by the intensity of her voice. "Jocelyn, please speak with the Thompsons about getting the decorations back. Chelsea, have some grace. You are not the only one who had a difficult day yesterday. Gerald, for the love of God, you need to treat *both* of your daughters kindly right now."

I put off calling Angela until the following Friday around lunch, when Mom finally got frustrated enough to threaten to come down to the shop and watch me call her. When I asked why she didn't just call Angela herself, she burst into tears and fifteen minutes later, I was calling the ex-wife of a man I'd slept with less than a week earlier.

"Hello?"

"Hi Angela. It's Jocelyn. Um, Jocelyn Miller."

"Oh! What a... surprise," Angela said. "Not that I'm not happy to hear from you, dear. Let me just, um, run upstairs."

I grimaced. "Isaac's there, isn't he?"

"That is true, yes. Just a moment." There were a few moments of the phone jostling and then the sound of a door closing. "I'm so sorry, dear. He was off work for the... well, anyway, now he's staying here for a bit. He's... he's having a hard time."

"I understand. I'm sorry to bother you, it's just..." I took a breath, steeling myself. "I know this is probably going to sound tactless and ridiculous, but Chelsea wants the decorations back and my mom said I had to call you to ask for them."

"Of course she does," Angela said impassively. "Well, she can have them. I have no use for them and Isaac is trying to get rid of anything that reminds him of Chelsea, which means he's down to two T-shirts and a few polos since apparently she bought the rest of his clothes, so he gave them all away."

Guilt rushed through me, so strong I felt my shoulders hunch forward. "Did he?"

"He'll be okay," Angela said. "You know, at the end of the day there's silver linings, and I suppose the silver lining here is that he's been reaching out to Derek quite a bit. I don't know how much you know about their, ah, situation, but Isaac never quite understood why we got divorced and now I think he's started to figure it out."

Derek. Of course. I winced again, almost nauseous, though that might have been less guilt and more really, really missing Derek.

"That's so good to hear," I said. "I hope they, you know, figure things out."

"Oh God, I hope so," Angela sighed. "It would be the best possible thing to come from this. If they can fix... well."

There was a slight thickness in her voice. If any more guilt rolled through me, I was going to get an ulcer.

"So, um, what's the best way to do this?" I asked. "I'm sure you don't want Chelsea to come by herself, and I doubt... I mean, it'll probably upset Isaac to see me, too, so..."

"Not as much as you'd think," she said. "I think he's sorry about everything. He feels bad he didn't listen to you."

Ulcers. I was definitely going to get an ulcer. "So, um..."

"Right," she said. "Sorry, dear. You know, why don't you give Derek a call? He could come pick the totes we have here up and bring them to his house for you to pick up, or he could probably... well, he probably wouldn't want to go to your parents'. He's, um, not a fan of your father, apparently."

I laughed weakly. "Yeah, they, um, got into it last weekend. I'll... you know, would it be too much trouble for you to give Derek my number? I just feel, um, bad calling out of nowhere, I guess."

"Oh, you don't have to worry about that at all. I'm sure he'll be happy to hear from you," she said. "But of course, I'll give him a call and let him know, dear."

I hung up and tried to force myself to eat part of the sandwich I'd brought for lunch. When my phone rang a few minutes before I had to go back to work, I'd barely picked at a quarter of it. The moment his number appeared on the screen, I sighed, dumped the rest of my lunch in the garbage, and slipped out the back door to take the call away from prying ears.

"Hi," I said.

"Hey, Joss," Derek said. "How's your leg?"

I laughed a bit. "Fine, thanks. Pretty much healed."

"Good, glad to hear it." He paused, the tension overwhelming. "Uh, so—"

"I know," I said. "Sorry. My mom—"

"Ange explained, it's fine. Don't be afraid to call me though, okay? Even after... you know. I don't want you to feel... uncomfortable, I guess."

"I wasn't worried about feeling uncomfortable, exactly," I admitted.

"Oh." He cleared his throat. "Fair point."

"I'm sorry," I said. "I shouldn't have—"

"You should have. Don't hide things, okay? Better to have the cards on the table."

My face was turning red. "Right."

"You're blushing, aren't you?"

I snorted. "Wouldn't you like to know?"

"I mean—"

"Don't answer that," I interrupted. "Let's just... let's figure this stupid decoration shit out."

"Good plan," he said. "So, you need the totes."

I thought of suggesting he leave the storage totes on his driveway and I would just make a few trips to pick them up, but as much as one part of me wanted to avoid Derek, another part of me was thrilled at the prospect of seeing him. He didn't suggest it, either. Instead, he said he would stop by Angela's on his way home and grab the other totes, and I said I would stop by that night and start bringing the decorations to my parents' place.

Nothing was going to happen with him, I told myself as I left work later that day. I was so certain that nothing was going to happen that I didn't even go home to shower or change before heading to Derek's. Going out of my way to go home and clean up would have been forethought, an intentional decision to make things more complicated.

When I pulled into Derek's driveway, the garage door was open. Derek was puttering around one of his motorcycles and looked up as I turned my car off. He looked good. Unreasonably good. The tattoo on his bicep poked out beneath the sleeve of his T-shirt and I wanted to reach out and run my fingers along the one on his neck. His jeans fit just right and knowing what was beneath them made it even more difficult not to blush.

"Hey," he said as I got out of the car.

"Hey." I tried to smile at him. "So, the totes."

"Straight to business, eh?" Derek said, chuckling. "Fair enough."

"What else am I supposed to do?" I asked.

"What I want you to do and what you should do are very different things," he said. "So what you should do is exactly what you did."

Oh good. I wasn't the only one struggling with the entire situation. I swallowed, not saying anything, not even able to look at him.

He cleared his throat. "So. The totes."

Together we loaded my car up, squeezing in as much as we could. It seemed likely I could get everything done in three trips, and I said as much to Derek as I closed the trunk.

"So you're going to do all three trips tonight?" he asked.

"Is that okay?"

"Probably better that way."

I nodded. "I'll be back in about an hour, then."

I drove to my parents, unloaded, then headed back. We reloaded the car, I drove to my parents, and unloaded. On a whim, just before heading back, I texted Derek.

I'm starving. Going to stop for a burger. You want anything?

When I got to the nearest fast food place, I checked my phone.

Hell yes. Thanks.

His order followed and I stopped in the drive-thru, picked up a couple of meals, and headed back to Derek's.

"You're a lifesaver," he said when I got out of the car holding the large brown bag. "I was just thinking I hadn't figured out what I was going to do tonight."

"I didn't eat much at lunch," I admitted. "I wasn't going to make it until I got home."

"Come in and eat," he said, motioning to the house.

"Is that a good idea?"

"No, but do you really want to stand in the driveway and eat?"

I didn't, of course, so followed him inside.

Our conversation was casual while we ate. We avoided all the heavy topics: the wedding, Isaac, spending the night together the previous weekend. We just talked about work and the new motorcycle Derek was planning on buying, little things that should have kept things friendly but distant.

It just seemed that no matter what Derek and I did, it was the wrong decision.

Instead of keeping things distant, it just meant we ignored all those reasons we were supposed to stay away from each other. We started making jokes, and then laughing, and by the end of the meal, I was trying to throw French fries into Derek's mouth from across the table.

"Yes!" I exclaimed as one finally went into his mouth, rather than bouncing off his cheek and onto the floor.

"I don't think one-in-six is that good of a track record," he teased, chewing the fry.

"Oh yeah? You think you can do better?"

"I know I can do better," he shot back.

"Prove it."

When he got the fry in my mouth on the first try, I groaned as he clapped his hands together.

"I win," he teased.

I laughed, chewing the fry. "It wasn't a competition!"

"Oh, it was," he replied.

"So what do you win?" I asked.

It was the wrong thing to ask. The words were almost visible, hanging off the tension in the air between us. Derek's face was somewhere between nervous and reckless, eyes boring into mine from across the table.

"I shouldn't have... this was a bad idea," I whispered.

"Terrible idea," he agreed. "But, uh... cards on the table? I've been thinking about you all week."

I pressed my lips together, willing myself to be strong, begging my heart to stop racing and my legs to stop tingling and my body to stop urging me to just drop the charade and kiss him.

"I have, too."

Derek sighed, brushing a hand against the scruff on his chin.

"I should go," I said after a moment. "I think that's probably for the best, right?"

He nodded. I stood up, collected the wrappers from my meal, put them in the empty takeout bag, and brought them to the garbage can under the sink. From behind me, I heard Derek stand up. The moment I turned around, he reached for me and I reached for him.

He kissed me hard, passion and longing entwined as we gave in yet again. His hands moved to my thighs and lifted me up on the counter in the faintest echo of our first kiss. It was different, of course; instead of a tentative, shaking hand touching his neck, I clutched him to me. Instead of standing in front of me, shocked but responsive, he pulled my body close to his and ran his hands along my hips.

"Just one more time," he murmured between kisses.

"Don't be stupid," I whispered, kissing him back. "It's never going to be just one more time."

He growled, his teeth tugging at my bottom lip. "You don't have to be so right, you know."

I chuckled against his mouth. Derek smiled, still kissing me, still touching me, but the urgency faded away until he rested his forehead against mine. His breath brushed against my lips.

"Isaac's been calling me regularly," he whispered. "Asking for advice, support, that kind of thing. He's pretty torn up."

I didn't respond, just let him run his fingers along my thigh as he thought.

"I've heard from my son more this week than I have any other week since Ange and I divorced," he continued. "That should make saying no to this worth it."

"It should," I agreed.

"So why doesn't it?" He pulled his face away from mine and looked at me, almost pleading. "Why can't I stop thinking about you, Joss?"

I shrugged helplessly.

"Isaac would never understand. I mean, shit, he thinks every woman I've been with since Ange has just been me trying to replace his mom. Add the fact that you're his ex-girlfriend... He'd be livid if he found out."

He had a point, but it was clear that it was going to be much harder for me and Derek to stay away from each other than we thought. I chewed the inside of my cheek thoughtfully.

"What if he... didn't?"

"No, he would be disgusted," Derek scoffed.

"Not that. I mean, what if he didn't find out?"

"What?"

I shifted nervously, staring at Derek's chin rather than into his eyes. "What if we just... you know, kept quiet about everything, but also... hung out every once in a while?"

"You want to sneak around behind everyone's backs and fuck, you mean."

My cheeks went red so fast I almost felt dizzy.

"Joss?"

"Yes," I whispered. "Yeah, I guess... yeah."

I had no idea what Derek was thinking. I couldn't bring myself to look at him, to see what I imagined was a look of disgusted indignation. He had to be judging me, I thought. He had to, because even knowing the risks, even knowing how badly it could hurt his son, I was still proposing that we... well, sneak around and fuck.

His hand moved up to my chin, nudging my face back to his. I closed my eyes, still unwilling to look at him, so I was a bit startled when his lips pressed against mine again. I kissed him back eagerly, urgently, letting him pull me close to him again.

"Is that a yes, then?" I murmured against his mouth.

"I've tried saying no to you," he mumbled back. "It's not working out so well."

I never made it back to my parents' with the third load of decorations that night. When Mom asked about it the next day, I told her it had started raining and I was tired and hungry anyway, so I went home instead of driving all the way back to her place. In reality, I let Derek strip my coveralls off in the kitchen and laughed as he ran his fingers along the lacy blue underwear I was wearing that day. I took his hand and led him to his bathroom, where he put those fingers to use in the shower by washing every inch of me.

Once he had, I returned the favour, though not quite as extensively as he had. I got distracted partway through and dropped to my knees in front of him, taking his cock into my mouth as the spray of hot water beat down on us. His groan echoed in the shower, a sound that shook through my body, and I glanced up in time to see him put one hand on the back of my head and brace himself against the shower wall with the other.

He finished in my mouth, panting as I swallowed every drop of cum, and tugged me to my feet so he could kiss me before dragging me to his bedroom. There, he returned the favour, pushing me on my hands and knees, licking my pussy from behind until I was shrieking and shaking as I gripped the sheets.

I didn't realize he was hard again until he moved behind me, the tip of his cock breaching my entrance as he slid himself inside my pussy. He gripped my hips, pounding me hard, and I slipped a hand beneath me to finger my clit as he did. When I came on his cock, he staggered, leaning forward so he could kiss the back of my neck and shoulders. Pulses of pleasure tingled through my body, little aftershocks and shudders each time he thrust into me.

He embraced me as he came again, an arm wrapped around my body and his hand cupping my breast when he finished. For a long, perfect moment, the feel of his breath against my back and his body against mine was all that mattered. He pressed his lips against me again before pulling out and moving to the side, wrapping his arms around me as I curled up against his chest.

"So how often am I allowed to sneak you over here?" he mumbled.

"How often do you want me?"

"Every day, if I could."

I chuckled, but Derek didn't. "For real?"

"In a perfect world, yeah." His fingers trailed enticingly along my arm. "In a perfect world, how often would you want me?"

"Every day."

"Are you saying that because you think that's what I want to hear?"

"Of course not," I said.

He chuckled. "Every day, eh?"

"Every day," I repeated. "Think you could keep up?"

I had to pull my head away from his chest for fear of getting whiplash, he was laughing so hard. Bemused, I watched as he wiped a hand under his eye.

"I could keep up, yeah," he said. "Don't worry about that."

"What's so funny?"

He kissed me softly. "Nothing."

"Are you saying that because you think it's what I want to hear?"

"Smartass," he muttered. "You really want to know?"

I nodded and he tightened his arms around me.

"I have a pretty high sex drive," he said. "Every day would be a dream come true. Realistically, though, I think that kind of frequency would make the whole 'sneaking' thing difficult."

"Why don't we just see what happens?"

I felt him nod before he kissed the top of my head. We spent the rest of the night in his bed, listening to the rain while we talked and laughed, until I fell asleep in his arms and slept more soundly than I had since the last time I had been there.

CHAPTER TWELVE

THEN

"Pizza? Are you for real?"

Isaac tried to smile. "We just thought it was, you know, more casual. It's just a chill get together."

Chelsea glowered at him. "Thanks for thinking of me. I'll be sure to enjoy the single slice of this I can have."

"Baby, you can have more than one slice."

"*Some* of us have a wedding dress to fit into, Isaac!"

"Hey now, it's no problem," I cut in. "I'll eat her share. It won't go to waste."

Isaac grimaced, but before he could say anything, Chelsea scoffed.

"You have a dress to fit into, too," she said through gritted teeth.

I took a large bite, chewing loudly. "Don't worry. My dress has way more wiggle room than yours does since the top is so baggy."

I thought she would glower at me or maybe tell me to stop being such a bitch. Instead, she smiled sweetly and patted my arm. "I admire you so much for that, you know. Not worrying too much about what you look like. It's super brave. I'm sure you'll find some guy who doesn't mind either... one day."

Rolling my eyes, I slid another slice of pizza on my plate and made my way across the room. For Chelsea, that was a pretty weak insult. I'd long since gotten over the biting remarks she made about my appearance.

Mateo was hosting a "get to know you" shindig for the wedding party. Well, that's what he said it was, at least. Only I knew it was actually another attempt at getting Isaac and Chelsea to break up, this time by trying to make her reveal that she was cheating on Isaac with her boss.

It was an asinine plan at best, but Mateo was getting desperate. He had enlisted the help of practically every sleazy douchebag he knew to try to catch Chelsea's eye. Not a single one of them managed to hold her attention for longer than it took to sneer and reject him. He tried to make the little things Isaac did that annoyed her a bigger deal, thinking maybe she would give up on the relationship. Isaac, unfortunately, was wrapped so tightly around her finger that he would move heaven and earth to change each time she snapped at him.

"It's like he's not even the same person anymore," Mateo grumbled to me one night.

"What about trying to get evidence of her cheating on him?" I asked. "Can't we, I dunno, catch them in the act?"

If she was cheating, though, she was careful about it. Even dropping in unexpectedly at her workplace didn't give us any leads and trying to dig up dirt about the boss she was supposedly sleeping with was useless.

My contributions to the break-up plan were minor. The only person I thought Chelsea might listen to was our dad, but he was wrapped around her finger even more than Isaac was. Still, I started going to dinner at my parents' more regularly and made little comments about Isaac not being good enough for Chelsea where I could. At best, Dad brushed them off. At worst, he just ignored me.

I think Mateo was disappointed by my inability to provide more help. He seemed to think I knew my sister far better than I did. That, and he seemed to think I was willing to go much further than I was in order to break them up.

"No way," I said when he suggested trying to catfish her.

"It's easy!" Mateo insisted. "We just create a profile on social media of some super-hot guy and—"

"She's a shitty person, Mateo, but she's not stupid," I said. "First of all, she'll see right through that. Second, if none of your hot friends have managed to seduce her in person, how is a Facebook profile going to manage it?"

I flat-out refused to plant evidence of an affair for Isaac to discover.

"What's going to happen when he discovers it was faked? Or if they catch you or me doing it?"

"They won't!" he said, exasperated. "You just need to—"

"I'm not faking it. Breaking them up through deceit makes us no better than Chelsea."

"Oh my God, what's worse, letting Isaac ruin his life or planting a little evidence?" he asked, but I stayed firm.

As it stood, over a month had gone by and we were no closer to breaking them up than we had been when Mateo first approached me. It was starting to look hopeless.

I settled onto the couch across the living room from Chelsea and Isaac, munching on the extra slice of pizza I'd taken. I didn't really want it, but I also didn't want Chelsea to have the satisfaction to think I was eating less because of what she said.

As usual, I was sitting alone. Chelsea's bridesmaids were her real friends; Isaac's groomsmen were all friends I had met while Isaac and I were dating, but who now found my presence as awkward as I did. Mateo was kind enough to me, but he had other things to worry about than keeping me entertained.

One of those things was trying to get Chelsea to slip up and admit she was sleeping with her boss.

There was no better way to describe it than cringeworthy. Mateo's questions were so leading and so obvious that Isaac should have easily figured out what was going on, but Mateo had been right. Isaac was a different person, and that person was so focused on his bride-to-be that he missed the glaring hints Mateo was dropping.

Chelsea, on the other hand, wasn't fooled. I had told Mateo she wasn't stupid, but he underestimated her at every turn.

"Well, of course I'm close with my boss," she said. "Dr. Karigan is a wonderful dentist and, well, I would consider him a friend. His wife is a lovely person as well."

"Oh, I didn't know he was married," Mateo said. "Do they seem to have a happy marriage?"

"What an odd question to ask," Chelsea said. "But yes, I believe he is madly in love with his wife. He's a very lucky man. She's so pretty and a very good mother, from what I hear."

"So he has kids, too. Wow," Mateo said.

"He sure does." Chelsea smiled at Mateo, though even from across the room I could see the iciness in her eyes. "You know, I am the luckiest person ever. I have a very kind and understanding boss, a wonderful family, including my sweet sister over there, and the love of my life right here with me."

Suppressing a gag caused by a mix of Chelsea's disgusting faux-sincerity and Mateo's horrible act that wasn't fooling anyone, I coughed. He glanced across the room at me, giving me a pleading look. Pleading for what, I didn't know. It was his own stupid plan, and I had no idea what he expected me to do about it.

Instead, I patted my mouth with a napkin and stood up. "Mateo, where's your bathroom?"

He looked exasperated. "Upstairs, second door on the left."

Smiling as pleasantly as I could, I brought my empty plate to the kitchen before heading up the stairs. I took my time in the bathroom, playing on my phone until I was fairly sure if I spent any longer in there, they were going to start wondering if I was sick. I flushed the toilet and was in the middle of washing my hands when the bathroom door swung open and crashed into me.

The person who hit me with the door gasped when I yelped.

"I'm so sorry! Are you okay?"

"Well, I just got my ass kicked by a door," I groaned, rubbing the spot on my arm that had taken the brunt of the force.

"Shit, I'm so sorry."

I looked at him. He wasn't one of the groomsmen, I knew that much. Curly hair, a slightly turned up nose, and a boyish smile looked back at me.

"Do you make a habit of just barging into bathrooms?" I asked.

"Well, it's my bathroom," he said.

"Oh. You're...?"

"Lawrence." He grinned and stuck out his hand. "Mateo's annoying roommate."

I chuckled and wiped my wet hands on the towel next to the sink before shaking his hand. "Jocelyn. Reluctant maid of honour."

"Oh. Having a hard time with Bridezilla down there?"

"That's my sister."

The muscles in his neck tensed as he grimaced. "Oops. Sorry."

"Don't be. She's a terror."

He burst out laughing. "Mateo kept insisting I could come down and have pizza with you guys, but I was like, dude, have you seen that girl? She's fucking nuts. No offense."

"Too bad. I could've used a source of entertainment."

He grinned. "Well, if *you're* inviting me..."

"Sure, why not?"

"Well, I was about to take a piss, so..."

"Oh, right." I laughed and moved out of the bathroom. "Come hang out if you want. There's still lots of pizza. The bride and her bridesmaids are all on diets."

"Aren't you too, then?"

"Nah. I'm the maid of honour, and I like pizza better than I like my sister."

He snickered and I slipped past him, shuffling close to his body as I stepped through the door.

"There you are," Chelsea said as I descended the stairs and stepped back into the living room. "I was starting to wonder what happened. Did the pizza not agree with your stomach?"

"Nah, I was just on a hard level of Candy Crush. But I ran out of lives," I replied, settling back into my lonely spot on the couch.

A few minutes later, Lawrence bounded down the stairs.

"Hey!" Mateo said. "You changed your mind."

"Yeah, some pretty girl invited me down for pizza. Sold it a little better than you did," he said.

"Pretty girl?" Chelsea repeated, frowning.

Lawrence grinned and gestured at me. "Yeah, that cutie over there."

My annoyance at being referred to as "cutie" was quelled by the look of shock on Chelsea's face. I suppressed a laugh and managed to smile as though I'd found the comment sweet instead of demeaning.

After all, Lawrence didn't know I didn't like being referred to as "cutie." I wasn't cute. I was short. There was a difference.

"Well, if you've met Jocelyn already, I think you know everyone here," Mateo said. "But just in case, everyone remembers my roommate Lawrence?"

"Sure do," Isaac said with an odd grin.

Lawrence helped himself to a few slices of pizza, grabbed a beer, and strode across the living room to sit next to me.

"So, Jocelyn," he said. "What do you do for a living?"

He took a huge bite of pizza and nodded excitedly when I said I was a mechanic.

"No shit!" he mumbled through a full mouth. "That's super cool."

"You think so?" I said, surprised. "Most guys think it's weird."

Lawrence shook his head. "Nah. 'We can do it' and 'girl power' and all that shit, right? Girls can be mechanics. I've got no problem with that."

I raised my eyebrows. "That so?"

"Yeah, of course." He grinned at me before taking another bite of pizza. "And you should get paid the same as anyone who does the same job, too."

I couldn't help but laugh. At least he was trying.

We chatted for the rest of the night. We had some common interests, mostly sports. Lawrence had played lacrosse growing up, as had I, and we both followed hockey almost religiously during the season. I wouldn't say we hit it off: he was nice enough, and we had fun, but there was no real spark there. Still, he made the night tolerable, and when I glanced across the room and caught sight of the annoyed look on Chelsea's face, almost enjoyable. In fact, we got into such a deep discussion about the upcoming NHL draft that I didn't realize everyone was leaving.

"Goodbye, Jocelyn," Chelsea said loudly from the door.

"Oh. Bye!" I said, waving from the couch.

"It was good to see you again, Lawrence," she said sweetly.

"Yeah man, good to see you!" Isaac said.

They left and I stretched. "Well, I guess I should get out of you and Mateo's hair."

"Are you kidding? No fucking way!" Mateo exclaimed. "Jocelyn, you're brilliant!"

I froze mid-stretch. "Uh... what?"

"Did you not see the way Chelsea was looking at you the *second* Lawrence started talking to you?" he said excitedly.

"What the hell are you talking about?" I asked, bewildered.

"Oh my God, you didn't even see it," he groaned. "Joss, she was boiling mad. Like snipping at Isaac about every little thing and couldn't keep her eyes off you two laughing over in the corner."

I put the pieces together. "No. No way."

"You said to me she must be bored because you haven't dated anyone since you and Isaac broke up," Mateo said, wagging a finger at me. "She would try it again, wouldn't she? If you were dating someone, she'd—"

"I'm not dating Lawrence on the off chance my sister might try to fuck him!" I blurted.

"Wait, what?!" Lawrence looked from me to Mateo, baffled. "You're... what are you trying to do here?"

Mateo sighed. "Jocelyn said she'd help me break Chelsea and Isaac up because Isaac's making a huge mistake, only we've failed so far, but if you were dating her, she would—"

"She wouldn't," I said. "There's no way."

"I can almost guarantee she would," Mateo argued.

"And then what?" I asked. "She does it to me *again* and that hopefully breaks them up?"

"Is no one going to ask if I'm into this?" Lawrence asked. "Because like, yeah, she's hot, but also, she's a total bitch."

Mateo turned to him, eyes flashing. "You owe me."

Lawrence groaned. "This is what you're cashing it in on?"

"Cashing what for what?" I said. "I didn't agree to this!"

"Lawrence owes me a favour for—"

"Dude. Did you think that maybe I just like Jocelyn and you're being kind of a dickhead?" Lawrence muttered.

Mateo froze. "Oh. Um..."

"Oh," I said. "I mean, you're nice, but—"

"Oh, thank God," Lawrence interrupted. "Because like, yeah, you're hot and everything, and I'd definitely hook up with you, but like I dunno if dating would be a—"

"Let's just not," I said. "Let's forget this conversation ever happened. I'm not doing it."

"Jocelyn, please," Mateo begged. "You don't even have to do anything. You just pretend to date Lawrence for a few months and let him do all the work."

"Wait, why am I doing all the work?" Lawrence asked. "Why am I getting dragged into this mess?"

Mateo raised his eyebrows. Lawrence stared back before sighing.

"Goddamn it. Fuck you, man, this wasn't what I thought you'd do."

"Is someone going to tell me why you owe Mateo a favour?" I asked.

"I got him out of a mess is why," Mateo replied. "That's all you need to know. It was a big mess, I saved Lawrence's ass, and now he's going to pretend to be your boyfriend long enough that Chelsea tries to seduce him and we get proof of it."

"I don't have to... you know, fuck her, right?" Lawrence asked. "Because like I said, she's hot, but—"

"You don't have to fuck her," I said. "We're not doing this."

"Yes we are," said Mateo.

"No."

"Yes."

"No!" I shouted. "You're asking me to put myself in the same position I was in when Isaac left me. Do you know how goddamn embarrassing that was? Do you know how weird it still is, how people treat me like a pity case because of them? Real or not, I don't want to deal with this again!"

"You don't have to," Mateo said. "All we need is for *Isaac* to see what she's doing. We just know Chelsea is more likely to go for a guy you're dating because... uh... well, because of whatever screwed up reason she has for going after your boyfriends. She's done it once, she'll do it again."

"She's done it more than once," I muttered.

Mateo couldn't have looked more excited if it was Christmas morning and there was an entire toy store beneath the tree. "She *has*?!"

"And what if it doesn't work?" I asked, ignoring him. "What if she doesn't—"

"Then you and Lawrence break up and we all go our separate ways, except Isaac, who will be destined to a lifetime of misery because of that spiteful cow."

"You know I don't care about Isaac that much, right?" I said.

"You used to," Mateo shot back.

I fell silent, stewing in my thoughts. Mateo moved across the room and sat on the coffee table in front of me.

"Please, Joss. You don't even have to do anything. Bring Lawrence to dinner a couple times, hang around Chelsea a bit, and let everything just go the way it would anyway."

The following weekend, I went to my parents' for dinner. Chelsea and Isaac were there, of course, and we were halfway through the meal when I got the chance to bring it up.

"...so you can come by on Saturday to finish making the place cards," Mom was saying. "Joss, if you could come help your sister..."

"On... Saturday?" I said. "Sorry, I have plans."

"All day?" Mom said.

"Well, sort of."

"What does 'sort of' mean?" Dad asked.

"I just... I was going out with someone. Hiking. We were going to leave in the morning."

"Were you?" Chelsea said suspiciously. "Or is this just another thing you're trying to get out of?"

"I'm actually going hiking," I said.

"With who?"

I bit my lip. "Just a... guy."

Isaac tried to hide the way his face lit up. Mom wasn't so subtle.

"A guy!" she squealed. "Oh my God, Joss, who is he? How long have you been—"

"It's not like that… yet," I said. "We just met, and we were going to hang out, see how things go."

"What's his name?" she asked. "Do I know him?"

"Um… well, no, you don't," I said. "But, uh, Chelsea and Isaac do."

Chelsea's eyebrows were as high as they would go. My face was turning red.

"Who?" Isaac asked.

"Um. Lawrence Pitt. Mateo's—"

"Mateo's roommate?!" exclaimed Chelsea. "Are you serious?"

"Why not?" I asked haughtily.

"When do I get to meet him?" Mom demanded.

I sighed. "If things go anywhere, I'll ask him to come by for dinner some night."

I spent the rest of the meal trying to ignore the sense of unease that fell on me. Whether it was from the fact that I was going through with this or from the way Chelsea stared at me every time I glanced up, I didn't know.

Chapter Thirteen

NOW

"If you keep getting visitors, you're going to need to hire your own assistant to handle them," Bretta said.

"What?" I plucked the earbud from my ear. "Who the fuck is visiting me?"

"Isaac."

I froze, staring at Bretta.

"I don't want to see him."

"Girl, I know it'll be awkward after what went down at his wedding, but it's the right thing to do."

I chewed the inside of my cheek. It wasn't what went down at the wedding that I was concerned about. It was more the fact that I had seen Isaac's father at least twice a week in the month that followed, though sometimes even more often than that.

It was unlikely Isaac had found out about me and Derek, but the fear was still there.

"Tell him to go," I said.

"I would," she said. "You know I would. It's just, he looks... I think he needs you."

"He better fucking not," I muttered.

"You know what I mean," Bretta said. "He's... have you seen him at all since the wedding?"

"No."

"Okay. I mean, I've met the guy, what, twice? But he looks, um, different. I think that's the nice way of putting it."

She was right: different was a nice way of describing what Isaac looked like. Older was another. Tired, jaded, pale, and lost delved into the not-so-nice ways of describing the broken man standing in the reception area of the shop. It was with a mixed sense of relief and guilt that I thought he didn't quite look so much like Derek anymore.

"Isaac," I said carefully.

"Joss," he replied. "You got a few?"

"Grab a coffee?" I suggested.

He nodded and I got my wallet from the back office. We were silent as we walked over to the coffee shop, speaking only to order, and still hesitated to talk once we had settled at a somewhat-private table in the corner.

Isaac looked bad. That wasn't a nice way of saying it at all, but he did. There was a tightness to his face, skin stretched over bone, the usual sweetness and hopefulness in his eyes faded to a stoic sense of deadened acceptance. It was my fault, I thought guiltily. If it wasn't for me, Isaac would have never met Chelsea in the first place, and if it wasn't for me, Lawrence wouldn't have been at the wedding. He would never have done what he did if it wasn't for me bringing them together.

"So," I said.

"I know it's probably weird for me to come see you," he said.

"Has there ever been anything normal about either of us?" I replied.

Isaac smirked. "Yeah, probably not. Still, sorry to... I dunno, drop in. My, uh... someone told me it might be a good idea to get some closure."

I knew that "someone" was the therapist he was seeing but didn't reveal that to Isaac. He'd want to know how I knew, and I'd have to admit

Derek told me while we were lying in his bed, pressed together after a particularly memorable evening that included me sitting on his face for what felt like hours.

"What kind of closure?" I asked instead.

Isaac cleared his throat. "About what happened. I'm holding on to a lot of, um, guilt."

I frowned. "Guilt?"

"Lawrence... he hurt you. And I hurt you like that, too. Only worse."

"Well, 'worse' is subjective." It came out less convincing than I had hoped.

"I mean, I guess," Isaac said. "I didn't... I never, you know, cheated or lied or anything. But I ended up with her, and I was so oblivious to who she was that I didn't see how she treated you or that you were right all along."

"You don't have to apologize or anything."

"Yeah, I do." He looked up at me, eyes determined. "I have to take responsibility for my role in the whole situation. What she did to me sucked, but what she and I did to you was... I have a lot of, I dunno, conflicting feelings. It's hard to feel sorry for myself when I feel like I put myself there, and I need to apologize because I wasn't innocent in the whole thing."

"No, but—"

"I'm sorry, Jocelyn." His voice was soft but earnest. "You warned me. You were far better to me than I deserved. You tried to put things behind you that I should never have asked you to put behind you. I've done nothing to deserve your forgiveness but—"

"Dude, it's fine," I said, shifting uncomfortably in my seat. "I don't hold any of this against you. I get it, okay? You thought you were doing the right thing. It was never... I don't feel like you ever did any of it to hurt me on purpose. Chelsea..."

He stiffened as I said her name and I coughed.

"Sorry. She, uh, she's the one who did all this. You shouldn't feel guilty about it, man. You... you fell in love with someone. You can't control that."

The smallest ghost of a smile flitted across Isaac's face, and a trace of himself seemed to settle back into his eyes. He paused, then chuckled as he shook his head.

"I've been seeing this, uh... you know, someone to talk to. About this stuff."

"You can say a therapist," I said. "That's not something to be embarrassed about."

He smiled a bit more. "Yeah. A therapist. He said to try talking to you, that it would probably make me feel better, and you know, I've been putting it off because I didn't... well. He was right, I guess."

"Glad I could help."

"You have no idea how much it means to me," he said.

I laughed uncomfortably. "Don't start getting any ideas here. Chelsea dates my exes. I don't date hers."

He winced slightly less when I said her name that time and even laughed a bit. "Yeah, no, I... I get that. I wasn't expecting—"

"I know. It was a joke."

"Okay." He smiled a bit more brightly. "Can we be friends? Like, is that asking too much?"

My hesitation didn't stem from not wanting to be friends with Isaac, but of course, he didn't know it was because I was sleeping with his dad, so that was how he took it.

"It is asking too much," he said after a moment. "Sorry. That's cool, it's not—"

"No, you just, uh, surprised me," I interrupted. "I just wasn't expecting—"

"I get it. That's still weird." He smiled and sipped his coffee. "It's okay. Just knowing we're on good terms is enough."

His visit shook me for the rest of the day. Bretta chalked it up to general stress, at first, but when I forgot to put an oil cap back on a truck before signing off on it, only noticing when she walked into the shop and asked where this oil cap came from, she pulled me into her office.

"What happened?" she asked.

"Nothing."

"Clearly it's not nothing."

I shrugged. "I just wasn't expecting to see Isaac, okay? It was weird."

"Jocelyn, you've worked here for years and you've never forgotten to put the oil cap back on. I know that because I've watched you give shit to other employees for forgetting to put the oil cap back on." She folded her arms across her chest. "What happened?"

"Nothing."

"Don't lie to me."

"He apologized and I forgave him. That's it."

"I don't believe you."

"Well, that's a *you* problem, not a *me* problem."

"No, it's a *you* problem because you're keeping something from me, and *me* don't like it." She frowned. "I mean, I. I don't like it."

Bretta stared at me, her eyes stony and determined. I held my resolve, folding my arms to match hers as I glared at her.

"He asked you out," she stated.

"He did not!"

"Okay, you hope he asks you out again because you want to get back together with him."

"I absolutely do not want to get back together with my ex who almost married my sister."

"Well, actually, he *did* marry your sister. It just only lasted less than a day."

I made a face at Bretta. "Exactly. So going out with Isaac? Not something I want, okay?"

"You say that, but I saw the way you looked when he got here." Bretta's face softened. "Joss, I'm not going to judge you for wanting to go back to him. I just want you to be happy and—"

"I don't want to go back to him!"

"—if that means you need to explore going back to Isaac, then fine. I mean, hey, maybe you guys just need to fuck agai—"

"Oh my God, Bretta, stop it!" I shouted, my voice cracking.

She stared at me. "Did you just yell at me?"

I swallowed hard.

"Joss, what happened?"

"I don't want to sleep with Isaac, okay?" My voice wavered.

"Talk to me." She leaned forward. "Whatever's going on, get it out of your head."

"I can't." I didn't know when I started fighting back tears, but my nose was twitching as I screwed up my face to prevent them from falling.

"Girl, you're scaring me. There's clearly more to this than—"

"I'm sleeping with his dad."

Her mouth was already open, half a word still floating out when she stopped speaking. I could only look at her face for a second before burying my head in my hands.

"You wanna repeat that for me?" she said.

"Not really."

"Okay, I will. You're sleeping with his dad?"

I made a soft noise of affirmation.

"Isaac's dad."

"Mm-hmm."

"Like, in a sexy way, not just because he's a good nap buddy?"

"This isn't funny," I mumbled.

She snickered. "I mean, it is a little."

"Bretta!"

"Okay, okay." She took a deep breath and let it out. "Question one. Um, *why?*"

"Because I like him." My voice was muffled by my hands.

"Question two. How?"

I snorted. "I know you aren't into guys, but do I seriously have to—"

"I'm glad you're not too upset to be a smartass. You know what I mean."

Sighing, I sat back, taking my head out of my hands.

"We were cleaning up after the wedding. We couldn't fit all the decorations into his car and I didn't want to wait at the church by myself, so I went with him to drop the stuff off at his house. I broke a vase, cut my leg, he patched it up and then I, um, kissed him."

"You kissed him?"

I nodded.

"And he...?"

I nodded again.

"Wow," she said. "And he didn't, like, have a problem with the fact that you're his son's ex?"

"Oh, he did. Does."

"Not enough of a problem to not fuck you, though."

"It's not like that."

Bretta raised her eyebrows. "No? He's taking you out to dinner, wants to meet your parents, would be proud to introduce you to people as his girlfriend?"

My chest clenched and I stared down at her desk, not responding.

"Joss, is he... being good to you?"

"He's not making me do anything I don't want to do, if that's what you're asking." I glanced back up at her. "If it weren't for the fact that everything is so fucked up already, he probably would do all those things. It's not just sex. I really like him, and he likes me."

"He is literally old enough to have a kid your age."

"Older, actually."

"What?"

"Isaac's older than me."

"And you don't see a problem there?"

I glared at her again. "Of course I do. It doesn't change the fact that I've never…"

I trailed off, but Bretta knew what I was going to say.

"You've never felt like this about anyone."

I nodded.

"That doesn't maybe have something to do with the fact that he's an older man who's giving you validation that you might be missing elsewhere?"

Her words were hurtful enough that I almost felt them. Shaking my head, I stood up. "I don't have to listen to this."

"Sit down," Bretta said harshly. I looked at her, shocked. "Joss, sit down. We're talking about this."

"And if I don't want to?"

"You need to. Look, I'm not saying this is super weird. It's not normal, but it's not… I mean, shit, I'm older than Leigh is. Not by *that* much, but she was only twenty-one when we met." She looked up at me, concern written across her face. "You're my friend, girl. I need to know you're safe and you're not being taken advantage of."

"I'm safe, and he's not taking advantage of anything," I said, settling back into the chair. "It's not like what you're thinking. Derek is a good guy. He's torn up about how this would affect Isaac, but he… I mean, I like… we like each other."

Bretta studied me. "You're in love with him."

"Fuck off, that's not—"

"Deny it all you want. It's obvious."

"I'm not… that's not even a possibility, okay? Even if everything was perfectly normal, we're talking a month here."

Bretta raised her hands defensively. "Fine. Don't admit it. If you say he's being good to you, I'll take your word for it, okay?"

I didn't say anything and she sighed again.

"Okay. So you're sleeping with his dad. Which explains why you didn't want to see him today. Why did he come see you?"

"To apologize," I said.

"Oh God. And now you're guilt-ridden so badly that you can't even remember to put an oil cap back on."

"Thanks. I needed to hear that."

"Am I wrong?"

I shook my head reluctantly. "If Isaac found out, it would ruin him. He and Derek weren't close for a very long time, but they are now. He'd think this was a huge betrayal. Angela would... I don't even know. I like him and I know he likes me, but I don't want him to lose his family over me."

"And your family?" she asked.

"Fuck 'em."

She burst out laughing.

"They don't... I mean, I told you what happened. I don't know what I ever did to make my dad hate me so much. They don't care about me."

"I've told you for years that your family treats you like shit," she said. "You'd still be devastated if they cut you out."

"I'd be less devastated if it meant I got to be with Derek."

"Shit, Joss." Bretta sat back in her chair, eyebrows furrowed. "What are you going to do?"

"Isn't that the million-dollar question," I mumbled.

Later that day, I had just finished work and was about to start my car when my pocket started vibrating. Very few people called me, so it was one of two people: my mom, or Derek.

If it was my mom, I'd be guilted into coming to yet another family dinner. If it was Derek, he was probably calling because Isaac mentioned he'd been to see me. Neither sounded like a conversation I wanted to have, but I checked my phone anyway.

Derek. It would have almost been better if it had been my mom.

"Hey," I said.

"You okay?" he asked immediately.

"Yeah. He told you?"

"Yeah. What did you say?"

I recounted my conversation with Isaac to Derek, skipping over the part where I'd told Isaac we wouldn't be getting back together. Of course, because it was Derek, he asked anyway.

"Does he want to, you know, give it another shot with you?"

"No."

"Are you—"

"Neither of us do."

Derek fell silent, but I knew what he was thinking.

"I would have said no even if you and I weren't... if this wasn't a thing. This... us... thing had nothing to do with that."

"You sure?" he asked.

"Positive."

"Because if I'm keeping you from being with someone better for you—"

"Don't, please," I begged. "You're not keeping me from being with anyone."

"You say that, Joss, but—"

"Derek, if it weren't for all the fucking drama surrounding us, I'd want to be with you. You know, like... properly."

It was a terrifying thing to admit out loud. I was sure Derek already knew how I felt. I knew how he felt. We both pretended like it was just sex, like it was a physical relationship and like that would be enough to satisfy us, but that was a lie. Still, it was the first time either of us had said anything of the sort out loud.

He didn't respond right away, leaving me to sit in my car with my heart racing and my palms sweating.

"Come over," he said.

"Now?"

"Yeah."

"I'm just leaving work. I haven't even—"

"Shower here. Then we'll have dinner. Watch a Doctor Who rerun or something."

"That almost sounds like a date," I said.

"It is."

"Is that a good idea?"

"Joss, when have we ever had good ideas?"

I bit my lip, as likely to cry as I was to laugh.

"I'll see you soon," I said.

CHAPTER FOURTEEN

THEN

"So, what do you do for a living, Lawrence?" Mom asked.

Lawrence smiled at her, his natural charm clear. "I work in pharmaceutical sales. Super boring, I know, but you gotta pay the bills somehow."

No one else at the table caught the momentary laugh in Isaac's eyes. I frowned, unsure of what was so funny.

"Understandable," Dad said. "You make good money, selling... pharmaceuticals?"

"Yeah, pretty decent," Lawrence said. "I've been thinking of maybe going back to school or something, maybe getting into chemistry or something like that. Something a little more cerebral, you know?

"You should be an accountant," Isaac said. "You're good at counting all that money you make."

"And be a boring old buzzkill like you?" joked Lawrence. "No thanks, I'm good, math nerd."

I closed my eyes, wishing I was literally anywhere else than at my parents' dinner table with goddamn Lawrence.

"So, what do you do, Mr. Miller?" he asked.

"I'm an accountant," Dad said impassively.

There was a moment of complete silence at the table.

"Well, if anyone was wondering just how deep in my mouth I could get my foot, it's apparently all the way," Lawrence said, chuckling.

Mom laughed far harder than she should have, a high-pitched chortle that rang in my ears. Dad grunted and ate another forkful of meatloaf, which was probably the best reaction any of us could have hoped for.

"Uh, what about you, Chelsea? You're a... what, again?"

"Dental hygienist," she said.

"That's super cool," Lawrence said enthusiastically. "So you like, clean teeth and stuff?"

"And stuff," she said. "So tell me, Lawrence, what's a guy like you doing with my sister?"

"Ouch," he laughed. "I've got that low of approval rating already?"

It was kind of sweet that he thought he was the one being disapproved of.

"Not at all!" Mom interjected. "I think what Chelsea meant is how did you two meet?"

"Well, Chelsea was there!" he answered. "Mateo is my roommate and they had some wedding party thing at our place, what was it, a month ago? Whatever. I ran into Jocelyn—"

"Your bathroom door ran into Jocelyn," I corrected.

He grinned. "Right, I hit her with the bathroom door. Not on purpose," he said earnestly to my dad. "I didn't know she was in there."

"Mmm," said Dad.

"Anyway, we got talking and she invited me down to have pizza, and before we knew it everyone was leaving and we were still sitting there! Figured if she liked me enough to hang out for a few hours, maybe she'd think about keeping me around."

"That's so sweet," Mom said.

"I'm just so surprised you brought him around this early," Chelsea said to me. "It's nice, honestly. Normally, you're so secretive about the people you're dating."

I couldn't tell if she was suspicious or simply making a comment. With Chelsea, it could be anything. She still wasn't over the dress debacle, and I knew the only reason I was still her maid of honour was because Mom told her she couldn't kick me out of the wedding party. Still, Lawrence's presence meant whatever fear she had about me going after Isaac was unfounded. At least, theoretically. She could have been actually happy for me, for all I knew.

"Well, Lawrence is... different," I said.

"Heard that a time or two in my life," Lawrence said out of the corner of his mouth to Isaac, who laughed.

The conversation fizzled out again, the sound of cutlery scraping against plates shrill in my ears. Lawrence ate another few forkfuls before turning back to Chelsea.

"So tell me more about this dental hygiene stuff," he asked.

"Well, you should brush and floss twice a day," she said boredly.

Lawrence laughed as though it was the cutest thing he'd ever heard. "You're pretty funny," he said. "Is it interesting work? Maybe chemistry isn't my thing. Maybe dentistry would be more fun. You'll have to tell me about it."

"I try not to talk about gingivitis and cavities at the dinner table," Chelsea replied.

I wasn't sure if I was grateful that she seemed disinterested in Lawrence or annoyed that it wasn't working. If she would just flirt back a little, maybe the whole charade could be done with. No matter what Lawrence did, Chelsea didn't seem to care. Isaac didn't seem to notice Lawrence's efforts to flirt with her, likely chalking it up to his usual level of charm.

After dinner, Lawrence remained seated at the table while I stood up to start clearing it. Isaac, who usually tried to pitch in and help clean up, joined me.

"So, you and Lawrence," he said when we were in the kitchen.

"Me and Lawrence," I repeated.

"I'm so happy for you," he said earnestly. "Really, Joss. I'm glad you're—"

"If you're about to say 'moving on,' don't," I warned him. "For your information, I moved on a while ago. Just because I don't bring people over doesn't mean I'm not dating."

He nodded in acknowledgement. "Fair. Do you want to invite him to the wedding?"

Fuck, I thought.

"Um, maybe," I said. "Like, probably, but that's still a while away."

"We'll save a spot for him. Or for, you know, whoever you might want to bring as a plus one." He shifted awkwardly. "This might not be my place, but—"

"If it's not your place, don't say it." I turned on my heel to head back to the dining room.

During the few minutes I had been out of the room, something had happened. I knew it the moment I walked in and saw Lawrence looking amused, Chelsea staring at him coldly, and Dad looking unimpressed.

"What's going on?" I asked, collecting a few more plates off the table.

"Your new boyfriend thinks Isaac and I make a strange couple," Chelsea said.

"I didn't say strange," Lawrence said. "I said you didn't seem all that similar and it was nice to see that opposites attract."

"You also said Isaac's a nice guy. What does that make me?" she asked.

Lawrence's eyes flashed playfully. "Well, just the opposite."

"So a—"

"A nice girl, obviously," he continued. "I mean, I'd say guys and girls are opposites, wouldn't you?"

"Do you know what the word 'opposite' means, Lawrence?" Dad said.

The rest of the evening did not improve, and when Lawrence and I were safely in his car and driving down the street, I groaned.

"I knew this wouldn't work," I said.

"Give it some time. I'll get it figured out," Lawrence replied.

"Give it some time?" I repeated. "Chelsea had zero interest in you—"

"Ouch."

"—you insulted my dad's career, you sounded like a total moron, no offense—"

"Uh, none taken?"

"—and now Isaac's saving you a spot at the wedding, so I have to come up with some story about why we broke up."

"Wait just a sec," he said. "You're so convinced this didn't work, but it's not like Chelsea started hitting on Isaac right away, is it? You said she even had a boyfriend when you and Isaac were dating."

"Sure, a 'boyfriend'," I said. "I'm ninety-eight percent sure it was just some guy she asked to come to dinner so she could take the spotlight."

"So we do it again," he said. "It'll be fine. Give it another try, I dunno, next weekend."

I sighed and stared out the window. Lawrence drove silently towards my apartment.

"I didn't know you were a pharmaceutical salesman," I said.

He snickered. "Well, sort of."

"What?"

"What do you mean, what? Mateo told you, right? I mean, fuckin' Isaac knows, he buys from me."

My stomach started curling. "Lawrence, what the fuck do you do for a living?"

He glanced at me out of the corner of his eye. "Uh... seriously?"

When I didn't respond, he sighed.

"It's a joke. What's another word for 'pharmaceutical'?"

The moment after I slammed the car door, I had my phone out. I was barely in my apartment when he answered.

"Hel—"

"A drug dealer, Mateo?!" I screeched. "You sent me to dinner with my parents with a fucking drug dealer?!"

"It's not that bad!" Mateo protested. "He just sells weed."

"Oh, he must be doing so well now that weed is legal," I said sarcastically.

"His shit is cheaper and better than the legal stuff."

"What the actual fuck? You didn't think that was an important detail to share? And *Isaac* knows, too?"

"Well, yeah, he buys his weed from Lawrence."

"Since when does Isaac even smoke weed?" My voice was getting more and more shrill.

"Uh, like, since high school at least," Mateo said. "How did you date him and not know that?"

"I don't fucking know! Why didn't he ever tell me?"

"I... I don't know, you 'd have to ask him."

"So that means Chelsea knows, and there's no way she's going to risk her fucking relationship with Isaac over some guy who sells illegal legal drugs!"

"Oh, Chelsea doesn't know," Mateo said. "Isaac refuses to tell her he smokes weed."

"You're joking."

"Nope. She made some comment about how gross she finds it and he's never mentioned it."

I flopped on my couch, tilting my head back against it. "And you didn't think that maybe we could just spill the beans to her and *that* might get them to break up?"

"No, it would just get Isaac to stop smoking weed."

"But—"

"Joss, come on." There was the sound of the phone shuffling. "Think about it. If Chelsea told Isaac the colour of his eyes annoyed her, he'd start looking into coloured contacts. If Chelsea told him she found accountants boring, he'd switch careers. So if Chelsea found out Isaac was smoking weed, what do you think he'd do?"

I grumbled, but had to agree.

"Look, I'm sorry I didn't tell you about Lawrence. I didn't… I thought you knew."

"Bullshit."

"Okay, you're right, it's bullshit, but does it affect anything? Your whole relationship is a lie."

"And what if it gets out, hmm? What then, Mateo?" I slumped forward, resting my head in my hands. "What about when my parents find out I'm dating a goddamn drug dealer?"

"They won't," he said. "And besides, he really is looking at going back to school. He's not making as much money now that weed's legal."

"You've got to be kidding me," I muttered. "Am I crazy? Is it me? Really, Mateo, be honest, because it feels like I'm the only sane person in all of this and that must mean I'm the crazy one."

"You're making a way bigger deal out of this than you need to."

"A way…" I paused, taking a breath. "Why does he owe you a favour?"

"What?"

"Lawrence. He's doing this because he owes you a favour. Why does he owe you a favour?"

Mateo sighed. "I might've bailed him out of—"

"Are you *fucking* kidding me?!"

"Joss, just let me—"

"No." The phone trembled against my cheek and I realized it was because I was so angry, I was shaking. "I'm done. Count me out and break them up yourself."

"Wait, before you—"

I hung up, chucked my phone onto the coffee table, and buried my head into my hands. Three times, I heard the phone vibrate against the table before Mateo gave up.

He kept trying: the next day he called six times and texted at least every half hour. The day after that, he had Lawrence in on it and they called so many times, my phone died while I was working. He gave up the day after that, and I pushed any thought of Mateo and Lawrence from my mind until dinner the following weekend.

"No Lawrence tonight?" Mom asked when I got there.

"Um, no. We, uh—"

"Oh no, you broke up *already*?" Chelsea asked from the living room.

"You seemed so good together," Mom said.

"That's too bad. I was looking forward to seeing him," Chelsea added.

"Yeah, sorry, Joss," Isaac said sympathetically. "I was rooting for you guys."

Chelsea rolled her eyes. "You're laying it on a little thick, Isaac."

He looked hurt, but tried to smile. I tried not to let it bother me, but it was like someone had kicked a puppy.

Fucking Isaac with his stupid...

"We didn't break up," I said. "Lawrence just felt uncomfortable after dinner last week because he thought you guys didn't like him, so he didn't want to cause any more issues."

"Well, of *course* we liked him!" Mom said. "Is he available? Call him, we can wait and—"

"Uh, not tonight," I said. "Maybe next weekend."

Chelsea grinned cheerfully from the couch. "I look forward to it."

CHAPTER FIFTEEN

NOW

GIVEN ENOUGH TIME, EVEN the strangest things can become routine.

Derek and I never talked about my admission that if it weren't for the obstacles in our lives, I'd want to be in a relationship with him. We didn't discuss being exclusive. He never asked me to be his girlfriend and I never said he was my boyfriend. We didn't talk about the hurdles, about the fact that the concept of "us" was steeped in bad ideas and questionable decisions.

It just happened. Unspoken and undefined, it became far more than it should have.

Weeks turned to months where I lived in two places: in real life, and in Derek's life. My routine became predictable. Fridays would roll around and I would go to Derek's after work. I didn't need to knock; I would let myself in and he would come to the door, taking me in his arms and kissing me the moment I arrived. While I showered, he would start making dinner, and I would help him when I was done. We would eat, talk, and clean the kitchen together, and the moment we were done, I was in his arms again.

We would spend most of Friday night in bed, wrapped around each other, cycling through waves of heated passion and quiet intimacy. My heart would ache as we talked, sometimes about trivial things like movies and how our week went, and sometimes about heavy things like family and memories we'd rather forget. Some nights, we would make love and fall asleep early; some nights we would fuck once, twice, however many times before exhaustion took over and we could barely move.

In the morning, he would wake me up early, his lips on my neck and his hands on my breasts as he nuzzled against me. Half-awake and wholly his, I would cling to him as he made love to me, slow and unhurried and every bit as intense as the night before. When we were done, he would kiss me and tell me to go back to sleep while he went out to do deliveries.

Some days he would be back before I woke up again. Other days, I would wake up and help myself to coffee and breakfast and sometimes even lunch before he returned. No matter when he got back, I was happy to see him, and he was happy to see me.

On Saturday nights we would cook together again, then watch most of a movie. One weekend, I brought my PlayStation over and got Derek addicted to video games; the next weekend, he had purchased one of his own. Always, things lead to the same place: Derek's bed, in his arms, holding him as he brought me to places of complete bliss again and again and again.

We only ever spent Sunday mornings together. Afternoons were reserved for getting ready for the week, or in my case, getting ready for dinner at my parents'. It was always hard to leave on Sundays, and before I even parked my car back at my apartment, there was a text message from Derek telling me that he missed me.

During the week, we would get together a couple of times, always on different nights. I didn't stay those nights, though. Going to work from his place in the morning felt like too much, which was funny, considering Bretta was the only person who knew about me and Derek.

"How's it going with him?" she asked one day over lunch. "Still... sneaking around?"

"Yeah," I said.

"How's Isaac doing?"

I smiled, though my jaw was tense. "Good. Derek said he's really come around and started putting his life back together. He helped him move into a new apartment last week. With, uh, Mateo."

"Mateo, the best man?"

I nodded. Bretta didn't know what Mateo had done. My guess was that Isaac didn't, either.

"So he's gotten over Chelsea?"

"Maybe. He's still talking to Derek regularly. They're going to a football game next week, even. Like, a father-son thing. Derek's so excited."

My voice cracked, the only outward sign of the guilt that was squeezing my chest. Bretta sighed.

"Is the amount of self-loathing you're holding over this healthy?" she asked.

"Oh, God no," I said.

"So why—"

"He makes me happy," I interrupted.

"How long are you going to keep this up?" Her voice was gentle. "Do you see a future with him?"

I shrugged, picking at my sandwich. "I'm not ready to give it up yet."

"The longer you wait, the more it will hurt when you have to."

"Well yeah, but maybe the longer I wait, the more worth it the pain will be."

Bretta snorted. "That was almost poetic, Joss. You really are a woman in love."

Every muscle in my body went stiff, so sudden and so thorough it might have been easier to just literally turn to stone. "Don't say that."

"What... love?"

"No one's used that word except you." My voice wavered, but Bretta didn't seem to notice.

"Sure. Whatever you say. I don't hear you denying it."

I tore off a piece of my sandwich and threw it at her, batting it away when she caught it and threw it back.

Still, her words echoed in my head the rest of the day, as much as I tried to drown them out. I put on my classic rock playlist and blared it, singing loudly until one of the other mechanics threw a rag at me and told me to shut up. I threw the rag back, flipped him off, and sang louder. Nothing I did stopped the reverberating sound of Bretta's voice in my head.

Love.

It was three months after the disastrous wedding. Three months of spending almost every weekend with Derek. Three months of heart-to-hearts and stupid inside jokes. Three months of thinking about him multiple times a day, wondering what he was up to, trying to hide a smile when my phone went off and it was a text from him.

Three months of guilt, knowing how much he was putting on the line to be with me, even secretly. Three months of knowing how much I had already done to hurt him and his family.

When I finished work for the day, a text message from Derek was waiting.

Come over tonight?

I swallowed hard, listening to Bretta's voice ringing in my mind.

I couldn't love him. Nothing good would come of it. Bretta was right: there was no future with him. I wasn't being fair, either. I might be okay with the inevitable hurt that would happen when things had to end, but Derek might not be. It wasn't fair to keep stringing him along.

My fingers tapped the response my head wanted to give, not the one my heart wanted to give.

Can't. Have plans, sorry.

Damn. Too bad. At least tomorrow's my favourite day of the week :-)

Of course it was. Everybody loved Fridays, but Fridays meant a lot more to me and Derek than most other people. And if Bretta was right about my feelings—which she was, as much as I denied it—it meant Fridays needed to stop being a special day.

The pain of knowing what I had to do distracted me at best, and had me on pins and needles at worst. I could barely focus on work, instead thinking of how I could explain to Derek that we couldn't see each other anymore. When I missed lunch and Bretta came in to check on me, she shook her head.

"Go home. You're useless," she said kindly. "We're not busy and it's pouring out there. Start your weekend early, get yourself sorted. And, Joss, you know if you need anything..."

"I know," I said.

"You must be really fucked up if you're not fighting with me on this."

My lips twitched. Bretta reached forward to hug me, second-guessed herself, and patted me on the back.

"I didn't mean for you to question whatever it is you and Derek have going on," she said. "You clearly care about him. I'm sure he cares about you just as much. It's hard because I can't meet him and let him know how badly I'll kick his ass if he hurts you."

I smirked, not quite able to laugh. "No, you were right. I needed to hear it."

"Wait, Joss—"

"Too late, you said I could go home early, I'm leaving, bye!"

She protested, but I was already out the door.

In hindsight, I should have stayed at work. The only thing I knew was that we had to end things suddenly, swiftly, and completely. Talking it over wouldn't work: we'd agreed a million times that what we were doing was a bad idea. No, the only way to do it was to grit my teeth and end it. If I had stayed at work, I would have at least had that as a distraction. Leaving early also meant that I heard my phone go off when Derek sent his usual after-work text, since it was sitting on my coffee table instead of in the back room.

I'm thinking spaghetti for dinner. Is an insane amount of garlic a total turn off if we're both eating it anyway?

Not thinking, I responded right away.

I can't make it tonight. Sorry.

Within seconds, my phone was ringing. I chewed the side of my cheek, face pained as I watched his name flash on my screen. When it stopped ringing, I waited for the inevitable ping of my voicemail going off, even though I'd told Derek a million times I hated checking my voicemail.

It didn't, though. Instead, another text came through.

What's going on? You're not at work?

I thought about not answering, but I couldn't bring myself to be that cold-hearted.

Not feeling well.

Let me come bring you something to eat then.

Not a good idea. I'll be fine.

He tried calling again. That time, I just sent it to voicemail instead of watching it ring.

Joss, please answer your phone.

I can't talk right now.

Tears were slipping down my cheeks. I brushed them away, angry they would dare to fall without my permission. Seconds passed, then minutes. I closed my eyes, sure this was the end of it, until he messaged again.

I don't play games and neither do you. If you're with somebody else, just tell me. I'll understand. If something's happened, just say so. Call me. Otherwise, I'm going to be at your apartment in 10 minutes to make sure you're not dead or kidnapped or something. If you don't want to see me again after that, I'll leave you alone. I just need to know you're okay.

I choked on a sob. Stupid Derek and his stupid compassion.

He answered halfway through the first ring.

"Joss?"

"I'm sorry," I whispered.

"Just talk to me," he said. "Please."

"I'm not dead."

"Okay. That's a good start."

"But I can't do this."

"Joss, wait—"

He tried calling twice more before giving up. The rain outside beat down faster, pouring down the windows in tumultuous streams as the wind picked up. I sat on the couch, watching it mindlessly, until my phone went off again about an hour later.

I'm not mad, okay? I'm scared. If I did something to hurt you or upset you or whatever... whatever's happened, please just tell me. The not-knowing is killing me, Joss. Maybe that's selfish of me but I care way too much about you to let things go like this. Swear to God, whatever you want to do, I'll agree to, just don't leave me in the dark. Just talk to me. Pl ease.

I was still processing the message when the next one came in, even though it was almost an hour later.

This isn't you. Whatever I did, I'm sorry.

The words ate at me. They broke me. What little resolve I had was shredded, dissolved, and poured out of me. I was barely aware of getting up from the couch and grabbing my keys, almost unconscious of the fact that I was getting into my car and driving to Derek's house until I was pulling into his driveway.

The rain had slowed, but it was still drizzling and grey when I got out of the car and walked to the back door. I hesitated when I was standing in front of it. Letting myself in didn't feel appropriate. Knocking, though... I had never knocked on Derek's door before.

As luck would have it, I didn't need to. He must have heard me come up, and before I could decide what to do, the door was swinging open.

I almost chickened out. Derek's face was a mix of concern and suspicion. There wasn't anger in his eyes, but the usual sparkle he had when he saw me wasn't there, either. His mouth was set in a straight line as he regarded me cautiously.

"What's going on?" he asked.

"I'm in love with you."

Derek was smart. He'd probably spent most of the night coming up with every conceivable possibility for the way I was acting. I already knew he thought I might have met someone else. He probably entertained the idea that maybe the "someone else" was Lawrence, or maybe even Isaac. He may have thought I was pregnant, or maybe that I was dying. There were a million different reasons he might have thought of to explain what was happening.

However, me saying I was in love with him was clearly not one of them.

"What?" he said after a beat.

"I'm in love with you."

My voice cracked and I burst into tears. Ugly, wet, horrible Kim Kardashian level tears. Without a second thought, in less time than it took to blink, Derek's arms were around me.

"Just breathe," he said. "Take a breath."

"I'm sorry," I whimpered.

"No," he said. "Joss, don't—"

"It's st-stupid," I stuttered into his chest. "This w-wasn't supposed to happen. I'm so sorry."

"Don't be."

"I c-can't... we can't..."

"I love you."

I wrenched myself out of his arms, stepping back to look up at him. "What?"

Derek stared back at me, his expression pained. "I've been in love with you since the first night you were here."

I collected myself just enough to process what he said.

"This is horrible," I finally sniffed.

Derek choked on a laugh. "Not quite the way I imagined this conversation going."

I couldn't help it. I giggled, a wet sort of bubble, and then we were both laughing. At some point, I clutched at him; he held me up as tears cut through the laughter.

"Don't cry," he murmured. "We'll figure this out."

"How can we possibly figure this out?"

His lips pressed against my forehead, then my cheeks, before finally finding my mouth.

"Haven't thought that far ahead," he said. "Come on, come inside. It's cold out here."

He pulled me in, releasing me just long enough to shut the door before kissing me again. I pulled myself against him, terrified of what would happen if I let go. Strong arms wrapped around my waist, holding me closer, pressing his body against mine.

It wasn't fair. The way he fit against me wasn't fair. The feel of his body wasn't fair. The taste of his mouth and the scent of his cologne and the way his hands gripped me were not fair. It wasn't fair to love him, and it wasn't fair for him to love me, and yet there we were in the entrance of his house, pawing at each other like we were starving.

The path to his bedroom was staggered, pieces of clothing falling behind us as we stumbled through the hallway. What should have been a short walk took ages, not that either of us minded. He pulled at my clothes, kissing me and touching me as I struggled with his shirt. When I finally got it off, he pushed me against the wall, trapping me against his body. His teeth grazed against my lower lip, his hands cupping my breasts over my bra before sliding down my bare stomach. He unbuttoned my jeans smoothly and slipped his hand inside, cupping my mound through my already-dampening panties.

I squirmed as he moved his hand back up so he could slip his fingers past the waistband of my panties, panting against his mouth when a finger pushed past my folds and into my dripping entrance.

"Fuck," he muttered. "Joss, you're so wet."

"I want you," I whispered.

He kissed me again, and again, and his hand moved against me harder. I moaned, fighting through the distraction so I could get my hands onto the buckle of his belt. Once I fumbled it open, I unbuttoned his jeans and pushed them down eagerly, eliciting a soft chuckle that turned to a groan as I cupped his quickly hardening cock through his boxers.

"What're you doing?" he mumbled when I nudged his hand out of my panties.

I didn't answer, just pushed him to the other side of the hallway before dropping to my knees in front of him.

After tugging his jeans the rest of the way down and pulling his boxers down to meet them, I wrapped my fingers around his cock. Derek groaned again, and another time when I replaced my fingers with my mouth. His hips moved forward just slightly, a restrained instinct as I took him into my mouth. A hand found the back of my head, resting against my hair as I began bobbing my head.

His cock slid over my tongue, hard and thick and throbbing. I pushed him deeper into my mouth, relishing the feel of him pressed against the back of my throat before pushing just a little further. Derek cried out and his fingers tightened in my hair, only just long enough for him to be able to grab it. I heard his head knock against the wall and glanced up, the sight of him with his head tilted back and his eyes closed one of the most beautiful things I could imagine.

Before either of us could get too far into it, Derek was pulling my mouth off his cock and tugging me to my feet.

"Bedroom," he growled, though he paused to push my jeans down and again to take my bra off before using his body to nudge me the rest of the way down the hall.

We fell onto his bed together. He guided me onto my back, bringing himself over me, his kiss lingering for just a moment before he moved to pull my panties down. I lifted my hips as he slid them over my ass, watching as he tossed them to the side carelessly. Large hands parted my thighs. He paused for just a moment to press his face against my pussy and dart his tongue between my folds, then he was nestling between my legs and pushing himself inside me.

Any tension left in my body dissolved as he buried himself in my pussy. With him inside me, I felt complete, like whatever pieces of me had been scraped and torn away were returned, like I was something. A soft noise left my lips as his pelvis met mine and he paused, his hand brushing against my hair.

"You okay?" Derek murmured.

"I love you," I whispered. There was a tightness in my throat, something threatening to overwhelm me.

He kissed me, his lips warm and soft against mine.

"I love you too," he whispered back. "So much, Joss. I love you so much."

That overwhelming emotion overflowed. Tears pricked in my eyes again, spilling as Derek started to pull out. He was pushing himself back inside me when he noticed and paused again.

"Don't cry," he pleaded.

"I'm not crying," I said stubbornly. "Keep going."

He laughed. "Demanding, aren't you?"

"Yes. But you love me."

"I do."

He began moving again, filling me, completing me. His lips barely left mine, murmuring softly as he brought me closer and closer to bliss, kissing me as he used his body to pleasure mine. I wrapped my arms around him, holding him to me, gasping when his pelvis brushed against my clit again and again.

Already little tremors were shivering through my body, quivers that pushed me closer and closer. I tightened my hold on him, my legs tensing, and Derek groaned.

"Come for me," he breathed. "Come on, Joss, come for me."

I couldn't respond, at least not with words. I responded by panting, by moaning, by losing my breath as he brought me to the very edge of completeness and held me there, dangling for a single, long moment before I felt the entire earth move and shudder. Then it was just us: just him, just me, and just blinding white light as my body spasmed. His lips were on mine, his breath hot against me, and I heard him go breathless.

"I love you," he said distantly, and then he was spilling inside me.

I felt every spurt, every twitch of his cock, eagerly accepting every bit of himself that he could give me. He stayed there for a long time. I couldn't bring myself to let go of him. I didn't want to lose the fullness he brought me. I just wanted to exist in that moment for the rest of my life. There was no worry in that moment, no problems, no concerns about how we could be in love when there were so many things against us.

It couldn't last forever, though, and eventually Derek kissed me and parted from me. I sighed, closing my eyes as he lay beside me and brought me into his arms, the reality of the situation rushing back into my mind.

"What do we do?" I asked sullenly.

"I don't know," he replied. "I want this to be a real thing, Joss."

"I do, too."

"So what's stopping us? What do we have to do to make this work?"

I buried my face against his chest as the rush of problems overwhelmed me again. "Too much."

"Let's start with the easier stuff, then." He kissed the top of my head. "No matter what happens with any of the other problems, the first thing people are going to question is the fact that I'm way too old for you."

"Fuck those people."

My head was jostled as he burst out laughing. "Okay, problem one solved."

I smiled, kissing a spot on his chest. "I don't care about that. Do you?"

"A little."

The answer surprised me, and I looked up at him. His lips curved into a small half-smile.

"I'm not going to lie to you," he said. "Most of the time when I look at you, I don't see a woman who's twenty years younger. I just see you. But sometimes I see the gap between us and I'm afraid to be the person who steals those years from you."

"You're not stealing anything. Do you think I'd be here if I didn't want to be?"

The half-smile grew. "I know you wouldn't."

"So problem solved."

He chuckled. "Okay, problem solved."

"What's the next problem?"

One by one, we began looking at all the roadblocks. We laid everything out, talking about what we might have to do, handle, or give up to be together. At the end of it all, only two stood out: my family, and his.

I thought figuring out how to deal with Derek's family would be the more complicated of the two, but after a few moments of thought, he shrugged.

"I'll call Ange," he said.

"What?" I gasped.

"She'll understand," he continued. "I'll explain it to her and she'll probably bust my balls a little because she friggin' adores you, but Ange is an open-minded person. She's also about thirty times smarter than I am. She'll have a good idea on how to break it to Isaac."

"You seem pretty confident about all that," I said shakily.

"I am."

"What if Isaac... you know."

He sighed, pausing while he thought.

"I'm not gonna lie," he said again. "It'll be hard. Isaac was barely civil to me for almost ten years. Any relationship we had was because his mom told him he had to. Now he wants to talk to me and... well."

"Is it worth it?" My heart hammered and I couldn't bring myself to look up at him to ask the question, let alone wait for an answer.

Not that it was a long wait.

"Absolutely," Derek said immediately.

"Are you... I mean, I don't want to come between you and him."

He was quiet for a moment before tilting my head up to look at him. I shivered unintentionally when our eyes met.

"You need to understand that I love you," he said. "A lot. Enough that I need to give this a chance, Joss. I love my son, but he also nearly cut me out of his life for..."

He stopped suddenly, the words fading out.

"For...?"

Derek shook his head. "For something he didn't understand. It doesn't matter. I need to see where this... this 'us' thing goes. What we're doing now isn't enough for either of us. Finding out what we could be together... that's what matters to me."

There was nothing I could say to that. All I could do was kiss him. When we parted, Derek brushed my hair off my forehead.

"What are we on, problem eight hundred and sixty-two?" he asked.

I laughed. "What's problem eight hundred and sixty-two?"

"What your family is going to think."

Any trace of a smile I had faded from my lips, happiness leaving my soul so completely and so thoroughly that my body went cold. I looked away from Derek again.

"Joss. We have to talk about this."

"I don't want to."

"I know you don't," he said. "But we need to."

I didn't say anything, choosing instead to pout and hide my face against his chest. Rather than laugh or scoff, he hugged me closely and kissed my head.

"I need you to tell me something," he murmured.

"What?"

He took a breath, hugging me just a little more tightly. "Your family... they're assholes."

I burst out laughing. "Yeah."

"Why do you still stick around when they treat you like that?"

He didn't ask it in a judgmental way. There was no malice in his voice, no condescending judiciousness. It was soft, quiet, curious more than anything. Still, it hurt, through no fault of his. It twisted inside me, a melancholy pinch, and I almost winced.

"They're my family," I said.

"Joss, I know, but the way they—"

"I know," I said. "I know what you see. You see my sister being... awful. Doing all sorts of crazy things to punish me. You see my dad doing anything he can to justify her behaviour because he loves her so much, and he barely seems to tolerate me. And you see my mom turning a blind eye to it, urging me to be the bigger person and to forgive them so we can still be what she thinks is a family. Is that right?"

"Uh, yeah. That about sums it up."

"What you don't see is that Chels and I were best friends growing up. Like, best-best friends. Or all the things Dad did for me, even if he never... even though I wasn't his favourite. And my mom? I love my mom. She's been on my side my entire life. She's always encouraged me. Like, when I said I wanted to be a mechanic and everyone laughed and said girls can't do that, she took my side."

He didn't say anything and I closed my eyes, breathing in the scent of him to calm myself.

"It's not so easy to walk away," I said. "I spent my whole life trying to impress my dad, and it's clear now that it's never going to happen, but it's so instinctual that it's almost a part of me. Mom would be devastated and she's... she's my mom, Derek. You don't understand. Faults and all, they're my family."

"You're right," he agreed. "I don't understand, not really, but... that explains more of it. So, what does this mean for us?"

"They accepted Chelsea and Isaac pretty quickly," I said.

"You don't sound convinced."

"Well, I'm not Chelsea."

"And that means...?"

I swallowed the lump that was building up in my throat. "I don't know what they'll say."

"And worst-case scenario?"

I sat up so I could look at him, so he could see what I hoped was a fierce sincerity in my eyes. "If I get to be with you, there is no worst-case scenario."

There was no more to discuss, and if there was, we ignored it. Derek kissed me again and I lost myself against him, running my hands along his body and pushing my fingers through his hair. We made love again, surrounded by only each other, safe in his bed where all that mattered was us.

The next morning, Derek woke me as he usually did, his hands caressing me out of a dream. He nudged me onto my back so he could slide his cock inside me, kissing me and telling me to go back to sleep after we finished.

"Won't be long today," he whispered as my eyes slid closed. "Just have a couple of stops."

"See you soon," I mumbled, and I was asleep before he even left the bedroom.

When I woke up again, it was to the smell of coffee. I smiled before even opening my eyes. Stretching and yawning, I glanced around the room as I blinked. Sun was streaming through the windows and I felt refreshed. In fact, I felt almost hopeful. Angela had always liked me; maybe that fondness would extend far enough to approve of me being with her ex-husband.

There was a strong possibility that she wouldn't, but still. She might.

I could hear Derek in the kitchen as I got out of bed. I considered walking out naked, but the air in his house was chilly as usual. I made a mental note to tease him about it, to tell him he could have had me walking around naked all the time but that I couldn't when it was so cold in here, before grabbing his bathrobe and tying it around me.

Barefoot, I padded down the hallway. Derek had collected the clothes we had left lying around the night before. I hesitated, wondering where he had put them, since my phone had been in the pocket of my jeans. A quick glance back into the bedroom showed they weren't there. Maybe he just left them in the kitchen while he made coffee.

"Are my jeans in here?" I asked as I rounded the corner.

If I hadn't said anything, I could have escaped. He was facing the coffee maker and wouldn't have seen me. I could have bolted back to the bedroom and hidden until I knew it was safe to come out.

But no. I had to speak. And he had to turn his head in surprise, not expecting to hear a voice, a female voice, a familiar female voice from behind him. His eyes met mine, not processing for a moment, not understanding, just bewildered.

"Jocelyn?" Isaac said.

My mouth dropped open.

"What..." His eyes trailed down, taking in the far-too-large bathrobe wrapped around me.

"Oh no," I whispered.

"What the fuck," he said quietly. Then, as realization set in: "What the *fuck*?!"

"It's not... I... Let me just—"

"Are you fucking my dad?"

CHAPTER SIXTEEN

THEN

"You've got to be kidding me. You don't actually believe that."

Lawrence grinned and shrugged. "Look, I'm just saying, there are plenty of eyewitness accounts..."

Isaac rolled his eyes. "Yeah, and they can all be explained. Even in the sixties, they said it was probably just a sandhill crane."

"You say that, man, but I fuckin' can't—uh, I mean, freakin' can't, sorry Mr. Miller—believe that someone would mistake a bird for a man with wings. And sandhill cranes aren't even native to Virginia."

"I mean, if it wandered out of its migration route, it could easily..." Isaac trailed off and shook his head. "Why am I debating this with you? How in the... how do you even know all this, man?"

"I'm telling you, Isaac. Sometimes, you just have to believe."

"In the Mothman."

"He's real, dude."

"Anyway," Mom said, confused. "I take it you two have seen *The Mothman Prophecies*, so let's take that off the list and pick a different movie."

"I'm not into horror anyway," Chelsea said, settling into the middle seat on the couch beside Isaac. He put an arm around her shoulder instinctively as she nestled into him, a bowl of popcorn on her lap.

"Me neither," I said. "What about something funny?"

"Oh, what about *Airplane!*?" Lawrence said.

"What's *Airplane!*?" Chelsea asked.

Isaac and Lawrence groaned in unison. Even Dad raised his eyebrows.

"It's got Leslie Nielsen in it," I said. "It's like a parody movie. You used to like Monty Python, right? You'll probably like this."

"Hmm," Chelsea said.

"She's right," Isaac said, nudging her. "You'd like it. Let's watch that."

"Shove over a bit," Lawrence said to me. "I'll sit in the middle. You can have the armrest."

Airplane! was the only saving grace in an otherwise-disastrous evening featuring Lawrence's fourth attempt at trying to fake-seduce Chelsea. I had no idea what he thought would happen by sitting next to her on the couch during the movie; Isaac was on the other side of her, and my parents were in the room. What he thought he would accomplish, I couldn't even begin to guess.

Movie night was Mom's brainchild.

"Well, the bridal shower is Sunday so we can't do family dinner," she explained the previous weekend. "So what about if everyone comes over for dinner on Saturday instead, and we can have a family movie night!"

"That's a great idea, Mrs. Miller," Lawrence said.

"Yeah," Isaac agreed. "I'm down for that."

"It's a plan, then," Mom said, beaming first at Chelsea and then at me.

I tried to smile back, but spending my Saturday night watching a movie with my family and Lawrence wasn't even a runner-up on my list of top hundred things that would be considered an okay time.

Despite that, I did enjoy the movie. I always did, every time I watched it. I didn't enjoy watching Lawrence lean over and whisper things to Chelsea, even though it wasn't like he was my actual boyfriend. It just picked at those old wounds: Chelsea, the hotter sister, giggling at the boys trying to compete for her attention while I sat squashed against the armrest.

I had to hand it to Lawrence: he did seem to be making some headway with Chelsea. At one point in the movie, he muttered something in her ear, and she snorted and slapped his thigh.

"You're terrible," she whispered.

"What'd he say?" Isaac asked, grinning.

Chelsea shook her head and Lawrence laughed.

"C'mon, tell me?" Isaac pleaded.

"It's nothing," Chelsea said. "Don't worry about it."

"Hmm," Isaac said, his grin fading a bit.

"Ah, don't worry." Lawrence sat back a bit and threw his arm over my shoulder. "I'll tell you later, Joss."

"Looking forward to it," I said, trying to sound less annoyed than I felt and failing miserably.

Chelsea glanced at me from where she sat, an eyebrow just barely arched. I smiled, or at least tried to smile, at her. It did no good: she knew I was annoyed. Unless I was imagining things, there was a small glint in her eye when she figured that out.

I reminded myself Lawrence wasn't really my boyfriend, that we were there for a reason, before taking a breath and elbowing him in the ribs. He turned his head, brows furrowed.

"Wha—"

I kissed him, forcing myself to linger for just a second longer than I wanted to, even though I wanted to linger for exactly zero seconds. When I pulled back, Lawrence had a mischievous smirk on his face.

"What was that for?"

"You know what it was for," I grumbled, then turned back to the TV.

He kept his arm around my shoulder for the rest of the movie, even when Chelsea leaned towards him to make another joke. He chuckled and muttered something back but didn't move away from me. It was the right decision. She looked mildly annoyed, and I knew we had struck a nerve.

The problem was Isaac. He finally seemed to realize that Lawrence wasn't just being his usual charming self, and a troubled look clouded his face. My stomach rolled and curled, and by the time the movie ended, I felt truly sick.

"That was great!" Chelsea exclaimed when the credits rolled.

"Yeah," Isaac said. "Hey, Lawrence, I was just thinking, Chelsea and I were wondering the other day if you were coming to our wedding?"

I pressed my lips together and Lawrence chuckled.

"Well, uh, not sure I'd been invited, dude."

"Oh," Isaac said, sounding surprised. "Sorry, I just assumed since you and Joss have been dating for a while now..."

"I, um, forgot," I said quietly. "I didn't think of asking."

"Sorry, I didn't mean to put any pressure on... we just need to, you know, finalize numbers. For the caterer," he explained.

"Well, hey, no pressure." Lawrence smiled and jostled me a bit. "You want me to come, I'll come, and if not, no hard feelings."

"Yeah," I said. "No, yeah, you should... you should come. If you want to."

Chelsea grinned and clapped her hands together.

"That's perfect," she said. "The pictures will look a lot better if Jocelyn has a date."

All I could do was hope there wouldn't be a wedding for him to attend. When we were driving home, Lawrence called me out on it.

"You probably should've invited me earlier. That was super uncomfortable."

"*You* were uncomfortable?" I shot back. "Jesus, I was half-sure you were just gonna mount Chelsea right there in front of everyone. Could have tried to be a little more subtle."

"Subtle? There's a month until the wedding and until tonight, there was no progress. None. 'Subtle' is out the window, Joss."

"All you're going to do is hurt Isaac," I said. "Did you not see the look he was giving you?"

"Did you not see the look Chelsea was giving you?" he replied. "She's falling for it. I did a damn good job tonight."

"This is crazy," I muttered. "This is absolutely insane."

"It's your family, not mine."

"No, I mean... whatever," I grumbled.

We didn't speak until we were nearly at my apartment.

"Why does she hate you so much?" Lawrence said.

"Excuse me?"

"Chelsea. Like, she's got zero interest in me as a person. I'm not an idiot, I can tell. But now that she knows it pisses you off, she's all over me. What in the hell kind of thing happened for you two to be—"

"That is none of your business," I said sharply.

"I mean, it kind of is," Lawrence said. "Seeing as I'm the one trying to seduce her and all."

"You're not supposed to be seducing her," I sighed. "You're supposed to be getting her to flirt back and be obvious enough about it that Isaac breaks up with her."

Lawrence turned into the parking lot of my apartment, parked, and looked over at me with his eyebrows raised.

"Are you that naïve?" he asked.

"Fuck you."

"No, seriously, Jocelyn. You think that's where this ends? With Isaac breaking up with her because she's *flirting*?"

My mouth dropped open, but nothing came out.

"If I was really your boyfriend, and you were gonna marry me or something, would you leave me just for flirting with another girl?"

"That's not the same," I said weakly. "Are you serious? You're going to try to…"

"No, not… no," he said. "I just mean, it's going to take a little more than a few inside jokes and gentle nudges. I don't want to fuck her. Maybe work out a situation where Isaac catches us making out or something."

Shakily, I walked up to my apartment. I didn't know why I hadn't considered what, specifically, Lawrence would have to do, but he was right. Isaac wasn't going to break up with Chelsea just because she was flirting. She had to do something to hurt him, to really hurt him enough to leave her.

I could only hope it would hurt him less in the long run than a lifetime with her would. The guilt rolled through me again and I found myself wishing I hadn't rolled my eyes in disgust at Lawrence when he tried to sell me a bag of weed before I got out of the car. Instead, I cracked a beer and sat on the couch, trying to convince myself I was a good person.

The rest of the month passed far faster than I would have liked. The bridal shower was followed by the bachelorette, the final fittings, and the last-minute decoration deliveries, florist appointments, and catering issues. My involvement in the wedding party was a blessing: I didn't have to spend as much time around Lawrence, watching him try everything he could to get Chelsea into a compromising position.

And he tried. Oh, did he try. He tried hard enough that Isaac called him out on it after dinner two weeks before the wedding, pointing out he was paying more attention to Chelsea than he was to me.

"Ah, Joss doesn't mind," Lawrence said. "She knows I'm trying to make a good impression."

"Is that what you're trying to do?" Dad said coldly.

Even Lawrence couldn't find a witty comeback, instead laughing awkwardly before raising his hands in surrender.

"Didn't realize I was being out of line," he said to Isaac. "Sorry. We cool?"

Isaac nodded graciously. "Yeah, man. Of course."

"This isn't going to work," I told Lawrence as he drove me home that night. "We're out of time."

"We're not out of time," he said. "I just have to rethink my strategy a bit here."

Unfortunately for me, the rethinking of said strategy involved a lot more PDA between me and Lawrence. Instead of Isaac catching Lawrence and Chelsea making out, his strategy was to have Chelsea catch me and him making out. It worked, a little: when we were at my parents' a few days later to finish putting together the slideshow of Isaac and Chelsea's relationship, Chelsea rounded the corner into the kitchen to see Lawrence pinning me against the wall, his hand under my shirt but a respectable distance away from my breasts.

"Oh!" she said, and Lawrence pulled back.

"Shit," he said, grinning.

The redness on my face wasn't fake. I was definitely embarrassed as I adjusted my shirt, unable to meet Chelsea's eyes.

"Well, if you're done, Mom wanted your opinion on a couple of pictures," she said uncomfortably.

"Yeah. Sorry."

"I think she might like me," Lawrence stage-whispered to Chelsea, who snorted.

"You're terrible," she told him.

He winked. "That's not what your sister said."

I almost gagged, but kept a straight face and walk back to the dining room with swollen lips and an unpleasant taste in my mouth. Whether it was from kissing Lawrence or from the guilt I was feeling, I didn't know.

Still, nothing happened. Chelsea never so much as teased Lawrence, even when no one was looking. Two days before the wedding, I called Mateo.

"I think we can safely say we failed," I said.

"Yeah," he said sullenly. "Well. Thanks for trying."

"He's going to be okay," I said unconvincingly. "Like, maybe... maybe it'll be okay."

"Yeah. Maybe."

I sighed. "I need your opinion. Do I break up with Lawrence now or after the wedding?"

"What?"

"Like, he doesn't have to come to the wedding. We could 'have a fight' and break up—"

"No," Mateo said, then paused. "No, he should still go to the wedding."

I frowned. "Why?"

"Just keeps the attention off us," he said.

"Really?"

"Mm-hmm. Besides, it can be kind of a thank-you. Free meal, open bar, Lawrence'll have a great time. Break up with him next week or something."

I shrugged. "Okay. Makes sense to me."

"Cool."

"I'm sorry, Mateo. I wish... well. I'm sorry it didn't work."

"Thanks, Joss. I'm sorry, too."

When I hung up, I lay in bed, staring at the ceiling for a long time.

CHAPTER SEVENTEEN

NOW

"It's not like that. Just let me explain—"

"Explain?" He laughed, shaking his head. "You and your friggin' sister are the same. 'Let me explain, Isaac, let me *justify* to you why I'm doing this horrible thing because for some reason, I think that'll excuse it'."

"It's not like that!" My voice was high-pitched, panicked, hardly sounding like my own. "It's not, I swear."

"How the hell can you explain this? You are *fucking* my *dad*. You *knew* how weird shit was between me and him and, what, you thought 'hey, Isaac's my ex-boyfriend, I should fuck his dad'?"

"No, that's not—"

"Not what? Not what you did?"

The panic in my chest was being replaced by anger. "If you're going to ask me questions, could you maybe give me the chance to fucking answer them instead of cutting me off?"

"Oh, excuse me," Isaac said sarcastically. "Go ahead, tell me why you think it's okay to hook up with your ex-boyfriend's father. I'm super interested in hearing that."

"You're being kind of a prick for someone who fucked my sister when he said he wouldn't."

"That's not the same. I wanted to marry your sister."

"Yeah, well, maybe I want to marry your dad. How the fuck would you know?"

Isaac laughed again, the sound dry and biting. "You know why I don't believe that shit? 'Cause I know what you did, Jocelyn. I *know* what you and Lawrence did."

It was like entering a building after getting caught in the rain. Not that warm moment of relief, but the moment that you realize just how cold you really were. Goosebumps rose on my arms and a chill spread through me, shivering across my skin, almost as painful as having plunged into cold water in the first place. I gaped at Isaac, unable to deny anything, knowing that any explanation I had wouldn't be enough.

"Yeah, imagine that," Isaac continued. "I come over here to talk to my dad after finding out my ex set up this whole elaborate charade to make me leave my fiancée, only to find out she's also hooking up with him. Crazy, right? How'd you manage the timing on that so well? Was he in on it?"

Derek picked that moment to barrel in through the back door, freezing as he caught sight of me standing across from his son.

"Oh no," he muttered.

"And you," Isaac said, turning to him. "What the fuck, Dad?"

"Now, just wait a sec—"

"No, you don't get to... no. You... that's my ex-girlfriend."

"You don't get to claim her," Derek said. "She has a name."

"I'm not claiming anyone, I'm just saying it's weird as shit for my dad to—"

"Weird? You hooked up with her and her sister!"

"That's different!" Isaac shouted.

"How?" Derek said. "How's that different?"

"I loved her!"

"And I love her. It's not like this is a onetime thing, it's—"

"Oh, so it's been going on for a while," Isaac said. "How long?"

"That's not—"

"How fucking long, Dad?"

"It's not important right now."

"How long?"

"Since the wedding," I said.

Both of them looked at me, shaking and helpless in the entrance to the kitchen. Isaac was the first to break the silence.

"Was he in on it, then?" he asked.

Derek frowned. "In on what?"

"No," I whispered. "And neither was I."

"Bullshit. You're so full of shit," he spat back. "He told me what happened, Jocelyn."

"What happened?" Derek asked.

"What was this, phase two of it?" Isaac continued. "It wasn't enough to end things with me and Chelsea. No, you had to go and just *really* make sure I understood how pissed you were. You couldn't just tell me? You couldn't say it?"

"It's not what you think," I said.

"Are you actually accusing her of being cheated on just to fuck with you?" Derek asked.

"I wouldn't put it past her," Isaac spat. "And I shouldn't have put it past you, either. After all this, I thought you had changed, and then you start fucking my ex-girlfriend—"

"Stop calling her that!" Derek snapped. "She is a person. She's not defined by who she is to you. Get that through your thick fucking skull. Her name is Jocelyn, and she is not yours."

Isaac didn't even acknowledge that he had spoken.

"I can't believe I started thinking you were different, Dad. What kind of creep fucks a girl twenty years younger than him and—"

"Watch what you're saying," Derek growled.

"—thinks it's okay in the first place? What is this, some kind of sick-ass mid-life crisis? You couldn't just buy a—"

Derek's face was turning red, the tension in the room caught behind a brittle dam that was seconds away from bursting.

"Isaac, back off."

"—Ferrari or something. I'm older than her! I'm fucking older than your goddamn girlfriend! It's not enough that you left Mom and ruined our family—"

"I didn't leave your mother!" Derek roared.

Isaac stopped, his mouth still open as Derek took a step forward. I shrank back, hardly able to recognize the people standing in the room with me. Isaac was almost grotesquely emotional; Derek's eyes were pools of hurt and frustration, his cheeks red and his eyebrows furrowed. He caught sight of me huddling in the hallway and his face softened, just a bit. Clearing his throat, he lowered his voice, but the anger was still soaked into every word.

"She left me, okay? Do you feel better now, huh? Do you want all the fucking details of it, too? All the shit that she and I agreed not to tell you or your sister because neither of us wanted you to think badly of the other one?"

Isaac sputtered. "No, I—"

"Too fucking bad." Derek's voice was tight, barely restrained. "There wasn't some secret affair or some goddamn conspiracy. It was the stupidest reason, okay? She had no sex drive. None. After Samantha was born, something happened. We went to doctors, tried to figure it out for years. They said that's just the way she was. And I stayed because I loved her anyway, very much, and I would've stayed with her no matter what, but she got it into her head that I wasn't happy. She felt like she was holding me back.

"She asked for a divorce for years, Isaac. *Years*. So long, Sam wouldn't've been old enough to remember it if I'd said yes the first time.

And I didn't. I said no, every single goddamn time, unless she could give me a reason that wasn't... that. When she finally said she was miserable because she felt so guilty about it all, we went to counselling, and when we got through that and they said the best thing we could do for each other was get divorced, we did."

Isaac was silent, staring daggers across the kitchen at his dad.

"That was it," he continued. "We wanted you and your sister to have parents who loved you, no matter what, and we agreed it was best to keep that shit between us. Ange wanted to go back on that when you started acting like a stuck-up brat but I'd rather have you think I was a dick than be mad at her. So get over it, okay? Grow up and get the fuck over it. Not everything is a big goddamn conspiracy to hurt you."

"I never said—"

"You're accusing Jocelyn of what, making her boyfriend seduce your fiancée? Do you know how crazy that sounds? You might not like that I love her, but I do, and if that's going to cause another rift between us, well, that's on you."

Isaac stared at him before turning to me. "So he wasn't in on it, then. This was all you?"

I looked at Derek, knowing it was probably the last time he was going to be the person on my side. My lip trembled as he looked back, so confident in what he was saying. I didn't know if my heart could handle breaking again, but I knew it was about to.

"This wasn't part of it," I whispered.

I'll never forget the way Derek's face changed at that moment. His face was red, eyes fierce, jaw set. He was every bit my defender, protective and stubborn as he argued with his son on my behalf. When I spoke, the first thing to change was his eyes. His mouth parted, he drew in a short, sharp breath, and his shoulders seemed to deflate.

"Part of what, Joss?" he asked.

"Oh, just that crazy plan she had of getting her boyfriend to break Chelsea and me up," Isaac said.

"It wasn't my plan," I tried to protest.

"You what?" Derek asked.

"It wasn't enough to just break us up though, was it?" Isaac said, turning back to me. "You had to humiliate me, too. You had to—"

"That's not what happened!" My voice shook, wavering so much that even I wouldn't have believed myself. "I swear to God, I had nothing to do with—"

"So you're saying you were dating Lawrence because you liked him?" Isaac said sarcastically. "I should've known something was up right away, Joss. You don't seem the type to date a drug dealer, though then again, I didn't think you were the type to fuck my dad either, so shows what I know."

"A drug dealer?" Derek repeated.

"I didn't know," I whimpered.

"You think I'm gonna buy you're *that* stupid?" Isaac snapped.

My cheeks flared red and I looked down. He wasn't going to buy it, even if it was the truth. I really was that stupid.

"You know, maybe I was wrong," he said. "You and Dad are perfect for each other. You're a lying little bitch, and he's a backstabbing creep. I'm done with both of you. Stay the hell away from me, okay? Stay the fuck out of my life."

The house shook when Isaac slammed the door behind him, leaving me standing in the kitchen. Derek looked at me for a long time.

"You set the whole thing up?"

"It wasn't like that, I—"

"Joss. Did you date Lawrence in the hopes that Chelsea would cheat on Isaac?"

Neither of them would let me explain. To get any answer in, I had to keep it short, and that meant there was only one thing I could say. Clinging to the smallest scrap of hope I had left, I nodded.

"Yes."

Derek snorted, shaking his head. "And this?"

"This wasn't part of it."

"I'm supposed to believe that?"

My voice cracked. "Yes."

He shook his head and my heart cracked, too. "You should leave."

"Derek, wait, please—"

"For what? You... how could you do that?"

"We just wanted him to see he was making a mistake," I said hoarsely.

Derek shook his head again.

"I ruined my relationship with my son because of you," he said. "Probably with Ange, too, once I tell her I said.... I'm fucked. You're as bad as your sister. The two of you are toxic."

He couldn't have said anything more hurtful. I didn't let it get to me until after I dressed, left, and drove myself home. When I got back to my apartment, I pulled the blinds shut, cutting off the sunlight before delicately sitting on the edge of my bed. It wasn't until I was there that I started to cry, my heart too shattered to simply be called broken, and I didn't stop for a long, long time.

CHAPTER EIGHTEEN

THEN

"YOU FUCKING *ASSHOLE*!"

"Whoa, wait a sec, Joss, just—"

I pushed Mateo back after the door swung open, limping slightly as I shoved my way into his house. Lawrence was sitting on the couch, looking alarmed.

"What the hell were you thinking?" I shouted. "You weren't supposed to fuck her! And at their *wedding*?"

"It got the job done." Lawrence was holding an ice pack to his eye, but moved it so I could see the bruise there. "Although yeah, I would have preferred that Isaac not kick the shit out of me."

"Why would you do that? At what point did it stop being about getting them to break up and more about getting into her pants?"

"It never did!" he protested. "Mateo said—"

"Dude," Mateo interrupted.

I whirled toward him. "You're joking. Are you serious?"

"It's not—"

"You planned this. The two of you planned this?"

Mateo sighed. "I mean, we had an opportunity, and we took it."

"An opportunity?" I repeated. "Are you kidding me?"

"Your sister was flirting with me, Joss," Lawrence said. "Like, she was laying it on *thick*. Kind of a freak, really. Who gets off on that kind of thing on their wedding day?"

I gaped at both of them.

"So it wasn't you just wanting to get laid," I said, then turned back to Mateo. "This was all part of the plan."

"He was so close to getting with her before the wedding. We were just running out of time. I figured if he was there and something happened…"

"Though you didn't bother telling me Isaac was a violent little prick," Lawrence muttered.

"Get over it," Mateo said. "You've been hurt worse."

"Are you serious?" I asked. "You humiliated Isaac, you humiliated *me*, you turned a horrible situation into an even worse one."

"It needed to be done," Mateo said.

"You don't think that was more hurtful to Isaac than just letting him have a normal wedding?"

"You know what, I don't like it any more than you do—"

"That's a fucking lie and you know it."

"Fine." Mateo glared at me. "Yeah, it was cold. Yeah, it was hurtful. But it needed to be done. He needed to see who she was."

"It wasn't all that enjoyable, if that's any help," Lawrence said. "She's kind of… pushy. And a sloppy kisser. Like, did you see her lipstick after we—"

"Ew," I said. "Don't need to hear that. And no, that doesn't help at all!"

"What's done is done," Mateo said. "Sorry you were caught up in it, but it's not like you came out looking like the bad guy, okay? You'll get over it."

"That's not the point!"

"She came onto me," Lawrence said again. "Like, plain and simple, Joss. She came up to me after the ceremony and was like 'hey, can I talk to you' and of course I was like 'oh yeah, for sure' and then next thing I know she's pulling me to the side and goes 'I want to do something crazy, you in?' and—oh, this was really fuckin' funny—I say 'depends, if it's you I get to be in, then yeah' and she says—"

"You have a strange definition of what's funny," I interrupted.

"I thought it was clever," Lawrence said. "Anyway, I barely did anything, and all Mateo did was make sure Isaac caught us. It's like he said, you didn't do anything. Just made sure I was there at the right place, right time, and bam. Though, your timing was a bit off, dude, if you could've given me like two more minutes to finish—"

"You're disgusting," I said. "And you, Mateo? You call yourself his best friend? You're sick."

"Oh, don't pretend you're all high and mighty now," he shot back. "You didn't enjoy slapping your sister?"

"Not the point," I said through gritted teeth.

"It is, a little, isn't it? You got all that sympathy. You don't have to worry about coming up with a fake reason to break up with Lawrence, and you have the satisfaction of knowing you got back at your sister for what she did."

"This isn't what I wanted," I said.

"What did you want, huh?" Mateo asked. "What did you think was gonna happen, Joss?"

"You could have at least given me a head's up," I said. "I discovered it at the same time as everyone else. You don't think that was awful?"

"Not really," he replied. "You would've stopped us. How many fucking times did you try to back out?"

"I'm telling Isaac," I said.

"No."

"Stop me. I fucking dare you."

"I don't have to," Mateo said, laughing. "You're seriously going to fess up to Isaac about the whole thing? Including your involvement in it?"

"I mean..."

"You come off just as bad as we do," Mateo said. "Whether you like it or not."

"I don't like it," I said. "And I never... I agreed to help break them up *before* the wedding. Not at it. Not after it. Before."

"He'll understand one day," Mateo said.

"I'm telling him," I repeated. "It's the right thing to do, Mateo. He deserves to know."

"What happened to your leg?" Lawrence asked.

I glanced down at the shorts I'd put on since the bandages Derek had put on my calf were had been rubbing painfully against my jeans. I'd driven straight to Mateo's after checking out of the hotel, telling myself the whole way that I was going to have a calm, rational discussion with him until he'd opened the door and I saw his stupid, smug face.

"I cut it," I said.

"On what?"

"None of your business, that's what."

"I heard Isaac's dad drove you back last night," Mateo said.

I raised my eyebrows. "Who'd you hear that from?"

"Angela. She was looking for you at the hotel this morning because I guess the church called to say there were a couple of bins left to be picked up. She thought you or Derek had taken them."

"We must have forgotten them," I said.

"She was also kind of wondering where you were," he continued. "Since your car was still in the parking lot, but you weren't answering the hotel phone. She even tried knocking, apparently."

"What are you trying to say here?"

"Nothing," he said. "I guess it's just a series of unrelated circumstances that look, you know. A little... strange."

He knew.

He didn't know for sure, but he knew enough.

"You're an asshole," I said. "Fuck you, Mateo."

He shrugged. "Sorry. You knew going into this whose side I was on. It's Isaac's, and it's always been Isaac's. I'm gonna tell him what we did, one day. When he's less upset, when he's had some time. I'm not a complete psychopath, you know."

"Close enough," I muttered.

"Look, Joss," Lawrence piped up again. "It's not as bad as you think it is. You think you have it bad? I lost a customer out of this. No way Isaac's going to keep buying from me."

"You're a moron," I told him.

"What? I'm gonna have to get an actual job soon. That sucks!"

Rolling my eyes, I turned on my heel and limped back to my car. Mateo rushed out after me.

"Don't tell him," he said. "Seriously, Joss."

"I won't," I said. "You're not giving me much of a choice, you blackmailing prick."

"It's for the best," he said. "Though... am I right? About, uh, you and...?"

"If you were, do you think I'd tell you, considering what you're doing to me?"

He had the decency to look ashamed. I got into my car, pulled out of his driveway, and made my way back home. My intent was to shut my apartment door, close all the blinds, and bury myself beneath a blanket on the couch, stewing in my own misery as I tried to forget what had happened.

Then, of course, my mom called, begging me to have dinner with a father who hated me, a sister who despised me, and her: a woman who would guilt me into doing anything she wanted.

CHAPTER NINETEEN

NOW

"ARE YOU SURE YOU'RE all right, sweetie?"

I glanced up at Mom, unaware that I'd been staring down at my plate with my fork in hand, not moving for long enough that it became suspicious. It seemed strange to me that she would notice that, of all things, considering how awkward that meal had been. Dad was silent as usual, but even Chelsea had seemed tense.

"Yeah," I said. "Fine."

"You're hardly eating," she said.

"Not feeling well," I replied. "Sorry."

"I hope you're not sick," Dad said. "Don't want to spread it around."

"No, I don't think so. Just a... stomachache," I said.

"Hmm," he said, and went back to his plate.

It wasn't a lie, either. My stomach was knotted, tumultuous one moment and frozen with anxiety the next. It had been since the previous morning when I had left Derek's. I spent the rest of the day in my apartment, crying on and off, watching TV and trying to distract myself. He needed space, obviously, and time. It would do no good for me to try explaining everything when he was still upset. Never mind that he was probably trying to deal with Isaac and Angela, trying to explain the situation and what happened, to salvage those relationships I had wrecked simply by being present. I had to let the whole thing settle a bit before I could even think of trying to explain myself.

I made it to about seven o'clock before I broke down and went to text him. The last message in our conversation was from him, and I burst into tears upon seeing it.

This isn't you. Whatever I did, I'm sorry.

Had that really only been the previous night? It was from barely twenty-four hours earlier. In that time, I'd gone from trying to break things off with Derek, only to end up telling him I loved him and spending the whole night in bed with him.

We planned what we were going to do.

We came up with a way to have a future, and before we could even try to live it, it was ripped away.

Well, not ripped away. The secrets I'd been keeping had come to light. I had no one but myself to blame for this.

When I stopped crying and could actually see what I was typing, I sent him a message.

I'm sorry. If you're willing to listen, I'd like to explain. I understand if you're not, but I swear I never lied to you about my feelings. Please give me a chance.

I waited for a few minutes to see if he would respond, but didn't expect that he would. A few hours later, I checked my phone again. Still no response. I plugged my phone in, went to bed, and barely slept. When there was still no response when I woke up Sunday morning, I knew what his answer was.

Instead of contacting Derek again, I texted Mateo to ask him what happened, why he couldn't have at least given me a head's up that Isaac knew. The response I got back from him was unsettling.

Isaac knows?!?!?!?!??!?!?!

I assumed that meant Mateo was being cut out of Isaac's life or that Isaac didn't know about Mateo's involvement. Either way, his response was useless to me. I sighed and responded, realizing very quickly that meant Lawrence was the one who screwed us over.

Yes.

My phone went off less than two minutes later.

"He's not at home," Mateo said urgently. "How'd you find out? Do you know where he is?"

"Um, from him, and no—"

"Maybe he's at his dad's," he mused. "He's been chatting with him a lot. If he—"

"He's not at Derek's," I said.

"How the hell would... oh." Mateo went silent. "You're joking."

I didn't say anything.

"You're not joking. Holy shit, Joss. You actually... after the wedding, you actually—"

"I don't need to hear this from you." My voice came out gravelly, the words scratching at my throat.

"No, no, of course not... wow." He fell silent again. "Uh, what the hell were you thinking?"

"Okay, I'm hanging up now."

"No!" he said. "I just meant... I mean, it wasn't like a... the wedding was months ago and you're still..."

"Bye, Mateo."

"No, no, wait!"

I sighed. "Make it quick."

"What did Isaac say? Like, what did he know?"

I explained what I could to him: Isaac had somehow found out, he'd clearly found out from Lawrence, and he was pissed.

"I don't think he knows you were involved," I said sullenly. "If he had, he would've said something, I'm sure. So, lucky you. You get to come out of it all unscathed."

"Well, that's not—"

"It's fine. I've already fucked up everything. Talk to you later, Mateo."

He protested, but I hung up and turned my phone off before burying myself under the sheets again. It was a testament to how horrible the weekend was that when the evening rolled around, I was looking forward to getting out of the apartment to have dinner at my parents'.

"Jocelyn!"

I glanced up, unaware I'd zoned out again. Mom looked worried beyond belief and Dad's eyebrows were furrowed.

"Are you on drugs or something?" he asked.

"No," I said.

"She's just upset because Isaac found out she set the whole thing up with Lawrence to get us to break up," Chelsea said casually.

It took a moment for me to process the words. When I did, I dropped my fork and looked at her. Chelsea stared back evenly, her mouth set in an unhappy line and her eyes cold.

"What?" Mom said.

"Do you want to tell them the story?" Chelsea asked.

"How did you..."

"Isaac told me." She laughed and shook her head. "That's right, you fucked things up so badly that Isaac called me out of nowhere to tell me what you'd done."

"It wasn't like that," I said.

"No?" she asked. "You were dating a drug dealer because you liked him?"

"What?!" Mom gasped.

"I didn't know he was a drug dealer," I said tiredly.

"Hmm. Just like you didn't know he was trying to sleep with me so Isaac and I would break up."

I didn't have a response to that. I stared down at my plate, wishing I was back in my bed, wishing I could go back in time and fix everything.

"Let me get this straight," Dad said. "You dated a drug dealer in the hopes that he would, what, seduce your sister so she wouldn't marry Isaac?"

When I didn't respond, he put his cutlery down loudly.

"I'm speaking to you, Jocelyn."

"It wasn't like that," I said again.

"What was it like, then?" Dad asked coldly. "If it wasn't like that, it must have been like something else."

"He flirted with me all the time," Chelsea said. "Remember the movie night? Every time I saw him? You knew the whole time, didn't you?"

"This is disgusting," Dad said. "I can't believe you, Jocelyn. I am so ashamed of you."

Ashamed.

I startled us all by laughing.

"That's nothing new," I said. "You've always been ashamed of me."

"Excuse me?"

"Don't act like you don't know." I looked up at him, glaring across the table. "Yeah, okay? I brought Lawrence around because we thought Chelsea might try something again. You know, just like she did with Isaac. Just like she did with—"

"Don't," Chelsea growled. "Don't you dare blame Cody on me. That was all you, you fucking—"

"Fuck off," I said. Mom gasped. "He was your fault, too. I've never dated anyone that you didn't try to fuck, Chelsea. You might be a goddamn princess, but at least have enough decency to own up to your bullshit."

"Watch your mouth," Dad growled.

I snorted. "Yeah, that's the problem here. I'm the problem here, always have been, right Dad?"

"You ungrateful—"

"Gerald!" Mom said warningly.

"Oh, that's not true," Chelsea said, not listening to our parents. "What about Mr. Thompson? I didn't try to sleep with him."

My face went red.

"Mr. Thompson?" Mom repeated. "Derek Thompson? Like, Isaac's—"

"Isaac's dad, yeah," Chelsea said. "He was so grossed out, Joss. I mean, after he stopped being disgusted that you would do something like that just to get back at him."

"That's not why I was... that isn't what happened," I said.

"You didn't sleep with Isaac's dad?" she asked.

"I... well..."

"Oh, so you *did* sleep with Isaac's dad."

"*Derek* was not someone I was just sleeping with," I said through clenched teeth.

"Jesus Christ," Dad said. "So you were... with his father. You were with his father?"

"And it didn't have anything to do with Isaac," I continued. "I never held any of this against him. The breakup thing? Yeah, okay, I had something to do with that, but that was about you, Chelsea. We didn't want *you* to marry Isaac."

"Who's 'we'?" she asked, but I ignored her.

"Derek had nothing to do with any of that. I lov... liked him. It wasn't to get back at anyone, it wasn't some big conspiracy. I had feelings for him. I... it doesn't even matter anymore. Everything's over."

"Jocelyn," Mom gasped. "He's got to be old enough to... well."

"Old enough to be my father?" I said sarcastically. "Great observation, Mom."

"Show some respect," Dad hissed.

"Or what?" I looked up at him defiantly. "What else can fucking happen to me at this point? When it rains, it just fucking pours, doesn't it? I can't date anyone because my sister will fuck anything that so much as glances at me with interest. I ruined whatever I had with Derek because of some stupid plan Mateo had because he could see right through Chelsea when Isaac couldn't. And you will never, ever be anything but ashamed of me. No matter what I do, Dad, you won't ever take my side."

"That's not—"

"I'm not stupid, okay?" I pushed my chair away from the table. "I get it. You love Chelsea far more than you'll ever love me because, what, because I wasn't a boy? Because she's perfect and I'm not? Whether or not Lawrence and I were really together shouldn't matter. She fucked my boyfriend, and you still said I was the one who should be ashamed!"

Dad's eyes flashed at me, redness creeping up his neck as a vein started to show through his skin. "You have no idea what I had to—"

"Gerald!" Mom hissed again. "Jocelyn, calm down—"

"Why do I have to be the one to calm down?" Tears were starting to collect in my eyes and at some point, I had stood. I didn't remember doing it. "Why did I have to be the one to be the bigger person, Mom? Why was I the one who had to give things up and put up with the way they treated me to 'keep the family together,' huh? You saw what they did to me, you saw how they… I mean, the wedding! Dad said he was leaving me there and you just went with him!"

"Joss, that's not—"

"You did! I was there, remember? Chelsea cheated on her husband on her wedding day and I was the one getting yelled at. I was the one expected to come to dinner the next day and let bygones be bygones. Neither of you ever even asked if I was okay. I was just expected to forgive and forget and move on."

"Don't speak to your mother like that," Dad growled.

"Don't tell me what to do," I shot back. "You… what did I ever even do to you, Dad?"

"I treated you both the same," Dad said.

"Bullshit! How can you even say that with a straight face? You have beautiful, smart, perfect fucking Chelsea over there that you were *so* proud of, that did *everything* right even when she was wrong, and then you have me. And no matter what I did, no matter—"

"You need to back off," he said.

I didn't listen. Tears were streaming down my face as I yelled, and just like the words I was yelling, I couldn't stop them if I tried.

"—what I tried, who I tried to be, you never treated me the same. I'm your daughter, too! I'm not the princess and I'm not a dental hygienist and I'm not, whatever, perfect like she is, but I'm not that bad, Dad. Why don't you love me like you love her? Why do you treat me like a fucking disgrace when you're supposed to be proud of me? When you're supposed to be my father?"

"Because I'm not your father!"

The words didn't hang in the air like a cloud, filling the room with shock and tension. They crashed onto the table, they splattered each of us, they burst into existence like ooze erupting from a cyst. I stared at the man across the table from me, his face red and his mouth twisted into a sick snarl, and realized I was staring at a stranger.

"What?" I whispered.

"Gerald," Mom choked, and she buried her head into her hands.

"I'm not your father," he repeated. "You're the product of Bianca being unable to keep her legs closed while I—"

He stopped suddenly, inhaling deeply through his nose to calm himself.

"You are not my daughter," he continued. "She told me it was a one-time thing, but you came along anyway. I wasn't about to raise my daughter in a broken family, so I stayed. I tolerated you. But *you* are not my daughter."

The silence was broken only by my mom's sniffling sobs, her head still buried in her hands. After a moment, Chelsea started laughing. To her credit, I don't think she meant to. The situation was absurd at best and horrific at worst, and I knew all too well how hard it was to suppress laughter in those situations. I'd laughed at her wedding when she'd slept with my pretend-boyfriend. It seemed only right that she laughed as I found out my entire life was a lie. Still, the sound of it echoed in my ears as I walked to the front door and picked up my keys and wallet.

"Joss," Mom cried, rushing after me. She caught up to me halfway down the driveway, grabbing at my arm.

"Don't," I said. "I'm done."

"No, you can't, you... family is—"

"That's not my family, is it?" I said. "I don't have a family."

"You do," she whimpered. "You have me, and Chelsea is still your sister, and Gerald... he'll c-come around and—"

"Mom." Any tears I had left had withered away, replaced only by numbness. "I'm never coming back here. I don't want to see any of you ever again."

She bawled as I walked away, and I didn't feel guilty at all.

CHAPTER TWENTY

BEFORE

"...HAPPY BIRTHDAY DEAR JOCELYN, happy birthday to you!"

I grin at the camera, my tongue poking through one of the gaps in my smile where a tooth hasn't quite come in yet, and wait as Mom takes the picture.

"Okay, go ahead," she finally says, and I blow out the candles.

"You missed one!" shrieks Chelsea. "That means you have a boyfriend!"

"Ew!" I squeal, blowing hard at the offending candle. "There, now he's gone!"

We giggle and Mom takes the cake to the side.

"Which piece do you want, Joss?" she asks.

"I want the pink flower!" Chelsea demands.

"I wanted the pink flower," I pout.

"It's Jocelyn's birthday, Chels, so she gets the pink flower," Mom says.

Chelsea sighs miserably, her forehead wrinkling as she squints her eyes and tenses her jaw. I'm only a year younger, but even I know what her fake-crying face looks like.

"She doesn't even like pink!" she wails.

"Jocelyn doesn't mind giving Chelsea the pink flower," Dad says. "We all need to learn to share."

"But it's my birthday," I protest.

"And it's very nice of you to give the pink flower to Chelsea, even though it's your birthday," Dad says.

I nod, confused, then grin again. "That's okay. I like the blue flower better anyway."

Chelsea grins and throws her arms around me.

"You're my favourite sister," she giggles. I kiss her on the cheek and Mom snaps another picture, one that she's sure will someday be perfect for a wedding slideshow.

"DID YOU SEE, DID you see?" I shriek.

"Yeah, Jossy, we saw," Mom says.

"You looked so cool!" Chelsea exclaims. "I couldn't even tell the ball was in your stick and then BOOM! You scored!"

"It's called a crosse," I say proudly, holding the lacrosse stick forward.

Chelsea takes it from my hands and examines it, posing with it over her shoulder. I giggle and correct her stance as she puts on a serious, dramatic face.

"Do I look the part?" she asks gravely.

"You'll be on the team in no time!" I say.

"Good game, Joss!" shouts the coach. I wave at him and turn to Mom. "Where's Daddy?"

Mom smiles and pats my shoulder. "He had to leave right at the very end of the game, but he said you did a great job."

Chelsea frowns.

"But he wasn't here," she says bluntly. "Mommy, you shouldn't lie."

"He was," she says again. "He was over at the other side of the bleachers because he had to leave so fast."

"But he saw, right?" I ask. "He saw me score the last goal?"

"Of course, sweetie. He saw."

Chelsea holds my hand as we walk to the car. I think she knows I don't believe Mom.

*"O*HMIGOD*!" squeals* C*HELSEA. "A brand new makeup kit! Thanks, Santa!"*

"I'm sure Santa says you're welcome," Dad chuckles.

I tear my package open next, silvery paper falling to the floor.

"Pyjamas!" I say, trying to match Chelsea's excitement. "Just what I wanted. Thank you, Santa."

"They're the right size, right sweetie?" Mom asks. "Santa knows you went through a growth spurt."

"Yeah," I say, even though I can already tell they're far too big.

"Joss, you gotta let me do your makeup," Chelsea says. "C'mere, I want to try this colour on you!"

I abandon the pyjamas next to the pile of wrapping paper and scoot across the floor to sit with my sister.

"Okay, but NO pink!"

"I DON'T WANT TO *wear her dress!" I protest.*

"It's your junior high graduation," Mom sighs. "You need to wear a dress."

"But I don't want to wear Chelsea's old one," I say. "It won't even fit me right, Mom."

"Just try it," she urges, and urges, and urges again until I put it on.

"See? That's not so bad," she says.

I look in the mirror at the hot pink monstrosity. It's too tight under my arms and skin pinches over the edges. The fabric pulls across my chest, and the skirt that hit just above Chelsea's knee the year before is halfway down my calves.

"It's horrible," I say. "This is so ugly."

"Uh, excuse me, I picked that dress," Chelsea says, her tone miffed.

"I mean it's ugly on me," I say. "Mom, please, can't I just wear something else?"

"Your dad said we don't have the budget to get you a brand-new dress," she says.

"Can I wear pants?"

"Well, it's a special occasion. I don't know if pants are—"

"What about, like, a lady suit?" I ask. "Like the boys would wear, but for girls?"

She sighs and nods. "I'll see what I can do, sweetie."

"CAN I ASK YOU something?"

Chelsea snuggles closer to me. We're far too old to be sneaking into each other's rooms to have sleepovers, but she's not just my sister, she's my best friend.

"Yes, of course."

"Promise you won't tell Mom and Dad?" I whisper.

"Pinky promise."

I glance at the doorway of her bedroom, just in case.

"Do you think Dad hates me?" I ask softly.

"Seriously?" Chelsea looks at me, shocked. "Why would you think that?"

I chew on the inside of my cheek, a nervous habit I picked up from chewing on my mouthguard during lacrosse.

"I don't know," I admit. "He just seems to act differently to me than to you."

Chelsea purses her lips. "I don't know, Joss. I guess I never thought about it."

"Maybe I'm just crazy."

She giggles. "Well, yeah, obvs, but if it's bothering you, that means it's important."

We both laugh and though we don't figure anything out, I smile as we fall asleep that night.

"I HAVE TO TELL you something," Chelsea says. We're sitting on the porch swing, lazily swaying back and forth.

"What?" I ask.

"I have a boyfriend," she whispers.

I try not to shriek and turn to her. "Chelsea! Dad said no dating!"

"I know," she hisses. "You can't tell anyone."

"Pinky promise."

She curls her finger around mine and smiles.

"Tell me everything," I hiss excitedly after she lets go. "What's his name?"

Her face lights up.

"His name's Cody."

CHAPTER TWENTY-ONE

NOW

"You look like hell."

"You sure know how to make a woman feel good."

Bretta pointed a finger at me. "I do, actually. Ask my girlfriend."

I tried to laugh, but nothing came out.

"Come into my office. Now."

"I'm fine, Bretta."

"You're a damn liar."

She shut the door behind me as I walked in, slumping in the chair across the desk without being told.

"What happened this weekend?" she asked.

I chuckled, shaking my head. "What didn't happen this weekend?"

"Uh... well, I sent you home early on Friday because you were so hung up on Derek that you couldn't focus."

"Right. God, was that only on Friday? Jesus."

"You're scaring me," Bretta said.

"Sorry." I shook my head. "Okay. Well, I tried ignoring him and that didn't go so well. I still ended up at his place."

"What happened there?"

"I told him I was in love with him."

Bretta winced. "And...?"

"He said he loved me."

Her face brightened. "Well, that's good, right?"

"Well, yeah. It was. Until we broke up."

Bretta's jaw dropped. "What?"

"Yeah, the next morning."

"Girl. You need to get the story out before I lose my mind."

I explained everything haltingly: Isaac's unexpected visit, his revelation about what Lawrence and I had done, the heartbreaking look on Derek's face as he found out what I did to his son. Then I had to backtrack and explain that part to Bretta, since I'd never told her about Mateo's plot or my involvement with it. I should have been in tears, but everything came out with a grim sense of numbness.

"You must think I'm a horrible person," I said.

"Not really," she said. "I mean, the fact that this plan worked says a hell of a lot more about Chelsea than it does about you. And I believe you when you say you didn't know he was going to... well, you know. At their wedding."

"I didn't," I mumbled. "Pinky promise."

"Okay. So... he was mad. He didn't believe you?"

I shook my head. "Neither of them did. Can't blame them, I mean... it looks bad."

"I'm sorry, Joss. That just sucks so much, but... well, maybe given some time..."

I shrugged. "Maybe."

She sat back in her chair. "That's not everything, though, is it?"

I shook my head.

"Let me guess... Chelsea knows too, and your dad was a dick about it."

"Well, yes and no."

She frowned. "Your dad wasn't a dick about it?"

I shook my head. "Chelsea knows. Her dad was a dick about it. But her dad isn't my dad."

Bretta stared at me, mouth dropped. I studied the edge of her desk.

"Do you know anything about changing your last name?" I asked. "'Cause... I think I might want to change mine."

"You're... he's..."

"He's not my dad and never has been," I said, and that was when the tears started.

Bretta was around her desk in an instant, wrapping her arms around me as I cried. I thought I'd run out of tears the night before while I played memory after memory over and over in my head, knowing they were all lies, every one of them. Apparently, like everything else, I had been wrong.

The worst part was, after the disastrous dinner, all I wanted to do was call Derek. He was the only person I wanted to talk to, the only one I thought might understand. I needed him more than I had ever needed anyone, and I'd lost him.

I'd lost everything.

Bretta was far more than a boss to me in the following weeks. She refused to let me go back to my apartment, instead insisting on driving me to her house. Leigh went to my apartment that evening after work and collected some clothes and toiletries, and both of them refused to let me so much as consider living anywhere but their guest room for the foreseeable future. I resisted, of course, like I always did, and it wasn't until Bretta threatened to put me on unpaid leave that I caved.

"Good," she said. "Now, you're on paid leave for the rest of the week."

I tried to insist that I'd rather be working, but she refused to hear it. As much as I hated to admit it, she was right to make me take the time off. I barely slept the first few days, memories swirling behind my eyelids every time I shut them, little moments long since buried that had resurfaced. With those memories came emotions I couldn't handle: the feeling of not being enough, the confusion of why, the desperate attempts at being better, stronger, faster, prettier. All the things I tried to do to impress the man I thought was my dad, not understanding why he never cared.

Mom tried to reach me. She called every day, usually multiple times a day. When I blocked her, she called from other numbers. At the end of the week, Bretta took me to the nearest mobile shop.

"She's got a problem with a stalker," she said to the employee.

"Let me see what we can do," he said, and I walked out half an hour later with a new phone number, free of charge.

If she really wanted to, Mom could have found me. I overheard Bretta tell Leigh that she had shown up at the shop that first week. Bretta told her in no uncertain terms to back off, and that if she was ever lucky enough to hear from me again, it would be on my terms and not hers.

I felt a little bit guilty when I heard that, but it might have just been that instinctive familial guilt I had from growing up with a mom like her.

The following week, I went back to work, but Bretta still insisted I stay with her and Leigh. The week after that, Leigh mentioned it was kind of nice having a roommate, and what did I think about maybe moving in permanently? I had no emotional attachment to my apartment, so I thought it was a pretty good idea. It seemed like an even better idea when we went there to pack up and I found the various notes and packages my mom had left.

Slowly but surely, I cut all ties. I stopped mourning the loss of my family and started accepting it for what it was: freedom. By the time a month had passed, I was almost embracing it. Bretta and Leigh helped me apply to change my last name, and though it would take a few months to be approved, the hardest part was deciding on a new name.

I eventually decided on Jones, partially because I didn't care what it was as long as it wasn't Miller, and because Bretta said it would be fun to call me JoJo. I thought Jocelyn Jones sounded like a comic book character or maybe one of The Doctor's companions, and since I didn't hate the nickname, Jocelyn Jones it was.

Things weren't perfect. I missed Derek horribly. I had only given my new phone number to a few people and considered texting him to tell him I'd changed it, but decided it was a bad idea. Once upon a time, I had told myself that to end things with Derek, I needed to do it swiftly, suddenly, and completely. As much as I missed him, I was fairly certain there was no way to repair things between the two of us.

That was okay. It hurt like a bitch and it was completely unfair, but it was my own doing. Derek deserved far better than what I could offer.

My new life wasn't perfect, but it was good. Bretta and Leigh became my family, and I had friends. For once, I wasn't worried about impressing anyone. No one told me I had to do things I didn't want to for their sake. Slowly, I was healing, and slowly, I was finding happiness.

So, of course, a little over a month after that horrible weekend, someone had to come along to pick the scabs off those wounds.

"Are you fucking stupid?" I was saying to one of the other mechanics. "You can't crawl into a car when it's on the lift just because you forgot the wheel lock key in the glove box. Take it off the lift so you don't kill yourself!"

"Jesus, Joss, it was just a question," he said.

"Nah, she's right," Bretta said, coming up behind me. "Don't be a moron, Travis."

He grumbled and walked away.

"I don't know about that one," I muttered to her.

"Me neither. Give it another week and we'll see." She tilted her head to the side. "There are some people here to see you. Don't be mad. I've thoroughly vetted them."

"Who is it?" I asked flatly.

"Joss, you should consider talking to them," she said.

"Who is it, Bretta?"

She sighed. "Isaac and Mateo."

I shook my head and put my earbuds in as I turned away. Bretta grabbed my arm and plucked one of the buds out of my ear.

"Hey!"

"I wouldn't even tell you they were here unless I was fairly sure it was a good idea to talk to them," she said. "Give them a chance."

"I'm done with that life," I said.

"That's why you still cry at night sometimes?"

My face turned red and she grimaced.

"Sorry. That was harsh. But, I mean, the walls aren't exactly thick, you know."

Sighing, I followed her to the reception area.

Mateo and Isaac both looked up as I walked through the door hesitantly. There were no other customers and I told the receptionist she could take a break, which she gladly accepted.

"Joss," Mateo said. "Can we talk?"

"What do you want?" I asked flatly.

"Maybe we could grab a coffee," he said.

I shook my head. "Say it here or leave."

He looked at Isaac, who nodded.

"Okay," Mateo said.

"So what do you want?" I asked.

"I thought we could both use some closure," Isaac said.

"I'm so glad you know what I could use," I replied.

He chose not to respond to that, probably wisely. "Mateo told me… about everything. The whole… what he asked you to do and everything."

I raised my eyebrows, glancing at Mateo. "Did he, now? And you're still good enough friends to come here in the middle of my workday to confront me together?"

"I was pissed at first," Isaac said. "But he had a point."

"I'm so glad he got the benefit of the doubt from you," I said. "Really, that's so considerate."

"Come on, Joss," he said. "I'm trying to apologize."

"Hmm. Weirdest apology I've ever heard, but sure."

He sighed. "I'm sorry for how I reacted about that, but only that. I should've let you explain more, and I should've been able to see that it wasn't... Look, when Lawrence came clean about what he'd done, I was pissed. I thought you... he didn't tell me you didn't even know about that part of it, okay? I wasn't thinking straight when we... saw each other."

"Well, sorry for my part in ruining your marriage," I said. "Are we done?"

"No," he said. "I'm still pissed at you."

"Oh, good. Well, thank you for coming to my place of work to inform me of that fact."

"I tried calling you, but you've blocked my number," he said.

"No, I haven't," I said. "I've changed my number. There's a difference."

He frowned. "Why'd you change your number?"

I stared at him. "Oh. I guess you only talked to Chelsea long enough to tell her your side of the story?"

"I haven't talked to Chelsea since... I just talked to her the one time," he said. "I thought she should know."

"No, that's fair. Well, I don't talk to her at all anymore. Any of them, actually."

His face fell. "Oh my God. Did they cut you out because—"

"No," I said. "I cut them out."

"Oh. I see."

"No, you don't," I said.

"Well, no," he admitted. "What did your parents, uh, say? About everything?"

"My mom didn't say much," I said.

"What about, uh, your dad?"

"I don't know what he said. He wasn't there."

Isaac frowned. "What happened to him?"

I shrugged. "No idea. But if you mean Chelsea's dad, he was reasonably disgusted, but that was more because I dared do something that hurt Chelsea."

"Wait, what?" Mateo cut in. "Your dad—"

"Chelsea's dad. Not my dad."

Isaac's mouth dropped open.

"You mean... wow, Joss. I'm so sorry. Who's your dad, then?" he asked, bewildered.

I shrugged. "Don't know. Don't care. That's not my family anymore. Anyway, you forgive me for being involved in Mateo's whole seduction setup, but not for all the other stuff, and you came here to tell me that because you don't have my phone number. Is that it? Are we done?"

"No!" Isaac said. "I still want to know why you did what you did."

"Why don't you ask your dad?"

"I did," he said bluntly. "He's pissed at you, too."

"Good," I said. "Thanks."

"Was it because of me?" he asked. "That's what I need to know. Were you with him because you knew it would hurt me?"

I laughed. Cackled, really. I laughed almost harder than I had in the entire month since everything had happened. Shaking my head, I tried to cover the fact that tears were collecting in the corners of my eyes.

"No," I said. "My world doesn't revolve around you, Isaac, okay? I don't give a shit what you do or what happens to you. Derek was never part of it. I didn't mean to... I never... he was there for me when the entire clusterfuck happened. He was there more than that, actually, a lot more. He was the one person in the world who was on my side."

My voice cracked and I coughed, trying to cover it.

"I never meant to sleep with him, and I didn't mean to keep doing it, and I definitely didn't mean to fall in love with him but I did, anyway. I would've stayed with him, if he'd have let me. The worst part about this whole fucking thing is that I know I hurt him and I can't fix it."

I looked at Isaac, still struggling not to cry, not caring if he saw it.

"It was never about you. And for the record, he was terrified of telling you because he thought you'd react exactly how you did. If you have to blame someone, blame me, but fix your fucking relationship with him, would you? He deserves it, even if you don't think so."

Isaac didn't seem to know what to say. "I didn't know—"

"Whatever," I said. "I have to get back to work."

"Wait, Joss—"

"It's been a month. I'm over it. Leave me alone, okay?"

"Let me just—"

I didn't hear whatever the rest of it was. I put my earbuds back in, turned, and let the door to the shop slam closed behind me.

CHAPTER TWENTY-TWO
BEFORE

Chelsea flies into my bedroom, looking panicked.

"I need your help," she whispers. "Please."

"What's wrong?"

She glances at the closed door. "Mr. Porter went golfing with Dad this morning and said he heard I was dating Cody Borowski, and Dad's livid. He's on his way home and he called Mom and she just told me."

"Oh no," I whisper.

"He's going to kill me," she whimpers. "He said no dating and I—"

"How does Mr. Porter know?"

"He said he saw us last weekend at the mall holding hands."

I think back. "Last weekend. When I was with you, right?"

She nods. "I think he must have seen us in the food court. I can't think of when else I was holding hands with Cody."

"Well, we just say we were hanging out," I say. "We were. Mr. Porter must have been mistaken."

She sniffles and nods, and when she starts crying for real, I hug my sister and tell her it's going to be okay.

"...IT'S NOT THAT YOU'RE dating him, Chelsea, it's that you lied about it," Dad says. *"I'm very disappointed in you."*

Chelsea looks at me helplessly across the dining room table. Mom's hands are folded on her lap as she listens to Dad give Chelsea shit for what feels like the first time in our lives.

"I'm sorry," she whimpers.

"I know you're getting older and boys are becoming interesting," he continues, "but I don't think you should be dating right now. In fact, I think you need to be grounded for a while, and—"

Chelsea looks broken. Dad's never spoken to her like this, he's never told her she's a disappointment, he's never ever punished her before. It's too much: I can't handle it.

"It's my fault," I interrupt.

"Joss, no!" Chelsea says.

"Excuse me?" Dad asks.

"She's taking the fall for me," I say. "Cody is my boyfriend. Mr. Porter must have seen us holding hands and mixed me and Chelsea up or something. I'm sorry, Dad."

He grounds me for a week, probably because he had to since he threatened to ground Chelsea, but it's clear he's relieved. Chelsea is annoyed because he's not as "disappointed" in me as he was in her, and I don't know how to tell her it's because "disappointed" is how Dad feels about me in general.

MOM SAYS CODY AND I can keep dating as long as we have a chaperone. Chelsea eagerly volunteers.

The three of us go to the water park one weekend. Chelsea packs two bathing suits: the one-piece she tells Dad she's going to wear, and the very small bikini she actually wears. I pack one bathing suit that has no strings and a lot of coverage.

"Let's go on a water slide," Cody says, tugging on Chelsea's arm.

"In this?" she scoffs. "I'll lose my top."

"Well, why'd you wear that, then? It's a water park, there are water slides."

She scowls at him. "I want to work on my tan. Why don't you and Jocelyn go?"

"I'm in," I say, grinning. "C'mon, let's go do the big one."

"...SO THERE ARE MORE *Daleks?*" I ask.

"Oh yeah!" Cody exclaims. "They're like, the main enemy, I guess. But this one is different, because Rose touches it, see? So it absorbs her DNA and gains compassion, but since they—"

"—can only feel hatred and anger, it's miserable!" I finish.

"Exactly!" He grins.

"Wow," Chelsea says, unimpressed. "This is a really nerdy show."

"No, it's awesome!" I exclaim. "I love it."

"Hmmph," Chelsea grunts. "Well, you two lovebirds enjoy it, then."

"Aw, come on," Cody says, putting his arm around her. "She's only my girlfriend around your parents."

"Yeah," I agree.

Neither of them needs to know how much I've started to like Cody. He's my sister's boyfriend, I tell myself. It's just a little crush. I'll get over it. Those feelings aren't appropriate.

"YOU'RE SUPPOSED TO WANT to spend time with me!" Chelsea hisses.

"I do want to spend time with you!" Cody protests. "Come to the game with me."

"I don't want to sit and watch a stupid football game," she pouts. "I wanted to go to the movies."

Cody tries to reason with her. "We went to the movies last weekend, and the weekend before, and you got to pick the movie both times. Can we do something I want to do this weekend?"

"Oh, so you didn't want to go to the movies and make out in the back row?" she says sarcastically. "Could've fooled me."

"That's not what I meant," he replies.

"Sure it's not." She rolls her eyes. "You need to put some thought into this relationship, Cody, because if you don't start treating me right, you're going to lose me."

She storms off and I'm left standing with Cody on the porch. He sighs and flops onto the porch swing.

"That didn't seem fair," I say.

"Nope," he says. "Wanna come to the football game with me?"

I glance at the house, biting the inside of my cheek. "Let me ask if Chelsea will mind, okay? She's my sister."

WE'RE ON OUR FEET, screaming.

"Go, go, go!" Cody hollers.

I don't know what position the player on the field is, but he's fast, far faster than someone on the defensive line usually is. I cheer along with everyone else as he avoids being tackled, spinning and breaking away from the rest of the pack.

"He's gonna do it!" I screech.

The clock is ticking down, he's seconds away from the end zone, and just a breath before the buzzer goes, the ref throws his hands up.

Touchdown.

"Fuck yes!" Cody screams.

We're jumping, arms in the air, screaming and hollering. I stumble, he throws an arm around me, I clutch at him and he kisses me.

I kiss him back.

We're not jumping anymore. We're not screaming. He's holding me, and I'm holding him, and my first kiss is with my sister's boyfriend and it's only when that thought floats through my mind that I pull back and gas p.

"CHELS?"

She's sitting in her room when I enter, terrified to speak to her. She looks up from her laptop, eyes cold.

"What?" she asks.

"I have to tell you something."

She laughs a bit. "Is it that you kissed my boyfriend?"

I feel the blood drain from my face. "How did..."

She turns the computer towards me. Someone has sent her a link to a video playing back highlights from the game. At the end of it, the camera pans over the celebrating fans, zooming in when it sees me and Cody with our lips pressed together.

"I'm sorry," I whisper. "Chels, I swear, it was a mistake and I... I came right here to tell you. I screwed up."

"You sure did," she says. "How could you, Jocelyn? That's my boyfriend."

"Don't hate me," I beg. "I'm sorry. I swear, it wasn't... I didn't mean to."

Chelsea isn't crying like I expected her to. She sits on the edge of her bed, clearly hurt, but not crying.

"I don't hate you," she says. "Honestly, I've been thinking for a while now that... well. You and Cody get along so well. Maybe you should be the one dating him."

"Not if it hurts you," I say. "Not if it's going to make you hate me."

She smiles at me. "I could never hate you."

I'm not sure what the look on her face means, but I trust her.

"So you... you think I should date him? For real?"

She nods. "I already texted him and said we were breaking up. Go for it."

"Thank you," I whisper, and I throw my arms around her. She hesitates before hugging me back, but I think nothing of it.

"WHAT DO YOU MEAN?" I ask, shocked.

Cody sighs. "It's just, I'm going away to university, Joss."

"But it's only a year, and then I'll be graduating too."

"I know, but... look, it's just better this way, okay?" he says. "I'm sorry.

I cry after he leaves, sitting on the porch swing with my head in my hands. Cody is my first love, my high school sweetheart, and now my first heartbreak. School in the fall was going to be hard enough with both him and Chelsea having graduated. Now he's not only not at school with me, he's not even my boyfriend anymore.

When Chelsea comes home, she finds me sitting on the porch swing.

"What happened?" she asks.

"Cody broke up with me."

"Hmmph," she says.

I expect her to sit with me, maybe hug me, but she pats my shoulder and goes inside.

"HOW ARE YOU DOING, *Jocelyn?*" *asks Kelsey, one of my friends from lacrosse.*

I smile at her thinly. "Okay. It's been a week. I'm over him."

"Wow," she says. "That's fast. What about Chelsea?"

"What about her?"

Kelsey frowns. "Well, I mean, did you forgive her, too?"

"Forgive her for what?"

Kelsey stares at me. "For... what happened at the graduation party."

I'm confused. I wasn't allowed to go to the graduation party with Chelsea and Cody. It was just for grads, and only the ones who were over eighteen. Kelsey's eyes widen as I remain silent.

"Oh no," she says. "He didn't tell you?"

"He just said we should break up because he was going away to university," I say. My voice wavers.

"Joss, I'm so sorry. I mean, everyone knows, but... well... Cody and Chelsea got caught sleeping together at the grad party. Lisa's parents kicked them out and everything."

"WHY?" *I ASK HER.*

She looks up from the magazine she's reading. "Why what?"

"Why did you have sex with him?"

Chelsea smirks. "Oh, get over it, Joss. You stole my boyfriend. I just got a bit of revenge."

My mouth drops open. "But I... I asked."

"You shouldn't have even asked in the first place," she says. "Who does that? He was MY boyfriend, and you are MY sister. Well, you were. That's not how sisters treat each other."

There are tears in my eyes as my heart breaks all over again, not by Cody this time, but because of him.

"I'm so sorry," I gasp. "Chels, please forgive me. I didn't know. I'm so sorry."

"No," she says. "I don't forgive you. You don't deserve it."

"Why didn't you just tell me?" I whisper. "I would never have... I wouldn't, if you had told me."

"Why?" Chelsea closes the magazine and sits on the edge of her bed. "You betrayed me, Jocelyn. You better watch out, because honestly? Now that I know I can't trust my own sister, if I like someone you like, I'm going for him. And since we both know you're a short little troll who looks like a fucking armchair, who do you think they'll prefer?"

She points at her door and I leave her room, wishing I could go back in time and just fix everything.

CHAPTER TWENTY-THREE
NOW

"Ma'am... ma'am! You... no, you *cannot* go back there!"

Bretta was talking so loudly that I could hear her over my music. Alarmed, I pulled my earbuds out and turned just in time to see the shop door fly open. Angela Thompson stormed through the door towards me with Bretta close behind, her face torn between being offended at Angela's impertinence and concerned at what, exactly, she was doing.

"Oh no," I whimpered.

There was nowhere I could run, and even if there was, there was no time. I was going to have to weather whatever Angela decided to throw at me. Given the look on her face, it could be anything from words to punches, and I braced myself as she flew across the shop.

"Angela, please," I pleaded.

"Come here," she demanded.

I tensed, tightening my muscles in anticipation of a complete smack down from my ex-boyfriend's mom... or was she better described as my ex-boyfriend's ex-wife?

When she wrapped her arms around me and pulled me in for the warmest hug I'd ever received, I was more disoriented than I would have been if she had just slapped me.

"I am so, so sorry," she said.

Over her shoulder, Bretta paused, seemingly as confused as I was.

"Um... what?" I asked.

"I'm so sorry, dear." She pulled back, her hands still on my shoulders as she looked at me. "Isaac told us about your family and about what you said to him yesterday and I just... my heart just broke for you, dear. I'm so sorry."

A nervous laugh bubbled past my lips. "Oh."

Her face softened. "You look terrified."

"I thought you were going to kill me," I admitted.

Angela dropped her hands from my shoulders, horrified. "Oh my God. Jocelyn, I'm so sorry. I didn't even... of course, that's just... I didn't mean to frighten you."

"It's okay," I said. "But, um, maybe we could move to the front of the shop before my boss loses her mind?"

"Oh, it's been lost for a while," Bretta said pleasantly. "But yeah, you should have PPE to be back here, so if you could maybe come to the front with us, Ms...?"

"Angela's fine," she said cheerfully. "I apologize. I just needed to let Jocelyn know how sorry I was to hear about everything."

"Angela," Bretta repeated, realization dawning on her face. "I see."

"Let's head up front," I said. "Or maybe I could take my lunch now, Bretta? Angela and I can go grab a coffee."

"That would be wonderful," Angela said.

Bretta led Angela back to the front of the shop while I ran to grab my wallet. When I returned, their heads were close together, both with serious expressions on their faces as they whispered to each other. As soon as I entered the reception area, they stopped and looked at me.

"That wasn't obvious at all," I said.

Angela blushed and Bretta just laughed.

"See you in an hour," she said.

"So, um... how's Samantha doing?" I asked.

Angela smiled and began talking about her daughter as we walked to the coffee shop. The small talk was almost surreal: after all the things I'd been through with her family, having a pleasant chat as we went to grab lunch together felt strange in its normalcy.

Still, it was an enjoyable strangeness. When we finally settled at a table in the corner of the shop with our drinks and sandwiches, I was almost sad that it had to end.

"So," Angela said firmly as soon as we were seated. "Let's talk."

"What would you like to talk about?" I asked, almost shy.

Angela smiled. "Relax, dear. Whatever happened with Isaac and Derek happened. Both of them are stubborn as hell and have a dramatic streak, but I think I have a fairly clear idea of what actually went on. I want to listen, okay?"

Swallowing hard, I nodded.

"Right. I guess that just seems weird. I mean, Derek is your... you know."

"I know," she said. "And Isaac is my son. And none of this is exactly straightforward, is it?"

"Yeah, I guess."

"Do you remember when Isaac introduced you? That day on the driveway?"

I smiled. "Yeah. Things were a little simpler back then."

Angela smiled back. "Yes, they were. But honestly, Jocelyn, the moment I met you, I just... knew. I cared about you instantly. Is the whole situation strange? Yes. But it's not... bad. Does that make sense?"

It didn't quite, but I still understood. "Yes."

We talked over everything while we ate. I told her about Mateo's idea and why I became involved; I told her how mad I was when I discovered what Lawrence had done at the wedding. As difficult as it was, I told her how Derek and I ended up together. It only grew more difficult when she started asking questions.

"So, the night before Isaac… let's say, discovered you and Derek… what happened?" Angela asked.

I bit the inside of my cheek. "He's told you, hasn't he?"

She nodded. "I still want to hear your side."

I sighed, staring down at the empty plate in front of me. "I told him I was in love with him."

"And were you?"

I laughed softly. "Yeah."

She paused, then leaned forward. "And are you still?"

My heart clenched painfully. I swallowed hard, staring at the plate in front of me.

"Jocelyn?"

Slowly, I nodded. "Very much so."

My voice broke just a bit. Angela kindly pretended not to notice.

"What about your family?" she asked, changing the subject. "What happened?"

Even Bretta didn't know all the details of what happened at that dinner. I had told her the gist of it, the main points, but not everything. I meant to give Angela the same kind of breakdown, but before I knew it, I was retelling every horrid moment in painful detail. She listened, a hand over her mouth, and when I finished by telling her about changing my name, she got up to come around the table and hug me again.

"I just don't understand one thing," she said after sitting back down.

"What's that?"

She studied me for a moment. "You said you and Chelsea used to be close, but you'd done something to upset her."

"I've never told anyone," I said.

"Tell me," she urged. "I think it's an important piece in understanding all this."

Reluctantly, I told her about Cody. I smiled when I thought of him, despite the way he'd broken my heart and how his presence in my life had revealed my sister's true personality. The smile faded when I told Angela how I'd met him.

"He was Chelsea's boyfriend," I explained. "He kissed me... well... we kissed, I guess, at a football game. While they were still dating. I had a crush on him and it just..." I stopped, sighing. "It was a bad moment. I went home and told Chelsea immediately."

"I see," Angela said.

"They broke up, obviously," I continued. "I asked Chelsea if she... well, if it would be weird for me to actually date him, since we were pretending to date anyway and since I really liked him. She told me to go for it."

"That was very, um, rational of her," Angela said. "Not what I expected."

"Well, rational in that it gave her an opportunity to get back at me. She slept with him after they graduated. He broke up with me, and that was that."

She winced, inhaling sharply through her teeth.

"It was my own fault," I said. "I betrayed her."

"Uh, not really," Angela said. "You asked her first, and she told you to go for it?"

"Yes."

"Then that's not a betrayal, Jocelyn. That's a cold, calculated little move on her part."

Her support meant more to me than I could explain. More than I could handle. Shaking my head, I tried to push down the lump that was swelling in my throat.

"None of it matters now, anyway," I said. "I'm done with them. In a couple of months, I won't even have the same name as any of them."

"What's the new name?" Angela asked. "If you don't mind telling me, that is."

I smiled. "Nothing too exciting. Jocelyn Jones."

"Makes you sound like a superhero." She grinned, then took a breath. "Joss, have you thought about talking to Derek?"

"He doesn't want to hear from me," I said.

"That's not true at all."

"Angela, he made it pretty clear—"

"No, he made some stupid statements while he was upset and now he regrets them, but doesn't know how to reach you, and wouldn't know how to fix things if he did," she said. "I'm not going to pressure you or tell you what to do, but Jocelyn, believe me. If you're willing to forgive Derek for being an absolute idiot and let him have a second chance, he'd beg you to take him back."

"I don't know about—"

"He misses you," she said. "Dear, I know my ex-husband better than anyone knows him. He was miserable before Mateo came clean with Isaac and now that he knows he was wrong, he's even more miserable. He asked Isaac if he had any way of contacting you. Other than coming to the shop, Isaac said he didn't, and it was almost impossible to get Bretta to even tell you Isaac was there."

I frowned. "Did Derek ask you to come here today?"

"Absolutely not," she said. "He'd be furious if he knew I had. I needed to see you myself and know that you were okay. Whatever happened between you and him, or him and Isaac, I still care about you, you know."

I almost started crying when she said that, and almost started crying every time I remembered her saying it for the rest of the afternoon. It didn't make sense to me that this woman who was so convolutedly connected to my life could offer me that kind of unconditional support.

My own mother couldn't do that. Why the hell could Angela Thompson?

"Joss?"

I jumped out of my thoughts, looking up at Bretta guiltily. "Yeah?"

"Leigh just called and said she's done work early." Bretta glanced around the shop, then came a bit closer. "If I give you twenty bucks for a cab, is it cool if I take off?"

"You're my boss, Bretta. You don't need to ask my permission."

"I'm also your ride, smartass," she said. "And your roommate, and it's been a while since Leigh and I have had the house to ourselves…"

I rolled my eyes. "That has literally not stopped either of you a single time."

She smirked. "I know. But this way we can do it in the living room."

I laughed and told her it wasn't a problem, shaking my head and shoving the cash she tried to give me for a cab back at her.

"It's like a ten dollar Uber," I said. "It's fine."

She tried to put the bill in my coverall pocket.

"Bretta! If it means that much to you, I'll take twenty bucks off my rent next month."

I could never quite remember if it was bad or good things that were supposed to come in threes, and I guess it didn't matter. I wasn't sure if Angela's visit was a good or a bad thing. It was just a thing. For me, it wasn't about anything happening in threes: it was that when it rained, it poured.

I sent the other workers home right at the end of the day, but took my time closing up the books and cash register since I figured Bretta and Leigh could use a little extra alone time. Just before ordering an Uber, I texted them both to say I was on my way home and would gladly put on headphones if they weren't done.

It was drizzling rain, so I waited in the shop. When the driver texted me to say he was there, I closed up, set the alarm, and locked the door. Just as I turned, I saw her.

"Please," she said, holding both hands up as if it would stop me.

Her handbag swung from her elbow and I stared, too dumbfounded to be angry.

"I have an Uber waiting," I said.

"I just want to apologize, Jocelyn." Her voice cracked and I looked at her, really looked at her.

I guess there was a reason I looked more like my mom than my dad... well, the man she'd said was my dad. As I looked at her that day, though, I couldn't even see myself in her. She was slightly taller, wore her hair longer than mine, and was always perfectly put together like Chelsea was. That day, she wasn't. Her eyes were red, her skin drawn, her hair was even showing grey, which was practically blasphemy in her mind.

"I miss you," she said tearfully. "You're still my daughter and... I'm just so sorry. What can I do to... I just want to be part of your life."

"I don't think that's a good idea," I said.

"Joss, I'm sorry, I am so, so sorry. Isn't there anything I can—"

"I accept your apology, Mom."

Her eyes lit up with hope, and I almost—not quite, but almost—felt guilty.

"But no," I continued. "You made your choice a long time ago, and you need to live with it now. Your family doesn't include me, okay? I'm done."

"Jocelyn, wait," she begged. "Joss, please, let me just—"

"Mom, if you love me at all, leave me alone."

She fell silent and I went to the Uber, apologized for the wait, and didn't look back as he drove away. I looked forward, only forward, and honestly... it felt good.

It felt right.

When I got home, Bretta and Leigh were back in their bedroom, if they'd ever actually left it in the first place. I jumped in the shower, mostly to clean off but partly so I didn't have to listen to them, though I likely wouldn't have been able to hear them over my thoughts anyway.

My mind was occupied with echoes of Angela's words mixed with my mom's visit. At first, it seemed simple. Mom wanted a second chance, and I said no. Angela said Derek wanted a second chance, and if I wasn't going to give one to my mom, why would I give one to him?

It wasn't that simple, though.

Mom had a lifetime of second chances, even if neither of us had ever realized it. My existence in itself was a second chance for her. She'd had every opportunity to protect me, to take me away from an environment that was painful to exist in, and she'd turned a blind eye to it until I'd finally left.

Derek wanted a second chance, but how could I give him one? I barely thought I deserved a second chance, and I was the one who wanted it.

I wanted him. We had hurt each other, but if I could forgive my mom for a lifetime of hurt, how could I not forgive him? What differed in the situations was me. With Mom, the only thing I was guilty of was being born. With Derek, I was guilty of much more.

With Derek, I was not the only one who had to forgive.

I stayed under the running water for far longer than I needed, staring blankly at the shower wall as I thought. Forgiving Derek and asking to be forgiven opened me up to even more heartache. Not doing so, though...

Before the water could run cold, I turned it off and got out. I towel-dried my hair, knowing it would be dry soon enough, and put on jeans and a Wonder Woman T-shirt. Bretta and Leigh were still otherwise engaged, so I left a note on the fridge and grabbed my keys.

I almost chickened out twice on the drive over. At one point, I pulled into a parking lot, fully intending to turn around and go home. I was so certain I was going to give up that I almost surprised myself when I turned out of the parking lot and kept heading in the other direction.

When I turned down his street, I slowed my car down, almost afraid to drive up to his house. What if he wasn't home, or worse, what if he had someone over? I almost chickened out a third time, intending to just keep driving past without stopping, but even from down the road I could see his car in the driveway and the overhead garage door open.

I parked on the street in front of his house, wiped my sweaty palms on my jeans, and got out of the car. Drops of rain fell on my face and shoulders as I paused a final time, looking up at Derek's house.

I couldn't give Mom a second chance. I was walking away from that life, leaving it behind me. It was time to find out what lay ahead, no matter where that path may go. It was time to move forward, no matter the direction, no matter the consequences. All I could do was hope Derek would be on the path with me, and if he wasn't, well, there were other paths to take.

The rain fell faster as I took a breath and started towards the garage. Halfway up the driveway, he looked up from the motorcycle he was working on and saw me striding towards him.

A few things flashed across Derek's face: surprise, amusement, a mild sense of unease mixed with a strong hint of embarrassment. He stood, wiping his hands on a towel he had resting nearby, and stepped around the bike. I couldn't help the pang of longing that went through me. He looked so good, like always, his hair just the slightest bit messy and the tattoo on his neck teasing me from beneath his collar.

"Jocelyn," he said. "What are you doing here?"

"I can go," I said, pausing.

"No," he answered quickly. "Don't."

"Okay." I stopped just inside the garage, a good distance away from him but out of the rain.

"It's good to see you," he said.

"You too."

I didn't miss the fact that his eyes flicked up and down my body before reaching my face. After a moment, he sighed.

"What, uh... what brings you by today?"

"You know Isaac came to see me."

Derek nodded. "He called last night."

"When did you find out about what really happened?"

"Mateo came clean a couple of weeks ago," he said. "I tried calling but... well, I thought you'd blocked me, but Isaac said—"

"I changed my number," I said.

"I'm sorry," he said. "Joss, I am so fucking sorry. About... I mean, obviously about not listening and thinking... I fucked up, okay? I'm sorry for that and I will beg and grovel if that's what you want. But what happened with your family, I'm so sorry you went through that."

I nodded sharply, not able to meet his eyes. "Thanks."

"When he called last night, Isaac said, uh, you told him to call me. To fix things."

I nodded again.

"Thank you," he said. "We've been trying to get past everything that happened, but that really... that helped a lot."

"No problem," I said.

There was a tense moment before he spoke again. "Can I apologize? For the rest of it?"

"Only if you'll let me apologize for my part," I replied.

"You don't need to."

"Yes, I still had—"

"No," he said firmly. "You've apologized. You've more than apologized. Okay? And it's accepted. Whatever part you had in anything, it's forgiven, okay?"

My chin trembled and I fought to keep myself from crying. "Okay. Thank you."

"Look, I don't expect that you'll even, you know, forgive me, let alone..." He trailed off, shaking his head. "I just need you to know I'm sorry. I didn't give you a chance to explain. I should've at least listened. Ange was so pissed when... well. I thought she'd, you know, be more uh... concerned about the fact that we... well. She wasn't. She was pissed that I let things go down the way they did. Knowing she would've approved of whatever it was we had... I was just so mad and I treated you horribly. You didn't deserve that."

"I deserved it a bit," I said quietly.

"No," he said again, and he almost stepped towards me before catching himself. "You didn't, and you don't. Whatever happens... you don't deserve to be treated like that."

I couldn't respond, so I just nodded.

"I'm sorry," he said. "Is there any chance you'll forgive me?"

"I don't know," I replied.

"That's fair, I don't—"

"I'm interested in that whole grovelling thing you were talking about, actually."

He laughed, startled, then eyed me cautiously. "Are you...?"

"Yes, Derek, I forgive you," I said.

The way his face lit up almost ended me. Still, it only lasted a moment before he looked worried again.

"Isaac said one other thing when he called last night."

"I find that hard to believe. I'm sure he said lots of things."

"Smartass," he muttered, and I bit back a smile. "Yeah, but one other important thing."

"What was that?"

"He said you told him you loved me, and that he believed what you said."

I looked down at my shoes. "You already knew that."

"Is it still true?" he asked.

"Yes," I whispered, still staring at my shoes. "Yeah, that's... yeah."

"Joss?"

I closed my eyes, waiting for him to laugh or send me away or tell me he was sorry, he couldn't forgive me *that* much.

"Yeah?"

"It's still true for me, too."

Hesitantly, I looked up at him.

"I love you, Joss."

"You're gonna make me cry," I whispered.

He looked halfway to crying himself. "Will you take me back?"

It was the moment I knew that "forward" wasn't just an option, it was *the* option. There were no secrets, no time limit, no pushing away feelings because of what other people might think. After everything, the rain had stopped, the clouds had cleared, and he was there; he was mine.

Tears spilled as I nodded and started towards him. He met me halfway, throwing his arms around me and lifting me in the air as he kissed me. It wouldn't have mattered if he'd left me on the ground; I felt like I was flying anyway.

His lips pressed against mine, warm and inviting, tasting so familiar and so good.

"I missed you," he whispered.

"Take me inside," I murmured. "Please?"

He didn't need to be asked twice. We were in his bedroom moments later, exploring each other like it was the first time all over again. His hands slid beneath my T-shirt, fingers skimming along my ribs and stomach.

"Off," he mumbled, slipping his hands out so he could tug the shirt up.

I laughed, feeling him grin against my mouth before parting from me just long enough to pull it up over my head. He wrapped his arms around me again, holding me against his body as though he was afraid I'd disappear if he let go. I clutched at him, winding my fingers through his hair and stretching up to kiss him until my desperate need to feel more of him won out.

I pulled away so I could lift his shirt up. He helped me remove it and went to embrace me again, only pausing when he looked down and saw my bra.

"I thought you hated pink," he said, fingers tracing the lacy fabric along my cleavage.

"Turns out I just hated it because my sister liked it," I admitted.

He laughed and reached for the button on my jeans. "Matching?"

"Of course. I have a bit of style, you know."

Grinning, he undid my jeans and slipped them down my hips, inhaling sharply when he saw what was beneath them.

"Perfect," he declared, and I'm sure my cheeks went the same colour as my panties.

If he noticed, he didn't say anything, just touching my cheek as he kissed me again. I trailed my hands down his chest, smirking as he shivered when I touched a sensitive spot on his ribs. Lazily, my fingers walked down his stomach to his belt, unhooking it and then unbuttoning his jeans. He groaned when I slipped my hand inside and wrapped my fingers around his cock, his knees almost buckling as I began to stroke him.

"I love you," he whispered.

"I love you, too," I replied.

He nipped at my lip, letting me go so he could push his pants off. As soon as they were down, he circled his fingers around my wrist, pulling my hand off his cock.

"Come here," he said, tugging me towards the bed. He stopped just long enough to take my bra off, then directed me onto my back and proceeded to worship my body.

I have no idea how long he was at it. His lips touched me everywhere, his hands gliding along my skin, tracing every inch of me until I was practically liquid beneath his palms. He kissed my breasts and lavished attention on my nipples, sending shocks of pleasure through my entire body each time his tongue circled one of the hard nubs. His fingers mapped the tattoo on my hip, followed by his tongue, making me squirm and shiver beneath him. By the time he pushed his face against my pussy, I was aching for release.

"Please, Derek," I begged. "I need to come."

"Yes, ma'am," he said seriously, and when he moved my panties to the side and dipped his tongue between my folds, my giggle turned into a low groan.

He didn't tease me. He didn't need to. I was a complete mess, burning with agonizing desire. Derek licked every inch of my pussy before focusing on my clit, bringing his tongue against it again and again until I was panting and trembling.

"Please," I gasped, squirming beneath him.

A finger slid inside me, followed quickly by another. I shook, almost at the edge, almost ready to explode. When I glanced down, I saw Derek looking up at me, his eyes sparkling as he sucked on my clit, adoring and reverent, and that was all I could take. My eyes slammed shut of their own accord, the entirety of my being at his mercy. I cried out, nonsensical gibberish in place of words, white light in place of vision, pleasure in place of any other sensation I could have possibly felt.

Slowly, I regained a sense of myself. Derek was kissing my pussy, nuzzling against the tender, sensitive areas while I caught my breath. When my fingers loosened in his hair, he carefully withdrew his fingers from inside me, kissed my mound a final time, and sat up.

"You're so fucking good at that," I gasped.

He laughed, the corners of his eyes crinkling as he leaned down to kiss me. I kissed him back eagerly, the taste of my pussy on his lips unreasonably erotic. Without speaking, I sat up, tucking my knees under me as I rose to meet him. I pushed on his chest, nudging him until he sat back so I could crawl onto his lap.

Chest to chest, his mouth didn't leave mine as I reached between us to guide his cock inside me. I felt him inhale when the tip of his cock breached my entrance, and felt him groan when I sank down on him.

"You're amazing," he breathed, his voice hoarse. "Joss, you feel so good."

I responded by rolling my hips, air pushing out of my lungs as I sank down on him again, and again, and again. He held me tight, his hand rubbing my back while I rode him, pressed as tightly together as we could get.

Even as I rode him, he focused on me and me alone. He touched and kissed and caressed anything he could reach: his lips were on my neck one moment and my shoulder the next, his hands cupping my breasts before embracing me, then sliding down to my ass and squeezing.

When we came, we came together. Derek's face was buried against my breasts and he cried out. I felt it vibrate through me, filling me as he filled me, surrounding my heart and claiming it as his own.

"I love you," he said against my chest.

"Me or my tits?" I asked, panting.

He laughed and pulled back. "You first. Tits second."

I giggled and he pulled me down on top of him, refusing to let go of me for even a moment.

"I need you," he said. "I'm never letting you go."

"I'll have to go to the bathroom or something eventually," I laughed.

He captured my lips with his. "I know. But you're mine, and I'm not letting go of you ever again."

I smiled, pressed my face against his chest, and fell asleep knowing he never would.

EPILOGUE

THE FUTURE

RAIN ON A WEDDING day is the best possible thing that can happen.

It takes the pressure off. So much time and money is spent trying to make sure every last detail is perfect, but at the whim of Mother Nature, it's gone in an instant. On Chelsea's wedding day, it poured in the morning and faded to a drizzle, and it was gone by the evening when the actual storm started.

On my wedding day, the sun shone in the morning. During the ceremony, a storm rolled in. The photos showed the progression: gathering clouds as I walked down the aisle, a darkening sky as we exchanged our vows, and the rain beginning to fall the moment the officiant instructed Derek to kiss me.

A few people expected us to rush, to kiss quickly and then scurry down the aisle. I wasn't going to let any amount of rain ruin that first kiss with him, that first moment of him as my husband and me as his wife. Bretta's cutting laugh filled the air as she leapt forward, snatching an umbrella from someone sitting nearby, and opening it over me and Derek as the clouds began to let loose. She was soaked moments later but let us have our moment as Isaac did the same for the poor officiant trying to cover her head with her folder of papers.

It was hopeless, honestly. Even with the umbrella, Derek and I were soaked. It didn't matter: a little rain couldn't dampen our spirits. We let our guests hurry away from the garden while we stayed outside, laughing and splashing through the puddles, Derek lifting me in the air and kissing me until the photographer insisted we had to have a couple of pictures where he could see our faces.

We obliged for one or two, then it was back to Derek holding me and kissing me and laughing with me.

He had proposed far too early: mid-October, at Thanksgiving, only a few short months after I'd left my family and only a couple of weeks after I finally became Jocelyn Jones. I had been so nervous, so incredibly terrified to attend. It was my first family holiday with no family, my first time truly meeting Derek's parents and his sister, and my first time seeing everyone in the same place at the same time.

My palms were sweating as he helped me off his motorcycle that unseasonably warm day.

"You're not nervous?" I asked.

"Nope," Derek said. "It's going to be fine, Joss."

I held my helmet under one arm and Derek took my other hand, leading me up the driveway to Angela's house.

Angela had insisted I invite Bretta and Leigh when she found out neither of them had family in the city, so at least I would have them there. I knew Isaac was bringing Mateo and Samantha was bringing her boyfriend, though I couldn't remember his name.

The scariest part, though, was the other attendees: Derek's parents, his sister and her husband, and Angela's parents. All of whom had been at Isaac's wedding, all of whom knew me as Isaac's ex and Chelsea's sister, the poor girl whose boyfriend had slept with the bride, and all of whom were going to meet me for the first time as Derek's girlfriend.

I was beyond nervous. Nervous was barely a memory: I was terrified.

Derek didn't knock, simply opened the door and called out a greeting.

"Hey, Dad!" Samantha said from the couch.

"Is that Derek?" Angela shouted from the kitchen.

"Sure is!" he replied.

"Thank God," she said, turning the corner from the kitchen. "That means Jocelyn's here."

"Ouch," Derek laughed. "I'm replaced so easily."

"Oh, don't be dumb," Angela said. "Joss, can you give me a hand? The microwave is doing that thing again and you got it working last time."

Derek took my helmet from me, kissing me on the top of my head. "Help Ange out, I'll introduce you to everyone in a minute."

Angela ushered me to the kitchen before I could even glance in the living room. Isaac and Mateo were standing near the refrigerator and I said hi to them awkwardly before turning to the perfectly functioning microwave, which had a dish of vegetables spinning inside.

"Um, I thought—"

"I know, it was a ruse," Angela said excitedly.

"What?"

"Mom," Isaac said, rolling his eyes.

"Oops," she said, giggling.

"What's going on?" I asked, confused.

I found out soon enough: Mateo and Isaac blocked me from going back to the living room, directing me to the balcony just off the dining room. Heart racing, I looked at Angela helplessly. She smiled, her eyes sparkling.

"Go see," she said simply.

As soon as I stepped onto the balcony, tears sprung into my eyes. It was October, too cold for any sort of garden to be flourishing, but flowers were everywhere. They were spread along the railing, piled on the table, and filling the wooden planters Derek had delivered that day so long ago. He stood among them, eyes sparkling with excitement, half a nervous smile spread across his lips.

Well, he stood only for a moment. As the door closed behind me, he went down on one knee and pulled the ring box out.

"I don't want to introduce you as my girlfriend and I said I wasn't going to let you go," he said. "Marry me, Joss."

A giggle and a sob seemed to mix together and bubble out of my chest. It had only been a matter of months, but they were the happiest months of my entire life.

"I'm not changing my name again," I said. "I paid good money for the new one."

He laughed. "You don't have to. Will you marry me anyway?"

"Yeah," I said. "I mean, yes. Of course."

When we went back inside, Derek took me straight to the living room.

"All right, everyone, sorry. Just had to take care of some business. I'd like you to meet Jocelyn Jones, my fiancée."

We spent the winter planning our wedding for the following spring. April rolled around with snow still on the ground, and the usual April showers became May showers. When our wedding day rolled around at the beginning of June, flowers were in bloom, trees were just budding, and it was beautiful.

"Your pictures are going to be perfect," Angela had declared that morning, only to grimace when she saw the clouds starting during the ceremony.

She was right though; they were perfect. Sure, our hair was matted to our heads, water dripped down our faces, and my skin was pale and covered in goosebumps, but none of that mattered. We were in them together, happy and in love, never letting go, and never letting that knot unravel.

Acknowledgments

My books would not be possible without some very special people:

My proof-readers, editors, and beta readers are extraordinary people who I am incredibly grateful to. Special thank you to Jason Caldwell, Nora Fares, John, and Chasten.

To Paul M, Kevin Matheny, centralsquareguy, KW, AG, PM, N, ED, KJ, MidNyt, RP, Caleb Waters, and all my incredible supporters on Patreon and in my Cheryl's Terrors group - thank you. Your enthusiasm, support, and belief in me means more than I can ever say.

I am lucky enough to be surrounded by friends and family who have read, supported, and encouraged my writing. To all of you, thank you, and I stand by what I said: you're the one who has to look me in the eye if you read something you didn't want to think about me writing! But also, thank you for not making it weird. I am so grateful for the special people in my life.

And finally, to the man I love more every single day: I love you. You're my everything. Thank you for standing with me, encouraging me to follow my dreams, and being my happily ever after.

ALSO BY CHERYL TERRA

Also By Cheryl Terra

Find all of Cheryl's books at cherylterra.com/stories

Aurora Flats Series

Fate and Fried Chicken

If You Can Series

The Boy Next Door
Kiss Me If You Can
Hold Me If You Can
Keep Me If You Can
Sleigh Me If You Can

Unicorn Confessions Series

The Unicorn Confessions
Unicorn For Sale
Death of a Unicorn

Love Across Canada Series

Get Over It
The Devil Made Me
Runaway
Finding Home

Standalones

When It Rains
Hearts at Play: Special Edition
One Little Question
What Happens In Vegas
Selfish Love
Another Last Call

JOIN THE CHAOS

Every hot mess deserves a happy ending.

Get exclusive bonus scenes, short stories, novellas, and more by joining my newsletter: **cherylterra.com/newsletter**▯

Find even more bonus content, early access to new work, and weekly updates that I sometimes actually do post every week on my Patreon (free tier available!): **patreon.com/cherylterra**